Nothing Got Broke

a novel by

Larry F. Slonaker

Published by

Sandra Kleven — Michael Burwell
3157 Bettles Bay Loop
Anchorage, AK 99515

cirquejournal@gmail.com
www.cirquejournal.com

The excerpt from "The Stranger Song" by Leonard Cohen, collected in *Stranger Music: Selected Poems and Songs,* copyright 1993 Leonard Cohen and Leonard Cohen Stranger Music, Inc., is used by permission of The Wylie Agency LLC.

Cover photo: Larry F. Slonaker

Book design by Carleen Dawn Photography & Design

Print ISBN: 979-888722852-5

A Note to the Reader

On behalf of my wife, Sandi, and anyone else scarred by the tales of our childhood:

The reader can be assured that the dog depicted in this novel comes to no harm.

—LFS

Contents

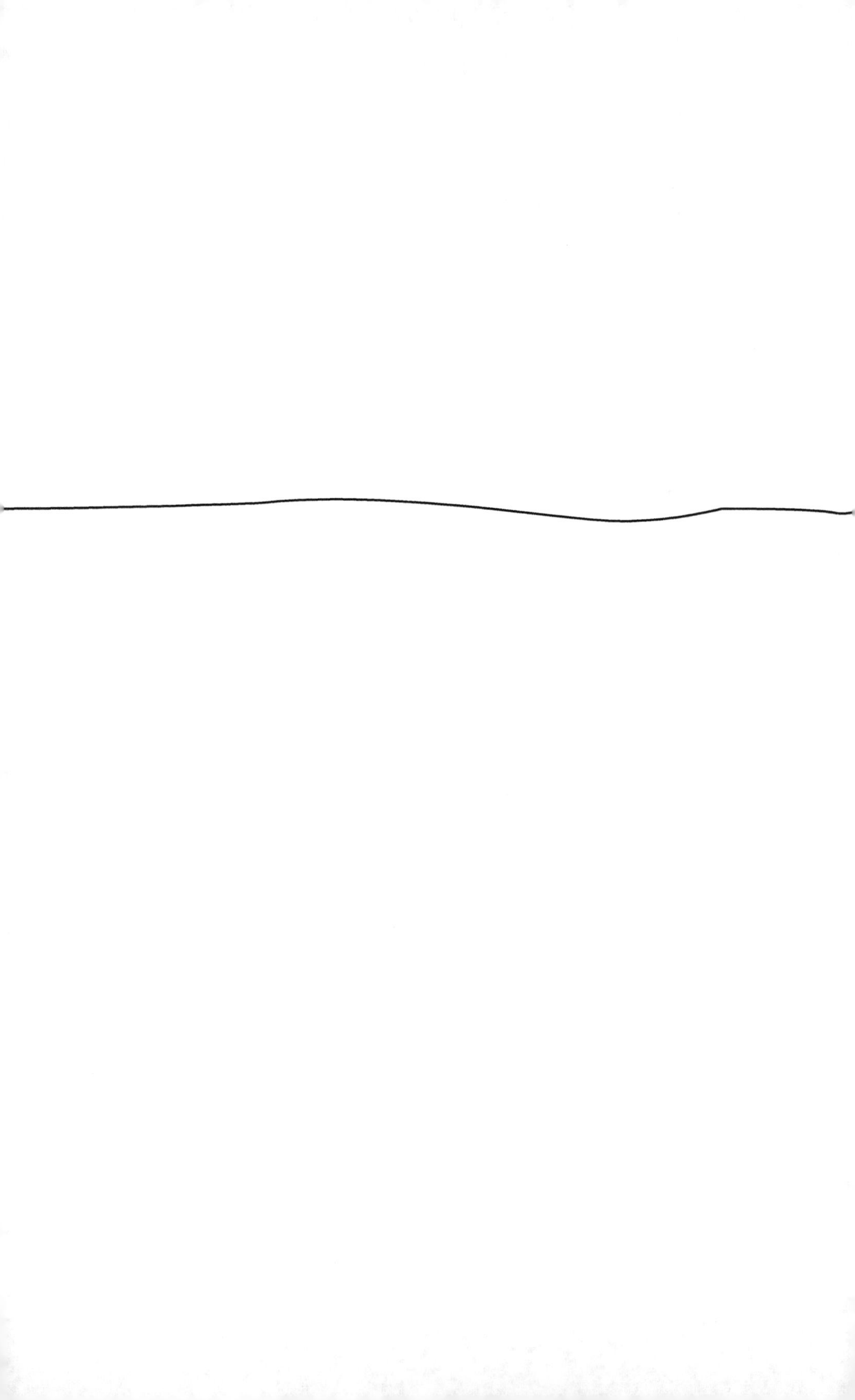

The Man in the Moon on the Man

August 1985

Here's what I can tell you about Rossiter at that time: He could report and write, seemingly with little effort, and always by deadline, just about any assignment at the paper—from a teenager's slaughter of his aged foster parents, to the rescue of a kitten stranded in a tree. But when it came to a domestic activity, he had a perverse compulsion to contort it…as one might twist apart and reshape a perfectly functional wire hanger into a makeshift snare, with the aim of retrieving some fumbled-away object behind the sofa or under the stove. The end result being something pretty much unrecognizable, as well as useless.

For example, there was this one lovely August day—which for a normal person might have been near-perfect—that preceded a sequence of events ending with him tangled in brush at the bottom of a ravine, hopelessly engrossed in the moon.

He and Jen had designated this as their date day, with a picnic in the hills. His pre-picnic assignment was simple: make two sandwiches. However. He found that the oddments of roast beef he'd been allotted did not lend themselves to the task. Neither did the romaine leaves and gooey tomato slices. Stuff kept falling out. It was like assembling some doodad manufactured in China; on completion, even after the punctilious following of directions, there were parts still sitting on the counter.

"Foodstuffs. Uncooperative," he grunted. Eventually he just pressed his palm down on the two top slices of bread, achieving what he deemed to be a manageable compaction. "Well…what does one say about this except, *ta-da*."

Jen, working beside him at the counter, assessed the end product. "Are you sucking at that just so you never have to do it again?"

"I believe the correct response to that would be, 'No.'"

She was mixing up a thermos-full of a recipe she'd seen the previous Sunday in the Herald's food section—red wine, seltzer, lime and bitters. He made a stab at a counteroffensive.

"Those ingredients don't seem to go together," he said.

She pointed to the folded sheet beside the cutting board. "It's from *your* paper. Isn't that what you call an unimpeachable source? Now, please don't distract me as I create."

"That is not an unimpeachable source. But OK, Julia Child."

He wrapped the sandwiches, then wandered to the kitchen table and sat by Jay, who was drawing on a torn-out sheet of notebook paper. "Hey, buddy. Whatcha making?"

"I don't know. Just a man."

"What's the round thing he's holding on top of his shoulders?"

"It's his head! Of course."

"OK."

Well…" Jay took a gray crayon to darken two circles toward the top of the round thing, and another in the middle. "It's not *really* his head."

"Ah. I thought not. What is it?"

"Guess."

"A beach ball?"

"On top of a man's neck? Ha. Guess some more."

"A tire missing some lug nuts?"

"Whaa-at? No!"

"OK, I give up."

"You do?" Jay glanced at his face to confirm he was giving up. "Okay.

It's the moon. See?" He grabbed his black crayon to further darken the circles. "The Man in the Moon."

"Oh, of course it is. So…the Man in the Moon is on the man's shoulders."

"Uh-huh."

"I always thought the Man in the Moon seemed surprised. I like yours better. He's more composed."

"He is?" Jay shifted the paper into a cockeyed angle, and pushed his glasses up for refined scrutiny. He squared the paper back up and sighed, shook his head, and grabbed a red crayon to make a series of slashes through the circle.

"Wait, what are you doing that for?"

"He's *supposed* to be surprised. Not deposed." More slashes. "This is not good enough for second grade. It looks like first grade."

"I disagree, but you're not quite in second grade yet, anyway."

"Tomorrow I am."

"Right, tomorrow. And you don't have to worry about how well your drawings measure up. You know, Penny and Jenny had Mrs. Simmons in the second grade, and they said she was their all-time favorite."

"They didn't say that."

"They really did. They had fun in her class. You will, too. Ask them when they get here."

"OK, I will." Jay sighed once more, heavily, and flipped the paper over. He began to draw a man again, starting with the trunk. "You can go ahead with your date day," he said. "I'm going to make a better Man in the Moon."

When the girls came, Rossiter enacted his customary mock confusion about who was who.

"Jenny, you've done your hair differently."

"I'm Penny, not Jenny."

"Jenny, a bit of wisdom from me: It's important to be comfortable in your own skin."

"Oh-my-god Mr. Rossiter," Jenny said. "*That's* Penny. *I'm* Jenny."

"I know you're only teasing me. It's fun to tease the old guy, huh? But

I'm fine with it. It's like we're bantering."

The girls, god bless them, did not recoil. Rather, with an exactly calibrated synchronicity, they turned to one another and rolled their eyes.

"Understood. We're done here," he said. "But Penny, Jenny, or vice-versa, can you please reassure Jay here about Mrs. Simmons?"

The girls sat on either side of Jay. "Great Man in the Moon," Penny said.

He jammed the sandwiches into a brown bag, and placed the bag, Jen's thermos, two plastic tumblers and a thin blanket into a backpack. He carried it to the bedroom, where Jen was sitting on the bed, putting on her hiking shoes.

"Jay's all worried about the first day of school tomorrow," he said.

"What else is new. He's a worrier, period. But in 24 hours he'll be fine. The girls loved Mrs. Simmons."

"I know. I told them to tell him."

"She's smart, she's nice, and she's good at what she does. What else can you ask for in a second-grade teacher?"

"I don't know. What if she were bosomy?"

Jen stopped mid-lace. "My god," she said. "I married a 12-year-old. Mister Child."

"I think it's fine for you to brag to *me* about it, but maybe don't do that with other people."

"Rest assured." She finished tying her shoe and looked up. "Hey, I know what." She had a sly grin. "Bring the pistol."

"Yes! To arms!" He held out his two arms, but she only curled her lip in distaste. So he pulled out the holstered .38 from the top shelf of the closet, and jammed it in the backpack beside the bag of sandwiches.

They walked in about a mile on a trail marked "Calero Open Space Preserve," then ducked through a gate onto an anonymous dirt road that probably was private. After another half-mile, they hiked up to the top of a hill to a grandly gnarled oak tree. He spread out the blanket under a long errant limb, and dug out their lunch. When they first drank the spritzer, they made faces at each other, exaggeratedly aghast, as if they'd just taken a swig of gasoline.

Three or four sips in, though, it didn't seem so bad. They drank it all, and devoured the sandwiches while admiring the view. When they finished, he lay down with his head in her lap, his hands folded on his chest. In the middle of the blue sky, he spotted what he thought might be a full moon, as transparent and ephemeral as a vitreous floater. He tried to make out the Man in the Moon, but could not. Too faint, and he could not quite fix his line of sight.

Their positioning, he decided, evoked a cinematic tableau. He cast their roles: he would be a William Holden type. Maybe a bit of a rake, vigorous, sort of cocky, but underneath certainly not a bad man. She would be a blonde, somebody like Gloria Grahame—pretty and good-hearted, but also no-nonsense. Probably somewhat scarred emotionally, and tough enough to have put that mostly in the past.

But after maybe a minute of lying there and concocting all this, he had to admit that Jen's thighs were not soft and inviting like a pillow. They were hard and unyielding. Like, say, a railroad track, or some other surface on which one would never lay one's head while sober. He sat back up and yawned. She patted his back and smoothed his hair.

"C'mon, show me your stuff, Deadeye."

"Yeah?" The dale lay wide open below them. No one was in sight.

"Yeah. Can you hit...what about that big rock over there?" She pointed to a gray boulder about 100 feet away.

"Maybe, but even if I hit it, how would we know? Here." He took the two plastic tumblers, one blue, the other red, paced off 10 steps up the ridgeline, and set them on the ground. Then he trotted back and knelt next to her. He took a napkin, tore off two half-dollar-sized pieces, chewed on them for a few seconds, and put them in his ears.

He held the torn napkin to her.

"Really?"

"Yes. You'll be sorry if you don't."

She tore off two more pieces and chewed them, making the same face as when she'd first tasted the spritzer, then delicately inserted the wads into her ears. "Ugh."

He unholstered the revolver and rose. He balanced, one foot forward, extended his arm and took aim, and glanced down at her. She cocked her head and crossed her wrists across her breast. "My hero."

His first shot kicked up dirt a foot or so above the blue tumbler.

"Whoop!" The wads in his ears muffled her voice. "Almost!"

He took aim again, and inhaled deeply. When his arm steadied, he squeezed off another shot.

This one struck about halfway closer, only below instead of above.

"Ross! Ha!"

She had a big smile. He couldn't tell whether she was derisive or impressed. Or maybe just excited. "OK, your turn."

She hopped up, took the pistol and squared herself to the tumblers. She squinted at them, frowned, then suddenly jabbed her arm in their direction, as if she were poking a door shut.

He couldn't tell where the first shot went. Nothing moved.

She said something. "Boo," it sounded like.

"Hold your arm steady."

"What?"

"Take your time. Aim. Like you did at the range."

Her second shot exploded the blue tumbler.

"Holy shit!" He stared at the spot where it had disintegrated. Bits and shards of blue glistened in the dirt.

She was laughing. "I'm the new Deadeye!" she proclaimed. She grabbed him around the neck and kissed him for a full five seconds, then whispered, "Race you back to the blanket!"

"OK…go."

She gave him a quick push to gain the advantage, and sprinted off. Her hair, a yellow dab, bobbed against the backdrop of the oak. She was waving the revolver high in the air, desperado-style.

As she neared the blanket she peeked back and slowed to a jog. "You didn't even try." She went into a backwards walk, and held both arms high in triumph. "The winner."

He took his time going to her.

"You need to reconsider the notion of a race," he said. "'I win' is a first-grade mentality. Think on more of a second-grade level. The order at the finish line is not the point. Because everybody's a winner in the end."

"Said the loser."

He groped for a response and, finding none, raised his hands in silent acquiescence.

1. Fort Shaw

I know that kind of man.
It's hard to hold the hand of anyone
who's reaching for the sky just to surrender.

—Leonard Cohen, "The Stranger Song" (1967)

CHICOLINI: Trentino!
FIREFLY: (Begins pelting Trentino with fruit) Trentino, hey?
Call me an upstart, huh?
TRENTINO: I surrender! I surrender!
FIREFLY: I'm sorry, you'll have to wait till the fruit runs out.

—"Duck Soup" (1933)

The town of Sun River was near-comatose. As I drove through, the only living creature I could detect was a dog drooping its bony frame over the front step of a shut-down gas station. After 20 hours of driving, I was feeling some internal disgruntlement that may have been hunger, but the prospect of buying Velveeta and Wonder Bread from the little grocery next to the gas station, and eating in the weedy parking lot, prodded me further down Highway 200, toward Fort Shaw, which was situated only about five minutes away. Its proximity suggested that maybe the original settlers of these two sparse towns had been confounded as to which location was better, or worse, and so in their bafflement chose to build in both.

As it turned out, Fort Shaw was livelier: twice as many dogs, one of them ambulant. As with Sun River, the town was bisected by the highway, which constituted its "Main Street." Fort Shaw did not appear to have any other paved roads. Halfway down Main Street there was a diner with an old 7-Up sign above the door. I slowed to see two pickups parked near the entrance, one black, the other white. Yes, just like the world! The black one had an American flag decal on the rear window and a bumper sticker that read, "Simms Tigers." I pulled into the gravel parking area, parking well away from the pickups.

I lowered the window of the 4-Runner I'd bought a month ago. A mild wind rustled through cottonwood trees across the street, moving some twigs about, randomly, like a sleepwalker pawing at socks in a drawer. Otherwise, very little to hear. My breathing and the faint hum of the world.

I got out, yawned, stretched, endured the fussing of the wakening ligaments and tendons. The air was drier here than in California. Something about the feel of the oxygen entering and drying my nostrils made me feel like I was elevating slightly off the ground, almost an out-of-body sensation…

I shook it off, and went around to the passenger side to retrieve my wallet from the mess of newspaper and bags. When I pushed the door closed, I heard an echoing slam from across the road.

A man and a boy were walking away from the side door of a garage. Presumably father and son. The man was powerfully built, and walked with a rolling gait…kind of simian-like. He had a halo of bushy hair and an equally bushy beard. The kid was maybe 10 or so, with the same bushy hair, but skinny. The man was speaking in a petulant tone but not loud enough for me to hear. The kid abruptly turned and jogged back to the front of the garage door. He hoisted it open, revealing an unfinished interior, in which miscellaneous junk surrounded a wooden frame contraption. It could have been a door sitting on two sawhorses.

The man was walking toward the shell of an old green VW Beetle. He bent over next to it, behind a pile of scrap metal that momentarily obscured him from vision. When he arose, he started walking back toward the garage with an engine block cradled in his arms. It must have weighed, what, 150 pounds? 200? But he walked casually and without any apparent effort. He set it on the makeshift bench with nonchalance—Gram setting the turkey down on the table at Thanksgiving—and uttered a gruff sentence, of which two un-Gram-like words were carried by the breeze: "…*fucking* thing…"

I gawked at all this a bit longer, anticipating that perhaps the man might return my gaze, but nothing came. So. Rather than stand there indefinitely to conjecture about how these two figured in the bob and weave of the cosmos, I went inside the diner.

Two guys wearing ball caps—one cap black, one white; who belonged to which truck?—sat at the counter drinking coffee. A middle-aged, wrinkly woman with a pencil behind her ear leaned on the counter from the other side, examining a bright yellow sheet of paper. The guys turned at the sound of the door opening, and briefly sized me up. I nodded a dude-to-dudes manly nod. They nodded back and returned to their conversation. Something about a high school trip.

The woman slapped the paper down on the counter. "If they can raise the money, it's OK with me," she said. "I wouldn't mind going myself."

I sat at the counter, six stools down.

"You ain't missing anything," said White Cap.

"Like you'd know."

"I been to San Diego."

"Uh, yeah. In the Navy. In 1972. Disco Dan."

Black Cap found this to be pretty funny. "Disco Dan," he repeated.

She walked down to me. "How ya doin' today, hon? Coffee?"

"Can I get a toasted cheese sandwich and a Coke?"

"I wish I'd had the chance to go to San Diego when I was in high school," she said. "Toasted cheese!" she called over her shoulder. There was an answering shuffle and the sound of a refrigerator door opening.

She set a plate and utensils in front of me and took a good look at my face. "Where ya headed?"

"Oh. Ha. I suppose to hell."

Silence. Perhaps this was not how normal people here spoke. I shifted. "I'm just going over around Crown Butte…Just headed there for a little time away." More silence. I attempted a reassuring smile.

Still studying my face, she repeated: "Crown Butte."

"Over there by Simms," said Disco Dan. "The *butte*. Jeez, Peg. You've driven past it a thousand times."

"OK. I just didn't know the name of it. Anyway, I thought that was the way to Missoula. I must've missed the signs that say 'To Hell.' "

I tried to play along. "Oh, that road isn't marked," I said.

"Not so sure about that." She set a Coke can and a glass of ice in front of me. "You've got a place over by the butte?"

"Yeah. It's just a shack. It's on the back side. My dad built it years ago."

"Oh. Hm. The back side, huh? What are you hiding from over there?"

I felt myself actually redden, as if she'd made an Aspergian reference to some physical defect that a polite adult would not point out…a hare lip, crossed eyes, a unibrow. I gasped out a pathetic, "Haha," and licked my lips, literally. I might as well have held my hands out to be cuffed.

Seeing I had nothing more, and maybe taking pity on me, she added, "I guess it's nice there, all right. Not especially scenic, though."

"That's all right. I'm not really into scenic."

She nodded, as if this were a wise attitude to have. Or, more likely, to politely indicate this wacked conversation should now end. She put the menu away and glanced down toward the Caps, teetering toward their safe gravitational pull.

"I like your calendar," I quickly said.

The calendar, hung on the wall above the cash register, featured a copy of a Charles M. Russell oil. It depicted several drunken cowhands riding crazily into a saloon, guns blazing, as their horses' hooves smashed through the planked walkway.

"You do?"

"Yes. Where could I get one, do you think?"

"Gee, I don't know. The bank in Vaughn gives them away at New Year's. I doubt there's any left."

"I'll give you twenty dollars for it."

The noise from the kitchen seemed to stop. One of the Caps snickered.

"Or…would that be too much?"

"Hon, if you want it that bad, you can have it."

"That's OK. I'm happy to pay for it."

"It's not worth no twenty dollars. It's a freebie. Nobody ever looks at it anyway." She pulled it off the wall and gave it a quick flip-through, seemingly verifying that it was in fact worthless, then brought it over and placed it on the counter. "There you go. Happy New Year."

"That's very generous. Thank you. Happy New Year to you."

She again looked toward the Caps. I groped for another topic. "And where's the fort?"

At this she actually smiled a little. "Oh. 'The fort.' Some fort. There's nothing left of it. When you walk out of here, on your left you'll see a gravel road going north. You go down that gravel road, and go left where it forks. You'll see the historical stuff and the house. That's all there is."

"Ah. The historical stuff. So, is there a lot of information on Shaw?"

"Shaw?"

"You know, Robert Gould Shaw…he's the 'Shaw' in Fort Shaw?"

"Mm-mm."

"Robert Gould Shaw was something of a Civil War hero for the North. Headed up a regiment of black soldiers. Matthew Broderick played him in the movie."

A synapse sparked in Dan's brain. "Ferris Bueller!"

"Oh, Ferris Bueller!" Peg said. "That's such a cute movie. What'd you say, what's the name of the movie in Fort Shaw that has black soldiers?"

"It's called, 'Glory.' It doesn't take place in Fort Shaw, though. They actually named the fort for him after he was killed in battle down South."

"Killed, huh? But his black soldiers beat the Rebs. Never heard of that."

"Actually, they lost that battle. It was more of a moral victory."

They soaked in this bit of trivia. Fort Shaw is named after this supposed hero, who got killed and whose soldiers lost the battle. And they made a movie about him. After a few seconds of cogitation, the silence of which felt awkward to the point of painfulness, Dan summed it all up. "No guts, no glory."

No one could contrive a rejoinder to this. Finally I said: "Maybe you should change the name of your town to Fort Bueller."

"Order up," came a weak cry from the back.

Peg motioned toward the two caps. "If we changed the name of the town, these two would never find their way home."

The two of them mimed vigorous agreement, their caps bobbing.

When I walked out, the stomach-grumbling I'd felt before was now transitioning to a different kind of gurgle. The cheese in the sandwich had been intensely, disturbingly orange. I took a couple of deep breaths. A faint, sweet, clean smell hung in the air. Sage. That helped.

The guy and the kid were still in the garage. The guy was hunched over the engine block, while the kid was behind him on his knees, fooling with something on the floor. Rolling it back and forth. Whatever it was, it was too small to see, but by the motion of the boy's hands, I could tell it was round.

The guy abruptly straightened and headed out, back toward the junk pile, talking without turning around. This time the wind was just right. I could hear him plainly: "Quit fucking around and throw that goddamn thing away."

The kid stood, scrutinizing whatever was in his hand.

"Hey!" the guy yelled.

The kid shrugged his shoulders, and carelessly flipped the object behind him, over his shoulder. A pebble or a ball of clay. A round shadow that disappeared into the ground.

2. God's Country

The boosters say it's a better country than it ever was but it looks like hell to me I liked it better when it belonged to God it sure was his country when we knew it.

—Charles M. Russell, letter to Bob Stuart,
March 10, 1913

My cabin was on the back side of the butte, so I couldn't see the gravel road a quarter-mile away that came out of Simms. But when vehicles drove on it in dry weather, they would kick up tattered sheets of dust. Sitting on the narrow porch that faced east, I would count off the seconds until it dissipated. Frankie knew I wasn't talking to him at these times. He might raise his head, just to be sure, then lay it down again.

Every once in a while, alerted by the hoarse whisper of rubber on gravel, I would fix my eyes at a spot where the sloping line of the butte melded into the prairie. At that spot I could discern the very top of a cattle truck or horse trailer going by in either direction. Just for a second. Those guys drove pretty fast.

I would try to visualize the scene inside the passing vehicles. In the first weeks after my arrival, they always were wearing plaid snap-button shirts, listening to country western music. Their black or white baseball caps nodded on the downbeat.

That was months ago. Now the imaginary riders could be anyone. Who knows who is driving from Point A to Point B, and why? They might be wearing those old-fashioned, military-style marching band coats—the ones with brass buttons and epaulets. They had Liverpudlian accents. But they couldn't be the Beatles because they were Russian. They were headed south, to the farmers' market in Helena, hauling blocks of fresh tofu. Or dynamite.

The scenarios changed, depending on my mood, my level of boredom, my nostalgia. The one consistency about the imagined travelers was a profound, grotesque contentment.

On a day in early October, nearing dusk, I heard the sound of an engine. It had rained pretty good a couple of days before, so there was no dust to foreshadow the vehicle until its top came into view. An RV? It was moving with unprecedented slowness. Maybe 20 miles an hour, if that. No one drove that slowly out here, unless they were having some kind of trouble.

"That's a little odd," I said. Frankie looked at me expectantly. "Odd," I repeated.

Maybe ten minutes later it was back, heading in the opposite direction. Moving even more slowly this time. Almost certainly an RV.

"Hm."

Gone. Five minutes later, back, but moving even more slowly. Within seconds Frankie was up, ears pricked, softly growling, but I already knew: They had steered off the gravel, gone over the cattle guard, and headed up the rutted roadway to my cabin.

In the past year not a single vehicle had come up that road, other than my own. "And of all things," I said to Frankie, "it's a fucking motor home."

When its flat nose came over the last rise, a hundred feet from the cabin, Frankie growled more loudly. I felt my own hair stand on end. "It's OK, boy. Tourists. They're lost."

The vehicle hesitated at the rise. I could make out two faces staring through the windshield. Unnerved astronauts facing the Martian landing spot. I advanced a couple of steps and tried to assume an unthreatening pose. The two faces turned toward one another, and back to me. Then the vehicle slowly resumed its progress, rocking comically to and fro in the rutted road.

Frankie barked.

"No," I said. "It's OK."

A woman was at the wheel; the passenger was a man. Their faces were a coppery glow in the direct light of the lowering sun. They couldn't have been going more than 5 miles per hour, but when they were 20 feet away, she hit the brakes hard enough to make them both pitch forward.

At first, they just sat. Everyone was suspended in the moment. I could see them both squinting at me. This lasted a few seconds, until suddenly, simultaneously, they started rustling about. The woman twisted around, yanking something from the back seat.

As they started to clamber out, Frankie growled again.

"Frankie. No."

She was a small woman, wearing a white ski jacket. She disembarked gingerly. Her exit was complicated by the fact that she was holding a fairly large basket wrapped up in green cellophane.

She lost a shoe as she stepped down. A black loafer. "Uh-oh," she said. Her downward line of sight was obscured by the basket. She poked her stockinged foot at the dirt. "Dang...." The guy came around to her side, but he didn't seem to know what to do. His left hand loosely cradled a green notebook or binder. He could easily have relieved her of the basket, but showed no inclination to do so. Finally she made contact with the shoe and slipped it on.

"Hi-ee," she called. It was a high, thin voice. "Hi!"

"Hi, there." It was the rare time of day when there wasn't much of a breeze, so I didn't have to call out. Although she was fully shod now, they weren't moving. She was eyeing Frankie, who measured maybe 12 inches from ground to shoulder.

"You can come on. The dog won't hurt you."

"Oh...he won't hurt us?"

"He's been trained not to attack anyone carrying baskets."

"Oh...he has? ...Hee-hee. He has?" This bit of nonsense seemed to embolden her. She started to stride briskly forward. The guy followed her lead.

"Yeah. Now, if you were carrying a zucchini, he'd kill you."

The path from the vehicle to me was on just a slight incline, but when they came up and stopped a few feet away, she seemed out of breath. "Whew."

She had Asian features. High cheekbones, smooth skin, dark eyes. Full lips. Maybe in her early 30s, hard to tell. She was smiling in a polite but not overly familiar way. The guy had features vaguely similar to hers, but broader and flatter.

"I left the zucchini inside," she said brightly.

"Thank god. OK, so, you folks are lost." I said this in what I thought might be received as a friendly or even avuncular tone. "…But the good news is, the way back to the highway is very easy."

"Oh, we're not lost."

"Really? You kind of drive like you're lost."

"Oh. Our directions aren't very good. Hey Duane—show him our directions."

Duane removed a folded-up sheet of paper from his breast pocket and handed it over.

I opened it to see a photocopy of a map, with handwritten notes beneath it. At the top it said, "From Great Falls airport to Crown Butte."

"Are you Mr. Rossiter?" the woman asked.

"Who?"

"Mr. Rossiter?"

"That name doesn't sound familiar."

"Really? You don't know the name—Rossiter?"

"I guess if you say it enough times, it'll start to sound familiar."

"Ah. Well, sir, my name is Thao Nguyen, and this is Duane Bistodeau, and we're from the San Jose Herald in California, and we're looking for Mr. Doug Rossiter."

"That much I've gathered."

"Mister…?

"Sam Gregory."

Thao Nguyen cradled the basket against her chest, and extended her right hand. I shook it; her hand felt soft but her grip was firm.

"Pleased to meet you, Mr. Gregory. Do you know how we might find Mr. Rossiter?" Her enunciation was distinctly clipped. She seemed quite at ease, but now, in contrast with her first greeting, the tone was almost formal.

"Since you're the journalist, I doubt I could give you any guidance of value."

"Of course. It's just that—I thought you may have heard of him because it appears there aren't that many people who live up in this area." She nodded toward the butte.

I reflexively looked over at the still, stolid mass. "That's very true. There's about 100 cows to every human in these parts. Now, if you were trying to find a certain cow, I know some folks who probably could help you."

She chuckled and shook her head.

"So, this guy you're seeking...does he wear sunglasses and a hooded sweatshirt?"

"Uh...not that I know of."

For the first time, Duane spoke. "We're not looking for the Unabomber. They already found him."

"Right you are. And just 50 miles west of here, at that. Maybe that's where your Mr. Rossiter is as well. Let's take another look at these directions."

This time I read the whole thing.

Take I-15 north to Vaughn. Exit on SR 200 toward Missoula. Go west about 20 miles, through a couple of little towns—Sun River and Fort Shaw. When you get to Simms, you'll find a gas station on the south side of the highway. It's the only one in town. There's a road next to the station that heads south. You'll see the butte right in front of you. Take that road about five miles. Look out on your right for a cattle guard (ask me if you don't know what that is). Go over that and stay on the road—it's hardly a road at all, but you'll be able to see it—till you get to his place.

"Actually, these directions are pretty explicit. They just took you to the wrong person. Where did you get this? Who wrote it?"

"My editor," Thao said. "His name is Edward Herbert. Do you know him?"

The wind was starting to pick up. Just like that. It was like the sound of an appliance—a fan or a refrigerator—kicking on.

"Sir, do you know him?

"Is that the guy who runs the John Deere dealership over there in Vaughn?"

"No...it's my editor in California."

"So it would seem pretty unlikely that I would know that Ed Herbert."

"Oh."

The bottom curve of the sun lay just on the horizon. Thao shivered.

"Cools off fast here," Duane said.

"Look, folks, I wish I could help you."

A gust shoved us. "Woo," Thao said.

"Yeah. The funny thing is, this is about the best time of the day. The wind blows pretty hard most of the time."

Duane shivered, too. He scanned the horizon. "Kind of bleak here, huh?" He pointed at Crown Butte. "That mountain or whatever you call it is impressive, for sure. But even that—it's like it's chopped off at the top. Like it's beheaded. It's not exactly God's country, is it?"

"You don't think so?" I surveyed the same arc of horizon. The contours of the butte were illuminated in the flat light. On its flanks, and below, the landscape was rounded and worn from the wind. "I always found it odd that God would make only a few places on the earth 'God's country.' With the rest, he just did a mediocre job. Or worse. Don't you find that curious?"

No answer.

"It just makes me wonder. Did he start off with enthusiasm, but eventually lose interest making the rest of it, do you think? The non-God's-country spots? It was like, 'OK, this part here is going to be *my* country. *God's* country. Um, and also this part here, the Grand Canyon, and this part, Victoria Falls or whatever. But the rest of it, I'm just going to make kind of half-assed. Like an unfinished garage."

"It's just an expression," Duane said.

"I know. You're right, I'm sorry. The thing is—" I signaled to the expanse. "Well, I actually kind of find this appealing. It's…what it is…it's what I would call an indifferent kind of beauty."

They obligingly looked around. When they were done, I thought I saw them glance for a second at each other.

"Mm-hm," Thao said. "I see what you mean."

"Really?"

"Mm-hm."

"Are you sure? As it came out of my mouth it sort of sounded like gibberish to me."

She chuckled uneasily.

"Look, folks," I said, "I wish I could help you."

"That's the second time you've said that, Mr. Gregory. So I guess you must really mean it. Right? It's going to be dark soon. Would you mind if we just parked here for the night?"

"What? You want to park that rig here?"

"Yes."

"Why would you want to stay here? It's not like you're stranded out here in the middle of nowhere. It's only a half-hour to Great Falls, and there are a hundred motels there."

"Really," she said.

"Oh, yeah. I recommend the O'Haire Manor, which is near downtown. There's this big piece of glass behind the bar, and it shows the interior of the swimming pool. You know, below the surface."

"That sounds very charming. But couldn't we persuade you to allow us to stay out here, amid the, uh—" She vaguely gestured around her. "The unspoiled wind. The music of the chirping…The charming music of the…"

"Crickets."

"Yes. The crickets. And that tiny moon." She pointed to the butte. A thin crescent moon dangled above it.

"God's Fingernail," I said.

"Really. I never heard of that," she said.

"Yes, he clipped it and forgot it and just left it there. Hey, honestly, the O'Haire is much more interesting. You can drink whiskey and watch the bottom half of women treading water. Or guys, of course. Whoever is in there."

"I'm sure it's fascinating. We'll be sure to stop there on our way back."

"There's really no point in your staying out here. It's an easy trip back to town."

"We'd like to stay, if you don't mind. Sir, I don't want to skirmish the issue. You're Mr. Rossiter, aren't you?"

"That must be someone else. Another man. Did you say 'skirmish'?"

She uttered a tiny sigh of impatience. "Duane, can you please give him the columns?"

Duane held out the green binder.

"No!" she said. He pulled the binder back and looked at her. "Sorry, she said, "I meant just the folder inside."

He extracted a manila filing folder from inside the binder, and gave it to me.

Inside the folder there were several sheets of paper. The top one had a clipping of a newspaper column glued onto it. The column heading read, "Doug Rossiter." Next to the letters there was a photo of a younger version of me.

I skimmed the first couple of paragraphs.

> **We go along** from one moment to the next, and one day to the next, because really, that's all the choice we have in the matter. But every once in a while something comes along and just grabs you in this assaultive way and makes you stop.
>
> Something happened at Whitman Elementary last week in Mrs. Simmons' second-grade classroom that grabbed me. It has not let go since.

"Yeah, OK, so?'

"Your hair was longer back then," Thao said. "Mr. Rossiter." She held out the basket. The cellophane made a crinkly noise. "This basket is for you."

I closed the folder, handed it back and quietly accepted the basket. It contained two bottles of wine, a block of cheese, crackers, beef jerky and some chocolate.

"Ooh. Hey Frankie. Treats."

Frankie's stubby rat-terrier tail cautiously twitched. He recognized his name, and he recognized "treats." But maybe not this basket thing.

"We got it from a grocery store by the RV place," she said. "They didn't seem to have any fresh fruit."

"This time of year, you can get some nice apples. From Washington." I pointed to the RV. "You have hot water in there, right?"

"Of course."

"And a shower?"

"Of course. So…you're probably wondering why we're here?"

"I give up."

"You do? You are Mr. Douglas Rossiter. Right?"

Nobody spoke. They just waited. I smiled at that. A reporter's trick. You just let the silence dangle there. For a lot of people, the extended silence is so uncomfortable, they'll start to talk. In spite of myself, I laughed. "There was a time when that's how I was known."

"Ah," Thao said.

"We have a letter for you, Mr. Rossiter," Duane said. He opened the binder again, withdrew a piece of paper and held it out.

"The pages just keep coming, don't they? Will you hand out the syllabus soon? Actually, I have a letter for you. It's the letter *Y*."

"Oh. Anyway, we'd like to give you this letter."

I put down the basket and read the letter.

Hey Ross—

Have tried every way I could think of to get hold of you. I knew you wanted to get away, but did not expect you to go all Col. Kurtz.

If you are reading this, it means Thao has found you. Sorry if it's an intrusion. Thao is a good reporter, & we wanted to do this story up there in Mont. I thought you could be of some help, if you were so inclined. I would appreciate it if you would.

Hope you are well. I won't go into updates here, other than just to say it's been quiet.

-EH

I returned the letter to Duane.

"I would love to be able to talk with you, Mr. Rossiter," Thao said.

"Yeah. And I would love to be able to fly…Wouldn't you?"

Duane stiffened. "They said you might be kind of hard to talk to. I wonder why."

"Exactly. *Y*? Get it?" As I bent to pick the basket back up, I thought: *So after all this, I'm still an asshole.* Touching the cellophane felt odd; it rustled in my grasp. "You'll have to forgive me," I said. "I tell you—it's been months since I had a conversation of more than 30 seconds with another human being. Clearly, I am suffering the effects. More accurately, you are suffering the effects."

I smiled at Duane, and fixed the smile until I saw his shoulders loosen.

"This might sound a bit weird," I said. "Would it seem just outlandishly bizarre if I asked if I could use your shower in the morning? I have not had a true hot shower in quite some time."

"Why, of course." Thao's tone suggested this request was entirely normal.

"All I have is this camping shower thing. The water doesn't get all that warm."

"But you are quite presentable."

"Oh…thanks, ma'am. I've done my best not to go entirely to pot." I attempted a titter, or what my imagination constructed as something that might pass for a titter. This effort was unsuccessful. What my mouth emitted was a sound hard to classify; it was a sound that might prompt an overly helpful bystander to initiate the Heimlich maneuver.

I pressed on. "A hot shower in the morning…that would be nice. Tell you what. How about we go in, out of the wind? Uncork the wine, have some cheese and crackers. Talk about your story."

3. Rocky Boy?

*I come from the West, where in a civilization founded on the mine
and the camp, we believe that the saloon and the theater has as good a
right to be open on Sunday as the church and the school. I come from
where we think that it is the right of every American to go to hell and be
damned if he wants to. That is not humor—it is the truth.*

—Charles Erskine Scott Wood,
speech at the Manhattan Club (1902)

The RV had a pull-down table, which was littered with newspapers and AAA guidebooks. Thao gathered up the materials and stacked them on a counter. She pulled off her coat, revealing a red turtleneck over a slender torso. I wondered if she was younger than I'd first guessed. "You sit there," she said, pointing to the bench at the table.

I set the basket on the table, removed the wine, and obediently sat across from her. She poked around in a paper bag and came up with three plastic cups, which she set down in front of us. The binder was gone, but she now had the manila folder, which she opened, setting it next to the basket. She adjusted it so that the papers faced me.

I ignored them, and appraised the interior of the RV. "This is nice. Big."

"Ha. Don't tell that to Ed. Really, it's not that big. Actually, it was one of the smaller ones. Duane said...." She looked toward the open door.

"I think he's outside taking pictures. Corkscrew?"

"...He said we should try to find something smaller, but I think this is fine. I don't think we have a corkscrew."

I reached in the pocket of my jeans for my knife. "It's a palace compared to what I've been living in, that's all. But in the unlikely event I have a conversation with Ed, I won't say anything to him about it." A conversation. I was having one now.

"Thank you. I'm sure your house is lovely. I'd like to see it."

"Really? Would you also like to stab yourself in the eye with this corkscrew?"

"I'm sorry?"

"I mean, my house—it's a shack, actually, as I think you've surmised. It's not going to be featured in *Sunset Magazine*."

It wasn't as though I was unfamiliar with my own voice. I talked to Frankie. Sometimes every hour of every day. And I had driven to the little towns along the highway now and then, and the people at the gas stations were willing to engage about the weather. But there was something unsettling about the sound clattering out of my mouth within this carpeted, insulated box.

"We're not fussy. In fact, it really is OK if you bring your dog in. I don't mind."

"He's fine. He had his treats. Would you mind if I opened the window a bit?"

"I've got it." She placed one palm on the table, and reached over to open the window above it. Overcoming any vestige of manners and restraint that may have lingered within me, I gawked at her chest as she stretched. She glanced back at me before I could turn my head.

Just slightly, she raised an eyebrow, then re-situated herself and tapped the paper. "So, Mr. Rossiter…." With this matter-of-fact resumption, I reestablished eye contact. Her irises were so dark I could not distinguish the pupil. Each was a single black orb. Again, she tapped the paper. "You're a very good writer."

The column heading—with a picture of my somber face—sat at the top of the page. When I first started writing the column, the paper had used a photo with a more genial expression. But when I wrote about anything even the least bit weighty, I worried that the joviality seemed insolent. So I had the header redone, going for a more impassive expression. Or an expressionless one.

"Kind of vacuous," I said.

"Pardon?"

"Look at this guy. Is this someone whose point of view you'd want to spend time reading?"

"I try not to make judgments based solely on the appearance." She had reverted to that clipped enunciation. "You're a very good writer."

"OK. Thank you. You are kind." I picked up the first sheet. "This one, as I recall, was a tale of despair and dissolution. But ultimately, of redemption." Then the second sheet. "…Or wait. Maybe that was this one?" I scanned the page. "Mm-hm-hm…Blah blah. Oh. I guess they both were. Yes." I pointed to the bottom of the column. "Ultimate redemption. I'm sure this third one was as well…Yep. First, there was a severe test. You could say it was a crucible. With tension that was almost palpable. No, wait. The tension *was* palpable. But it too was ultimately a tale of redemption."

She patiently waited for me to finish. "I may have missed those parts. I didn't see anything about that. Certainly, no redemption. Especially not in the third one."

"I guess you are right. Maybe that was the problem." I shuffled the pages. "But aside from the thematic deficiencies, any particular reason you picked these three columns?"

She put her finger on the header of the top one. Her finger was smallish, perfectly shaped, with a long unpainted nail. "They were all written in first-person."

"Ah." I put them down, side by side. "Pardon my saying so, but that doesn't strike me as plausible."

She started to speak, but stopped.

I pushed the pages aside. "Never mind. I'm rude. Who's to say anyone should have to be plausible, anyway?" I began to work on the cork. It was a pinot from Enz Winery, from down in San Benito County. "This is a pretty obscure wine."

"Yes, Ed warned me you might be…brusque. He also suggested this particular wine."

"He has a good memory. You taste this, you know where it comes from. I mean, you can tell by the taste, the grapes are grown in a distinctive soil. Lime. You can't get that up here, that's for sure. You came prepared."

"Yep, I did. We both did."

I poured the three cups half-full. "Why did you get an RV?" I raised my cup to her, and tasted it. Just a little. And swallowed. "Oh. That's good."

"We plan on traveling around quite a bit for our story."

"But there are motels here. There are lots of motels."

"So you've said. You seem to be quite an advocate of them. We're not just going to the tourist destinations. The story is beyond the tourist destinations."

"Okay…."

"The theme is the uninhabitability—" she said the word slowly and carefully—"of the West. How large parts of the West can't sustain all these little towns. It's too arid. It's a water issue. So, we are traveling around to some of these little tiny towns. Where the population is dwindling…all the young adults moving away…"

"Why Montana? Parts of Montana are doing very well. Rich people are moving to Bozeman in packs. Droves. Whatever the term is for the groups that rich people travel in."

"We're looking at the part of Montana without the trees."

"Still. It's not really a new story."

"Yes, it is. For us."

"No offense. It just seems like a big investment, sending two staffers all this way, taking all this time, renting an RV, for a story that the L.A. Times and others have already done."

The open window allowed a mild breeze and the sound of the crickets to flit inside. Thao put her coat back on.

"The cold doesn't bother you? There's lots more to be done on the topic, Mr. Rossiter."

"Yeah. Cold does bother me."

"For example, how does all this affect California? One, the thousands of Californians who cashed in their housing equity and relocated to these inland Western states. What happens to them when the water evaporates? And two, how all this might eventually lead to a reverse migration, back into California. Which isn't really ready for more people, if you haven't noticed. Nobody's done *that* story."

Duane came in with a camera. Thao shook her head at him. He placed it on a counter.

"You guys are a team, huh?" I asked.

"Just for this assignment. Duane has some relatives up here. So he knows the area a little."

"Really. What part do you know?"

"Up around Havre. I don't really know it that well. We just visited a few times when I was a kid."

"Ah. Speaking of arid." I pushed one of the cups of wine toward him. "Rocky Boy?"

"No thanks." He crossed his arms and leaned back against the counter, nudging the camera with the small of his back. "Rocky Boy. The reservation? No, not Rocky Boy. Havre."

"Ah. Right." He was short and slight, with close-cropped black hair, and a slightly flattened nose. "I wouldn't have taken you for Chippewa. I'm thinking, more like a gatherer tribe. One of those California mission tribes."

"My grandmother was native American. From here. Havre."

"Native American, right. But which tribe?"

"I don't remember."

"Really."

"Yeah. I'm not that into tribes."

"That's hard to believe. Everyone is interested in tribes, in one way or another. What about you, Thao?"

"My family comes from near Saigon."

"From which you were expelled by the tribe from the north."

"Sort of…I guess you'd say. Anyway. The point is, we're a team, as you so aptly point out. For this assignment."

I refilled my cup. "If I may be so bold. I'm getting a bit ahead of the two of you, but I haven't had a decent plastic container of wine in…god. Months." I lifted the cup to each of them. "Apologies for going off-track. You are a team for this assignment."

"Yes. For which we had hoped you might assist us."

"Understood. You know, the fact that you are so eager for my help does not exactly inspire confidence in your reportorial know-how. I mean, I don't know much about your story topic. Uh, clearly, neither do you. But that being the case, usually one seeks out the experts in the field, as opposed to someone who's living *in* a field. Who doesn't even have the social skills to conduct a friendly conversation."

"You are doing just fine," Thao said. "And I do have experts to talk to. I was more hoping you could help us with—you know, how the land lays. Because you live here."

"Yeah, I live here. Along with 800,000 other people. But, 'how the land lays'…you mean the lay of the land?"

"Right, that's what I meant. How the lay of the land is." She pointed to her chest with her thumb. "ESL."

"I never would have guessed."

"I bet you would have."

She was taking hummingbird sips, and the cup I'd offered to Duane was untouched, but the wine tasted too good for me to resist. "Where are you headed, exactly? The Hi-Line? Havre, up that way?"

"Yes. The Hi-Line. To the east. Where the train goes."

"So you'll go through Prague. Actually, that's kind of funny." I stopped there. When they said nothing, I added, "Kind of funny, in a way."

A sensation, somewhere below my belly. I had not felt it in months. Longer. In fact, since moving into the shack, I had only been reminded of the feeling on those random occasions when Frankie was onto the random gopher or a rabbit. But that was only in an observational sense. *The dog is experiencing excitement.* Was I having that sensation now?

Or. Maybe. It was just the unaccustomed effect of the wine.

Either way, I had started. "Speaking of tribes. There's a story up there I always thought the Herald should do."

"Seriously?"

"Yeah. As long as you are going to be there, you should do it."

"Seriously." She rustled around for what seemed barely a second or two, and a notebook and pen materialized in front of her. "What is it?"

"Oh, do not ask, 'What is it?'"

"No?"

"It's got nothing to do with water."

"That's all right. We're flexible."

"I am getting that impression."

"So what's the story?"

"OK. You've never heard of Charles Wood, have you? No. Well. Charles Wood was a very prominent figure in the South Bay in the '20s and '30s."

"Really." She was dutifully taking notes.

"In fact, do you know the cat statues in Los Gatos?"

"Those big white statues next to Highway 17?"

"Right. He commissioned those sculptures. They were built as the sentries to his home."

"Really. Is that why they call it Los Gatos?"

"I think maybe the town was already called that. Anyway, he was well-known in the South Bay. He's obscure now, of course, but I think he was one of the most fascinating figures in the history of the American West. He was a very accomplished lawyer…well-known writer… an advocate for women's rights. Way ahead of his time. Plus, he'd been an Army officer who participated in probably the most famous campaign of the Indian wars."

I abruptly stopped. Was I talking too loud? This stupid box deadened all the sound. She was writing, trying to keep up. I didn't hear the crickets anymore.

"Sorry," I said. "I get a little excited."

"No, this is fascinating." She reviewed her notes; her nose crinkled. "Please go on."

"During that campaign, Wood was involved in recording one of the most venerated speeches in American history."

"Oh, that," Duane said. "'Hear me my chiefs.'"

"Yes. 'Hear me my chiefs. I am tired.'"

Thao again examined the page. "I don't know that speech," she said. "It's venerable?"

"It's only about the third-most famous speech in American history."

"Really?"

"In the canon of complete speeches. Not just a phrase or two, but think of whole speeches. One, Gettysburg Address. Two, MLK, 'I have a dream.' Three, Chief Joseph, 'Hear me my chiefs.' Unfortunately, its authenticity is somewhat suspect—that's where Wood comes in—but it is famous nevertheless."

"Must not be that famous," Duane said. "Thao's never heard of it."

"Wait, I think I have. Yeah. It does sound familiar."

"The battlefield where the speech was given is right by Prague," I said. "You could do a travel story on it. Bonus for the Herald. They love shit like that. They send you out to do this piece about water, and you toss in a bonus travel piece. Funky little Western town. Kitchen-sink museum. Connection to the Los Gatos 'cats' guy for a local angle. Where to stay, where to eat, what to see."

"Duane, we could pitch it to Sherry! I know she'll love it. The man who built the cats in Los Gatos, and the third-most-famous speech ever."

Duane looked at her, and she at him. He slowly nodded.

"How do you spell it?" she asked. "P-R-A-I-G?"

"No, it's spelled like the city in Europe. Pronunciation Americanized. Speaking of which—if you go about this right, you could include the context of the real story, which is how the U.S. totally and completely fucked over Joseph and his people, shoved them into ruination, and walked away from it all without a shred of remorse."

Thao studied her notes and made a face. Apparently there was nothing there yet about anybody fucking over anybody else.

"Interesting. That's part of the story?"

"Absolutely, it is."

"Then will you help us?"

"Help you…?"

"Help us do the story about Charles Woods and the Indians."

The crickets were going again. Maybe they hadn't actually stopped.

Suddenly, in fact, they seemed very loud.

"OK."

"You *will?*" She slapped the folder on the table. "Oh my god, I was hoping you'd say that!"

"He's kidding us," Duane said.

"No. I'm not kidding. I would love to go to Prague with you for a couple days and help you do that story."

"Why?"

"Duane! Who cares! Because he's interested in the story. *Obviously.*"

"Yes, Duane. I'm interested in the story. And it just happens to be one hell of a story, and it can't be told enough. You of all people should know that. And, I've been there, and I'd like to see it again."

"'Hear me my chiefs.' It *does* sound familiar," Thao said. "This is going to be great. Oh, Sherry is going to love this idea." She tapped the notebook. "Charles Woods. I'm going to call her tomorrow."

"Charles Wood. Charles E. Wood."

"Wood." She wrote it down carefully, and underlined it.

God's Fingernail had sunk behind the butte. I edged carefully through the darkness, following the sound of Frankie's soft panting and the faint shimmer of his coat, back to the cabin.

When we got inside—Frankie politely stepping aside and allowing me in first—I struck a match to light the lamp on the table. It was not brilliant, but it emitted a buttery glow that was enough to read by.

Frankie went straight to his dog bed, where his blue rubber bone lay. He plopped down beside it and emitted one of the most expressive articulations in dog-speak, a long sigh, which translates simply as *"Finally."*

4. Not a Person of Interest

Every battle makes me wish more and more that the war was over.

—Robert Gould Shaw,
letter to his father (Sept. 21, 1862)

The columns were clean photocopies of newsprint. Rather than just print them out from the electronic archive, she had bothered to retrieve the actual newspapers from storage, cut out the columns, paste each one onto a sheet of paper, and neatly mark the date to the side. She then had photocopied those pages.

I shuffled through them and saw they were in chronological order. In the first one the header showed me clean-shaven, with poufy hair. It was dated September 1985, the era of poufiness.

What the hell. I started to read.

We go along from one moment to the next, and one day to the next, because really, that's all the choice we have in the matter. But every once in a while something comes along and just grabs you in this assaultive way and makes you stop.

Something happened a few days ago at Whitman Elementary in Mrs. Simmons' second-grade classroom that grabbed me. It has not let go since.

Piecing together some information from Mrs. Simmons, the dispassionate police report and the impassioned report of my son, who is a student in that classroom, I have learned this is what happened:

The school's annual open house was held on Friday, and the public had been welcomed to visit and view the students' handiwork, so the classrooms were open.

I was there. I viewed the students' Crayola'd self-portraits hung up on corkboard. I said hello to Mrs. Simmons, and we chatted briefly about Jay. Based on early impressions he is categorized as a good student with a lot of potential (a description that is shared, I'm pretty sure, by nearly every other student at Whitman) but somewhat prone to being distracted. (Not unlike his old man, poor kid.)

But on the whole he's shown himself to be a good boy, and a good citizen of the second grade. For example, he volunteered to help monitor and maintain the classroom terrarium. A terrarium, as I understand it, is a learning device designed to illustrate the ways of the natural world, i.e., that living things tend to sleep, move about occasionally—if they are biologically so enabled and inclined—and seek to fulfill an unending urge to eat other things (often living) for sustenance. (That's most of how the world goes. For second-graders, anyway, that is enough knowledge for this stage of their lives.)

I had already known about Jay's role, because about two weeks into the school year, he came home and made this announcement: "I take care of the terrium. The terror-ium. The tuh-ROR-rium."

He went on to explain that the terrarium temporarily housed a tortoise, by the name of Horace, on loan to the class from Mrs. Simmons' brother. It was important to note he was on loan, Jay cautioned, because tortoises should not be confined for extended periods. Horace, age 25, required clean water every day, and it was Jay's job to see to it. He had done so faithfully, up to the time of the open house.

Perhaps you anticipate the rest; maybe you read about it. Briefly: Three teenagers are accused of having hidden in the school on the night of the open house, sometime before the evening ended. After all the visitors had left, and the rooms closed for the night, they emerged and vandalized Mrs. Simmons' classroom.

The damage they inflicted was as unimaginative as you might expect. They left obscenities and crude drawings scrawled on the white board...feces on the desk of Mrs. Simmons...the Crayola'd autobiographies in tatters on the floor...and poor Horace, plucked from the terrarium and dead on the floor

They had shattered his shell with some heavy object.

I found out about all this the next evening when I got home from work. Jay was both distraught and indignant.

"Horace is DEAD!" he spluttered as soon as I was in the door.

"Oh, no. What happened to him?"

"They KILLED him. Those bastards!"

I had never heard him use the word before. But I suppose that is the whole concept of school. Kids learn new vocabulary there.

We talked over what had happened at length. I tried to make him understand that whoever would do such a thing was actually a person to be pitied. He had a sickness in his brain. Of course, the sickness did not justify or excuse the act, not one tiny bit. But it was very unusual for someone to act this way, and he did it because there was something wrong with him.

Now, it was up to the school authorities and the police to find the person. Maybe they would punish him; but we would hope they also would find a way to help fix his sickness.

"I hope they find him so they punish him," Jay said.

OK. For now Jay is stuck at Point A, "find and punish." Maybe it will occur to him later that it would be good if whoever did this would, Point B, be cured of their sickness, too. Or, maybe he didn't really buy into the idea that they are really sick. Maybe they are just bastards. Evil bastards, that's all.

As the adult in this scenario, I have to place my faith and support in Point B. For now, though, I find myself, like a 5-year-old child, dwelling on Point A.

And that is where I have stopped.

I shuffled that page to the back, and started reading the next one. The date was almost 10 years later: April 14, 1995.

Many readers of this paper—let's just say many people, period—would find it unremarkable that I've been characterized as "not a person of interest." To this I am resigned. However, to have to read it with one's own eyes, in one's own newspaper… well, that's different.

The official declaration can be found in a news story that appears elsewhere on this page. The story is headlined, *Columnist / interviewed / in slaying*. Here's the gist: I was interviewed by detectives of the sheriff's department yesterday. A security camera at an east San Jose convenience store revealed that my car was in the parking lot at the same time that slaying victim Jack McMahon was inside. This was just two hours before he was killed on Feb. 28.

The police detective in the news story, Robert Causey, responded to a reporter's question by saying (and Mother, please avert your eyes), "We interviewed Mr. Rossiter, but he is certainly not a suspect in this case. He is not a person of interest."

It may be relevant to note here that I've interacted professionally with Causey in the past, which actually sort of adds to the hurt. Nothing against him, of course. He's just speaking in the law enforcement lexicon familiar to him. That's what I'm telling myself, anyway.

So, given the consensus about my uninteresting-ness, why am I bothering? As it turns out, there was much excitement in the news meetings of the day yesterday, as the Herald's Brain Trust earnestly mulled whether my cop-shop session should be conveyed in a news story, this column, or both.

In the end they decided on both. I would be encouraged to "address the issue head-on" (a task you'll notice I have successfully evaded up to this point).

"It's a great chance to give people some insight into the criminal justice process," said Ed-the-editor, with the sort of feigned conviction that has elicited promotions in newsrooms all across America, and, in earlier days, fraggings of lieutenants in Vietnam. "You can give an inside glimpse of how it works."

No, I can't. After a 15-minute discussion, during which I was twice offered a Coke, and one of the officers was interrupted with a call from his daughter, who'd locked her keys in her car, I must reveal that I still don't know how it works.

In summary, the entire experience was pretty boring. But I am getting paid to write more, so here goes:

I was contacted by phone on Tuesday by Causey, who told me about the video. He set up an appointment to interview me, at the place of my choosing. I chose his office.

I arrived early, and from my seat off to the side, spent the next half hour watching a succession of entrances and exits by glum, bedraggled or aggrieved visitors. Remarkably, the woman who dealt with all this behind the counter maintained the same cool demeanor throughout.

When Causey came to escort me within, I was almost reluctant to leave. He noticed this, and assured me genially that I could come back any time to observe. "It's more or less the same routine every day," he said.

We were joined in his office by a second detective. They showed me a frame from the video of the parking lot, and I verified it was my car. Then came a series of frames showing McMahon, both outside and inside the store. The ensuing conversation, according to my recollection, went like this:

Detective: "Do you remember seeing Jack McMahon at the station?"
Me: "Yes."
Detective: "Really?"
Me: "Yes."
Detective: "Well, do you remember what was he doing?"
Me: "Yes. He bought some stuff, then he came out and smoked a cigarette."

Detective: "Did you see him interact with anyone? Talk to anybody?"

Me: "Wouldn't that show up on the surveillance video?"

Detective: "Probably, but we're just looking to corroborate."

Me: "No. I don't recall his talking to anyone.

Detective: "I noticed you never did get out of your car."

Me: "Nope, I didn't."

Detective: "Why not?"

Me: "I didn't need anything in there."

Detective (pause): "I know how that goes. Been there, done that...And then, it looks like you left right after he did?

Me: "Yeah. As I said: I didn't need anything there."

The two of them nodded, knowingly and reassuringly. They asked one more time: Was there anything I could remember, anything that I saw, anything that seemed noteworthy? I thought for several seconds (because I could tell they really wanted me to) before I answered: No. I could not recall anything noteworthy about it.

The two cops escorted me out, thanked me sincerely, apologized for the inconvenience, and said goodbye. And that was it. Sorry, folks. Sorry, Ed.

As the news story relates, the police have little information about McMahon's death. I've heard some sentiments that, given his sordid past, it's just as well. But I think we all have to concede that his death, and everything that preceded it, make for a sad and disturbing story. The case presents an interesting quandary, in that Mr. McMahon—who would never have been mistaken for a model citizen—should be entitled under the law and by virtue of our better natures to a full and earnest investigation of his death.

I mentioned something to that effect to the officers as I departed. Although they seemed to agree, I thought they were perhaps humoring me, and may have felt what I had to say was neither profound nor insightful.

Which, let's face it, is exactly what you'd expect when dealing with a person who is not of interest.

The third column was dated three weeks later.

This day always loomed in my mind's eye, the day I would have to announce that I can no longer write. That I'm done.

That it's over.

"Loomed" seems like a good word (although I now am

at the point where I no longer really trust my judgment about what is or is not a good word. I'm just sort of tooling along now, blithely and numbly, leaving it all up to fate and happenstance, like a drunk driver). But when I think of something looming, I envision a block-like and stolid mass, vaguely menacing. Something one sees out of the corner of the eye. Something that causes one to avert one's eyes, actually.

I have been averting my eyes for some time now, until ultimately I faced the looming mass, and written upon it, in large words, was: "You can no longer do this."

I'm sure the question will arise among you (you people who have been so kind and generous to read these columns, and I sincerely thank you for having done so) as to whether this is somehow connected to an incident from my recent past. The answer is no. At least, I don't think so. But that's just it. I am thinking right now along the lines of, "Nothing is connected to anything."

And that, my friends, is the problem. When nothing is connected to anything, you can't write anymore. All the words that once connected themselves into sentences now seem to just slip randomly through my fingers.

Or, put it another way: I look back at all the words I have written, and they are like the product of a child's sparkler on the Fourth of July. Waved recklessly around in the darkness, they fizzed into life for just an instant...and then immediately became nothing.

Ladies and gentlemen, through all these years and all these columns, each time I dutifully wrote enough to fill the allotted space. One column, on today's shrunken news page, equals about 900 words.

I'm sorry. I don't have that many words anymore. I can muster only this meager amount. They will have to fill the vacant space below with something else, e.g.: It's going to rain. A lady took fertility drugs and had triplets. Someone lost a heroic battle with cancer. A dog that got lost on a family camping trip found its way home one year later.

Any of that would be better than this, huh?

Goodbye and thank you.

Editor's note: Doug Rossiter has resigned from the Herald to pursue new interests.

I laughed out loud. I'd forgotten about that last line they'd tacked on regarding my new interests. In his sleep, Frankie raised one ear, and groaned.

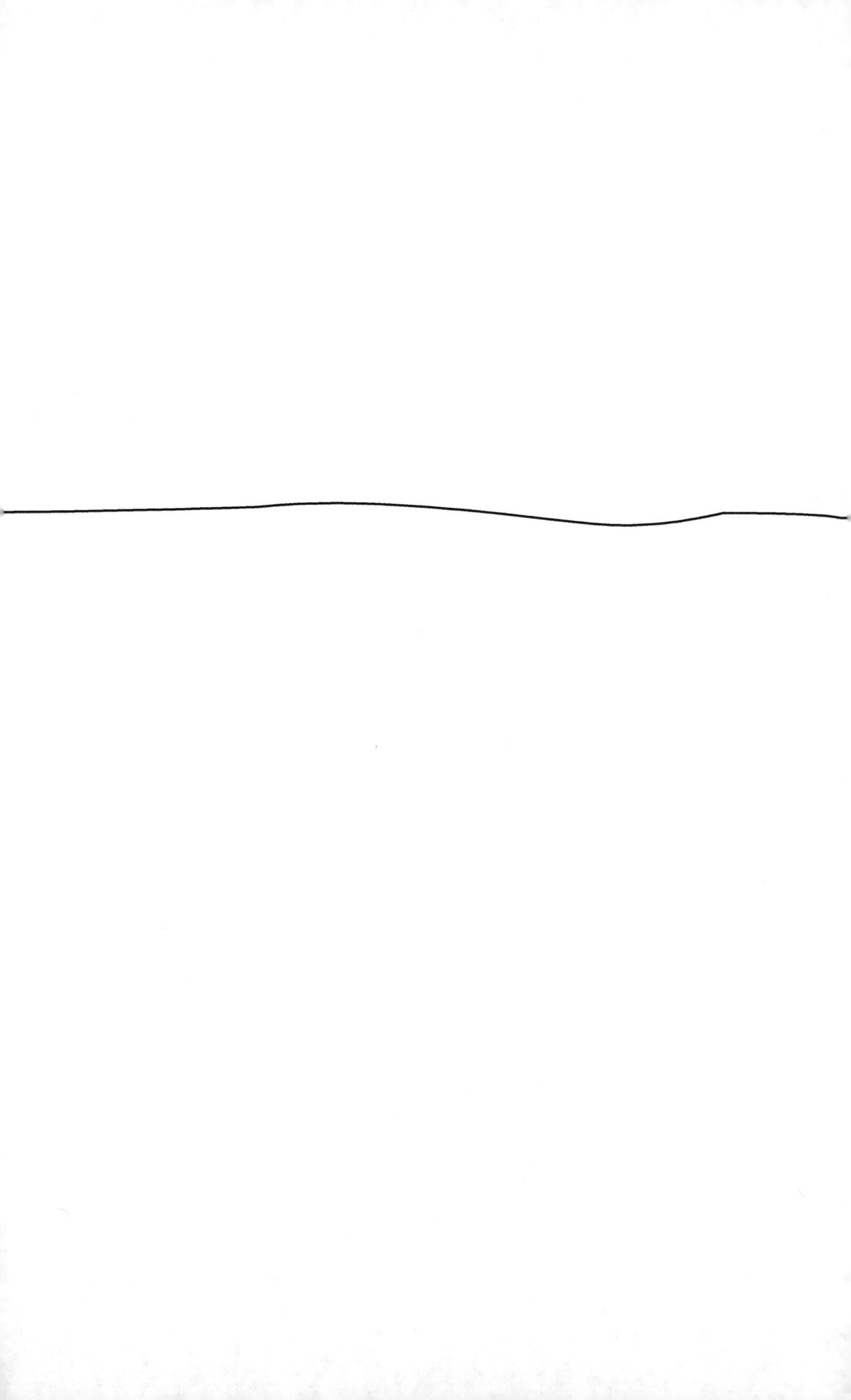

Jacky McMahon

September 1985

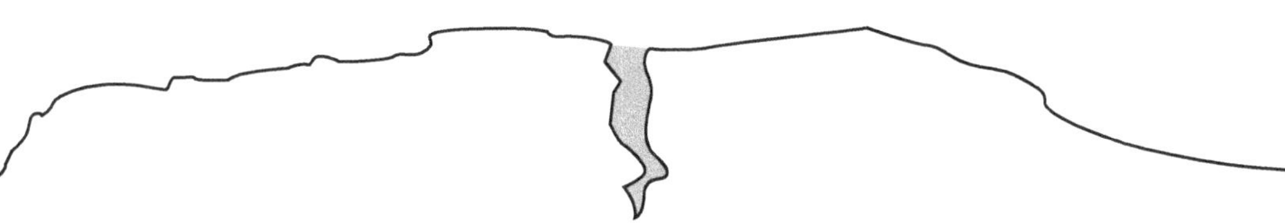

For all of his errancy and outright bumbling, it must be conceded that Rossiter possessed, within a limited arena, a certain knack. Thus, he was able to extract the name of the kid from Mrs. Simmons herself. Class had been dismissed about 20 minutes earlier, but a few students still lingered, discussing what twigs and bark should go into the new terrarium. It would house a chameleon. Mrs. Simmons was arranging a stack of papers into three sections, vigorously tapping each section into symmetry.

"I understand they made an arrest," Rossiter said.

"Yes. Big surprise. I had both Jacky McMahon and his brother in the third grade. They were the worst kids I ever had. The worst."

"Oh, yeah, Jacky McMahon. I think I may know him. Kind of a tall skinny red-haired kid?"

Mrs. Simmons was unwary, or maybe just distracted. "Jacky McMahon?"

"Right…Jacky."

"I haven't seen him in six or seven years, so I don't know if he's tall and skinny, but he's certainly not red-haired unless he's dyed it. He was as blond as you could be."

"Oh. I must be thinking of someone else."

She finally extracted one sheet of paper with math and reading assignments detailed in neat printing, and handed him that along with two books. "When he's ready. No rush. I know he'll catch up in no time when he's ready."

He took the paper and books.

"Why don't you take some books from the table in the back, too? Time goes by so slowly in the hospital. Take *Make Way for Ducklings*. He's way past it, skill-wise, but he loves it anyway."

"Sure…when he's ready."

"You could read it to him."

"Yes, I will."

"Will you give him a kiss for me?"

"Uh…of course."

He went to the back of the room, and blindly grabbed a few thin books from a stack. As soon as he got back to the office, he called the DA's office for Blasingame, who worked a lot of juvenile cases. Blasingame extracted an assurance from him that no, of course it was not for publication, then provided a few details. McMahon was only 17, but he'd been arrested several times already. Blasingame remembered one case in which he'd started a fire and burned down a shed, and another when he shot several cats and dogs in the neighborhood. First he was using a BB gun, then a bow and arrow. Rossiter vaguely remembered that a story about this had run in the Herald. There had been a photo of a big white cat, crippled by an arrow still sticking out of its hip.

The cops knew it was McMahon who vandalized the classroom because he had dropped a wadded-up piece of paper in the wastebasket by Mrs. Simmons' desk. It was a clumsily altered prescription made out to McMahon's mother, on which he had tried to change "Elavil" to "codeine."

Within a few hours after arresting McMahon, the cops picked up his two accomplices—both 13, both former students at Whitman, neither with a prior arrest. All three were being charged with trespassing, malicious destruction of property and animal cruelty.

When Rossiter got back to the office, he checked the files and public records, and found McMahon's address, but nothing specifically on the kid. He dug out the files on the cat attacks. It was from three years back. The unnamed suspect had been finally caught in the act by some guy in the neighborhood, who held him until the cops came. He was convicted of cruelty to animals and a couple of lesser charges and sent off to juvy. No other information.

On an afternoon two weeks later, when he was lying on the bed in the guest room, Rossiter heard the phone ring. It rang for a long time; when it stopped he could make out Jen's faint voice. A few seconds later she knocked on the door.

"Are you here?" she asked.

He put his hand over his eyes. Was she really asking him that question?

She knocked again. "Ross. Phone for you."

"Who is it?"

"Some attorney."

"Who?"

"I don't know who. Somebody Binghamton."

He got up, lumbered wordlessly past her at the door, and went to the phone in the master bedroom.

"I'm really sorry about your son," Blasingame said.

"Thanks. I appreciate it. How did you get my home number?"

"Your editor. How are you doing?"

"Me?"

"Yeah. How are you?"

"I'm OK. What's going on?"

"I just wanted to tell you that Jack McMahon's out. Released to custody of his mother."

"When's the hearing?"

"I don't think a date has been set yet."

"Good. Thanks for letting me know."

"Sure. Hey, let me know if there's anything I can do."

"Can't think of anything, but thanks."

He went to the closet and randomly removed a shirt. Jen came in and went to a chair by the window. She picked up a book lying on the cushion and sat, placing it unopened on her lap.

"Going out?"

He was fumbling with the buttons. "Hmm? Oh...yeah." The collar was askew; he had inserted a collar button into the top hole of the placket.

"With your shirt like that?"

"I don't care."

She opened up the book and opened it. "OK. Bye, then."

"Yeah, bye."

The house was in a postwar tract in east San Jose off of White Road. Many of the houses did not have visible numbers, but he found the place with no trouble. There was an incongruously large palm tree in the tiny front yard, and the house number had been spray-painted in white on the trunk. He parked across the street, mulling over whether to go to the door. There was nobody around. The only person in view was about five houses down, at the corner—a little girl standing by the street sign, drinking from a green can of soda. She was a skinny little thing, very blonde, wearing shorts and flip-flops.

He assessed the house. It needed paint. The weeds needed to be mowed. There was a waist-high chain link fence around the front; the partly open gate appeared to lack a hinge. Still, the house was not much different from the others on the block, aside from the palm tree with the spray-painted numbers.

A motion down the street caught his eye. The little girl was scurrying back in Rossiter's direction. She abruptly stopped two houses down and dodged behind a car parked on the front lawn. From his vantage, he could see just her ankles.

A school bus stopped at the corner, and one kid got off. He had long blond hair that covered most of his face. Baggy jeans, untucked flannel shirt. He came around toward the back of the bus and started moving in a slow shuffle toward Rossiter.

As the kid passed the house with the car on the lawn, Rossiter could see the two girl's ankles shifting back and forth. The top of her head came briefly into view, and she peeked through the windows.

50

The kid got as far as the house with the palm tree, and kicked the gate further open. Rossiter could not get a clear view of his face.

The little girl came out from behind the car, and started to run, as much as the flip-flops would allow, in the opposite direction, still carrying her soda. She got almost to the sidewalk when a sudden bang came from the house. The kid came crashing out the front door. "Bran-day!" he yelled. "Bran-DAY!"

He was on her within seconds. She squealed. He took a fistful of her hair and began to drag her back. She was bawling. When he got to the sidewalk, he wrenched the can from her hand. He was saying something but Rossiter couldn't make it out. And she kept saying, between wails, "I didn't!" He raised the can and poured its remnants on the top of her head. There was still quite a bit left.

Rossiter honked his horn, started his car and quickly pulled out. Both of them gawked at him. The kid still had her by the hair.

He pulled up to within a few feet and rolled his window all the way down. "Hey, what the hell. Take it easy."

"She's my sister. Who the fuck are you." He tightened his grip on her hair; she gasped.

Rossiter stared at him. A scar curved along his left eye.

"I didn't touch no Atari!" Her hair was as blonde as his. She was maybe seven or eight years old.

"Fuck you didn't."

"C'mon, let her go," Rossiter said.

"Fuck you."

Rossiter pulled up so close that he could reach out the window and grab him if he wanted to. "Let her go. Jacky."

McMahon met his gaze for a moment before he pushed her to the ground. She yelped as she braced with outstretched hands. "Fucker!" She barely touched the asphalt before she sprang up and ran to the passenger side of the car. "Fuck you!" she said. "Stupid!"

McMahon gave her the finger, and did the same to Rossiter. "Who're you. MacGyver? Button your shirt, why don't you." He dropped the soda can—it was Mountain Dew— and headed back toward the house.

The girl was still standing at the passenger window, staring wide-eyed at Rossiter, breathing through her mouth, her face wet.

Rossiter leaned over to roll down the passenger window. "Are you all right?"

"Uh-huh."

"Where's your mom?"

She shrugged.

"Can you go somewhere else right now?"

She started to open his car door.

"No, sweetheart, I don't mean with me. Can you go to one of the neighbor's houses?"

She turned her gaze to her own house. McMahon had stopped near the gate. The girl pushed the car door closed, but not hard enough to shut it all the way. Dutifully, she pulled it back open, and with two hands pushed it shut. Her eyes were pale blue-gray.

"I'll wait here," he said.

She didn't move.

"OK?"

After a few more seconds she backed up two steps; then she trotted off in the same direction she'd been heading when McMahon chased her down, toward a house at the end of the block. She went to the door and let herself in. Rossiter slowly drove down the street, looking in his rearview mirror. McMahon stood motionless at the gate.

5. Street to the Sky

*A good deal of cheap wit has been expended upon a
fanciful story that I published an order or wrote a letter
or made a remark that my 'headquarters would be in the
saddle.'*

—Major-General John Pope, *The Century
Magazine*, Vol. XXXI (1886)

I awoke early, well before dawn. The mornings were getting cooler. I didn't feel it below my neck, under the down sleeping bag, but my nose and cheeks were a bit numb.

Outside the sky was clear, and a good hard frost scrunched under my shoes. There was the sound of that, and Frankie sniffing and panting. An early gasp of light was just enough to disclose the hulking presence of the RV, sitting there in cold silence.

They probably were still conked out, but I went the extra few yards to the outhouse, instead of pissing wherever. Company means you use the facilities, even if you're not in anyone's line of sight. "See? I'm not crazy yet," I whispered to Frankie.

When I got back, I started a fire in the old cast iron stove, and mulled over whether to put on a fresh shirt and jeans. It would be a while before the room heated up, so the prospect of changing clothes was not appealing. Anyway, I hadn't done anything more strenuous in the past couple of days than take my usual walk up to the top of the butte. Still. People of the civilized world might think differently about such matters.

"But on the third hand, or in your case, paw...Wouldn't it make more sense to change *after* the shower? Life when you deal with these people is very complicated, buddy."

Nevertheless. I pulled on the fresh clothes.

About a half-hour after sunrise, as I was stirring a pot of oatmeal, Frankie told me someone was approaching. This was followed by a knock, quick and emphatic. It was Thao, stamping her feet, her arms folded. In addition to the white ski jacket, she was wearing a red wool hat. "Brr! It is so cold!"

I gestured toward the stove. She bustled over and held her arms above it, like a diver at the lip of the pool. "I wasn't sure I had the right address."

"Eh?"

"The numbers you have tacked up on your front door. Is that a joke? 1231 what?"

"What?"

"Twelve-thirty-one what street?"

"Oh. Street to the Sky. It's an old Indian name."

"You actually have an address here?"

"How else will Dick Clark find me when I win the Publishers Clearing House Sweepstakes?"

"Good point. Whoo. This stove is warm. Oatmeal, huh?" She removed her jacket and hat and placed them on a chair at my little table. The act seemed to free a subtle perfume. I thought it might be my imagination, but then I noticed Frankie, immobile and trance-like except for his twitching nostrils. Her hair was tied back in a ponytail. She was wearing a white sweatshirt emblazoned with the letters UCSC, and a pair of sweatpants. I had never seen sweatpants like these; instead of being baggy, they declared the shape underneath them.

"Jesus."

"What?"

"The oatmeal. I need to cover it and get it off the stove. Duane not up yet?"

"Yes, he's going to cook up some breakfast for us in the RV. Speaking of which, bad news. The shower is not working."

"Uh-oh. Maybe a line froze." I poured coffee into my least chipped blue-and-white Currier-and-Ives-design cup and presented it to her. "Sorry, I don't have cream or sugar."

"Thanks. What a lovely cup. That's what I said, the line froze, but Duane said he didn't think so because there's water running to the sinks." She took a hesitant sip. Her lipstick left a vague pink mark. "Gosh, that's really strong coffee, isn't it?"

"Oh...it is? Would you like tea instead? I think I have some somewhere..."

"No, it's fine. We have coffee in the RV, anyway."

"Ah. Well, when it gets a little lighter we can take a look at the water situation. Anyway, I don't need to take a shower in your RV. I'm kind of embarrassed that I asked."

"Embarrassed? Why? It's a small matter. I'm just sorry we can't accommodate you."

"It's really no problem. I do bathe otherwise."

"Yes, you mentioned that. You actually are a bit sleeker than we'd expected. Your hair is so short. You shave it, huh?" She surveyed the room. "Your house is nice and clean, too."

"It's easy to keep things neat when you have so few."

"Just one room. Not quite as spacious as your house in San Jose, is it?"

"You've seen my place in San Jose? I guess you looked me up on the tax rolls."

"Oh, I just drove by one day on my way somewhere. It's nicely kept up. I assume by the renters."

"Good to know."

"…And oh my. You have a lot of dog food. And beans. Are those cans all beans?"

"Every one. It's the breakfast, lunch and dinner of champions."

"Doesn't seem like the healthiest diet."

"Yeah. But when you mix the beans and the dog food, it's a nutritionally complete meal. *And* it's delicious."

She pursed her lips. I wasn't sure if she was smiling, or suppressing a smile, or frowning.

"I don't really eat the dog food," I said.

"That was my presumption."

"Or if I did, it was only by accident.…OK. I didn't really."

"I thought not. You seem to be keeping up your civility."

"I do my best with civility. Also, civilized behavior. Not to parse that too much. And diminish your compliment, which was entirely well-meaning."

"Hmm... I don't think I know what you're talking about." She brought the cup back to her lips, in just the same spot as before. "Do you?"

"I'm about 90 percent certain you don't know what I'm talking about."

She again pursed her lips although not quite in the same way as before.

"Whoops," I said. "That was ruder yet, wasn't it? Not quite sure what's wrong with me, other than..." I gestured to indicate the four walls. "Like I said: I'm really not fit for company. As you can see. I live an isolated life." I pulled out the chair. "Wouldn't you like to sit down? We should talk a bit. I read over the columns last night."

She sat and crossed her legs. Her feet, in neatly tied red sneakers, were tiny. I could have fit one in my palm.

"They were really interesting," she said. "You were really upset when the turtle died, huh?"

"Tortoise. Horace the Tortoise."

"Right."

"So, tell me: What are you up to?"

"Pardon?"

"What are you up to?"

"I heard you, I just don't understand the question."

"You've been at the Herald how long...maybe a year? You must've come along not long after I left, right? What about Duane? He's relatively new, too? Did he come with you?"

"We started at about the same time, but we didn't know each other before."

I pointed to the folder sitting on the table. "How is it that you chose these particular columns when you decided to come looking for me? And no bullshit about they're all written in first person."

"Did that sound like bullshit? I'm sorry. We weren't quite sure how to approach you, or what to say. Ed said that you might not be all that inclined to be cooperative. I didn't want to put you off, is all."

"I'm not put off. I just want to know what you're doing."

"OK, that's fair. Full disclosure. You're something of a legend in the newsroom. People thought highly of you. And then, how you left and all. Mystery Man. So I did a little research on you."

"Full disclosure, how much research? Aside from digging up my property records."

"Oh, whatever I could find in the library. So I know...." She uncrossed her legs, and sat forward at the edge of the chair. She lowered her voice. "...I know the basics. Your son and all."

"I suppose his obit was in my file?"

"I'm sorry, I didn't mean to—"

I waved my hand, as if, magician-like, I could make the matter disappear. "Don't worry about it. Look, don't tell me you came all the way up here to do a story about me."

She walked back to the stove. "It's a little weird to sit when you are standing. It makes me feel like I'm being cross-examined." She held her hands out again.

"Are your hands still cold?"

She pulled them back. "No."

"Are you here to do some other story, too?"

"Why, is there some other story, too?"

She smiled. It was the same smile she had worn the day before when she first walked up to me. I stared at her until the smile faded.

"Lady, no offense, but you're in my house, and your RV is parked out there on my property, so enough with the fucking coyness for just a minute, all right?"

Frankie jumped up from his bed and trotted to my side. "It's OK, buddy," I said.

Her eyes went from Frankie to me. "Fine," she said. "This is why we're here: We're doing a story on dying towns of the West." That clipped tone again. "Ed told me about you, that you know the country up here, and you might help us. I did some research on you and I thought it would be interesting to find out more about you, too. As I told you, Ed told us to tread lightly and feel you out. And why those columns? They do provide some insight into your life and character, wouldn't you say?"

"Frankie. Go lie down." Frankie padded slowly back to his bed. "Here are two pretty straightforward questions. Let's see if you can give me straight answers. Want to try?"

"Yes."

"One: Did you used to be a cops reporter?"

Brief pause. "Yes. At a weekly."

"Which one?"

"The Alum Rock Journal. In East San Jose."

"I know where it is. Courts, too?

"Sure. If you do cops at a weekly, you do courts."

"OK. And two, does Ed know what you're really doing here?"

"I'm honestly not sure what you mean."

"Did he assign you to come up here to do a story about drying-up towns in the West, and nothing else?"

"We agreed that if there are other stories we come across, we can take those on as well. As you said, it's expected on a trip like this."

"Did he know what else you thought you might bump into?"

"No."

"Well. OK, then."

"'OK'? Really?"

"I said, 'OK.'"

"And that's it? You're satisfied?"

"Do I appear to you to be someone who's satisfied?"

She laughed. "No. Are you still coming with us?"

"Sure. Why wouldn't I?"

"Based on the conversation we just had in the last two minutes, I'd say you are having doubts."

"When you stop having doubts, you are dead. Until that time, I can manage a few doubts."

"Don't get me wrong, I'm thrilled you're coming. I'm just wondering why."

"It's like I said. I want you to do this story. And I want to see the battlefield again. That's part of it."

"What's the rest?"

"Let's just let that unfold, shall we?"

"Sure. I'll be honest with you. You intrigue me."

"Oddly, I find that flattering."

"Why is that odd?" After waiting just long enough to determine I wasn't going to respond, she began to survey the room again. "Bookcase. Nice. And the sink—you pump water right in the sink. From the ground? Interesting." Her gaze stopped at the C.M. Russell calendar and clock above the sink. "You check off the days. Like a prisoner? And your clock is wrong. Also weird. Anyway. I guess we should go see how Duane's doing with breakfast."

"Oh, thanks, but...."

"Come on, join us. He's making enough for three. It's nothing special. Not beans or anything. Bring your oatmeal if you'd rather."

I handed her the white ski jacket. "I have some of the local honey, too. Pretty good cook, Duane is?"

"I have no idea. We're about to find out."

The interior of the RV smelled overpoweringly of bacon. Duane, standing at the stove, spoke over his shoulder. "Morning. Excellent timing."

"I know!" Thao said. "Duane, Mr. Rossiter brought oatmeal and the local honey."

"Sounds good." He motioned at the stove. "You can keep it warm here."

"Mr. Rossiter, do you want to try some of our coffee?

"'Mr. Rossiter.' That sounds strange to me."

"How about we call you 'Ross,' like Ed did," Thao said.

"I guess, if that works for you." I took my blackened pot to the stove and set it gingerly onto the adjoining counter. "This oatmeal is probably too cold for you to eat now. But you could use it for…well, for instance you could use it to glue stamps onto an envelope, if you didn't want to lick them. Or possibly for self-defense. If you needed to blind someone, you could hurl it in their eyes. Anyway, this honey is still good. You just scoop it out with a spoon."

"I'm not really anticipating the need to blind anyone today, but thank you. Why don't you have some bacon and eggs with us? Duane made some for you. Save your oatmeal for when you do your mail."

"Thanks. I'm not much in the way of eating meat. It sure smells great, though. You came well supplied."

"We picked up a few things when we got the fruit basket."

The oatmeal was bland but actually still warm enough to mix with the honey. I dawdled with it as they made it through their elaborate meal, which was complemented by ketchup and tabasco, toast, and huckleberry preserves they'd bought in Great Falls. They declined my honey. "I never saw honey that you scoop out with a spoon," Thao said. "It looks good, though."

She ate my share of the bacon and eggs. Each time she added food to her plate, or a condiment to the food, she'd proclaim its deliciousness with, "Mm!"

"Where do you put all that?" I asked. "You can't weigh a hundred pounds."

"I know, I'm eating like a pig. Something up here, the air or something, makes me so hungry."

As they finished, and I drank coffee, they laid out the plans for the day. First, back to the Great Falls RV rental to resolve the water issue. Thao seemed certain this would be a quick, straightforward process. Since it was about two-and-a-half hours from Great Falls to the Bear Paw Battlefield, there would be plenty of time to get there by evening. She offered assurances that it was fine for Frankie to come with us.

"No," I said, "it's too complicated. There's an animal-rescue lady in Vaughn who took in his siblings. She told me she'd dog-sit him any time. If I can borrow your cell phone I'll try calling her."

"You're welcome to try, but I haven't been able to get a signal out here."

"Ah. I'll just call when we get to Simms, then."

"We have some time, right?" Duane asked. "This is a good time to make some pictures around here. I'm starting to see some possibilities in that mountain."

We stepped out of the RV to see the butte still glowing in the dawn light. Duane clicked off some shots. "Striking," he pronounced. "When you really look at it. I think I'd like to gain some altitude."

"You mean, climb the butte?"

"Not necessarily all the way. That would take a while, wouldn't it?"

"It would only take you maybe 20 minutes to reach the top. Depends on how fast you go. It's a steady climb, but not too steep. Once you reach the top, you could walk around for hours. It's very flat. And the views are quite striking."

"Aren't there snakes?" Thao asked.

"Not this time of year. But in the summer, I wouldn't go up there without a pistol. There are rattlesnakes up there as thick as my forearm."

"Ooh."

"I doubt that," Duane said.

"OK. At least as thick as your neck, though."

Thao made an appraising glance at his neck. "Really?"

"Yep. That would be about a Number 2 pencil. Duane is built like the Indians who were on the cross-country team at my high school. Also the ones sitting on the sidewalk outside the Mint Saloon in Great Falls."

"What is that supposed to mean?"

Thao quickly placed herself between us. Duane's face was entirely visible above her head.

"Oh, no offense, none at all," I said. "Merely an observation. Anyway, no snakes up there now, but I hope you have hiking boots, because there's cactus up there year-round."

"We came prepared for anything," she said. "I want to go up, too."

"Sure. But listen, honestly, be careful up there. It's generally a nice safe hike, but watch where you're going. There are a couple of places where it opens up into deep ravines, with really rough thickets and rocks below."

"Of course, we'll be careful."

"I'm serious. If you fell into one of those ravines, no one would find you in a million years."

Duane snorted. "Hey, Thao, maybe if you fall in, you'd come out in Vietnam."

I guessed this was supposed to be funny, but he still seemed miffed. I thought it odd that he was directing his miff at Thao instead of me. But she merely uttered a dismissive "Pff" to him, then said to me, "Directions, please?"

"You'll find a deer trail about a hundred feet to the west of here." Thao looked to the east, almost directly at the rising sun. I lightly grasped her shoulders and turned her around. "That way. You follow it to a rock outcropping almost all the way to the top. You'll know it because there's a pine tree growing out of a crack in the rock. As in, straight out of the rock. You can't miss it. The trail branches at that spot. You will be facing the same way you are now. Take the trail that switches back, to the north—in other words, to the right. It's just a little ways to the top. The other one kind of skirts the top and winds back down, so you don't want that one."

"So…not that one, Duane. Are you following this?"

"You can't get lost," I said. "You can see my shack the whole way up. Just take the trail to the rock with the tree, and go right."

After they headed back to the RV, I returned to the shack to throw some clothes and travel stuff into a bag, and picked out a crumpled card from my wallet. Maysie Puppy Farm. I held it out for Frankie to examine.

"You'll play with the other dogs. It'll be fun, buddy." I noticed movement outside my small single window. Thao and Duane were starting their trudge up the sketchy trail. She had changed into jeans. She was in the lead, talking, pointing at something on the ground.

I passed the time just sitting on the floor next to Frankie. He knew something was up, and studied my face to try to understand what, but after 10 minutes the stillness overcame his canine will, and he dozed off. They were gone maybe an hour. Frankie surfaced from his sleep to announce they were coming back. I checked the pot of water on the stove—still warm—cranked some fresh water out of the pump and splashed it on my face. I opened the door to see them trudging the same way as before, with Thao in the lead, still talking, though I could not make out the words. They'd both taken off their jackets and tied the sleeves around their waists. Somewhere on the trip she had donned sunglasses with oversized lenses, and a baseball cap.

"Hey, you made it. Welcome back."

"Whoo. Nice hike. What views!"

"Glad you enjoyed it. C'mon in."

They halted in unison, standing maybe twenty feet away. Duane had his camera cupped in his left hand. "Can I get a shot of you there at the door?"

"Well...OK. Sure. A heroic pose, or...?"

"It's OK to just stand there."

Thao grinned broadly. "Cheese!"

Her face was just teeth and oversized sunglasses. I thought, *insect.*

"I normally don't."

"This will work," Duane said. He quickly squeezed off six or seven shots.

"You don't smile?" Thao asked. "Really?"

"I don't remember. I'm sure there are times when I have. Do you want to get out of the wind? We're pretty much ready to go here, whenever you are."

The fire was dead, but they undid their jackets anyway. "You weren't kidding about the views out here," Duane said. "The wind really clears the sky, doesn't it? You can see forever."

"Past forever," Thao said. "And everything is so vivid. The mountains, the clouds. It almost looks artificial. Like a cartoon."

"An interesting perspective," I said. "We've come to the point where we associate vividness with artificiality."

"It's like getting eyeglasses for the first time. All of a sudden, the world is clear. Huh, Duane? The vistas are so intense, it almost hurts your eyes. And there's kind of a smell in the air…what is it? I can't describe it."

"The grass, probably. Trees. Dirt."

"Hm."

Duane was reviewing the room. "Spartan." His tone conveyed approval.

"Oh, this stuff? I got it on sale at Bed, Bath and Beyond."

He studied the clock. "Dang, is it really half-past-noon? Is that Mountain Time?" He checked his wristwatch. "Dude, your clock is way off."

"It doesn't work."

Thao was facing me, her sunglasses still on. "You don't really need a clock out here, do you?"

"Sure. Every house needs a clock. To tell you time. Speaking of which, shall we get going?"

"Yeah, we should go. I want to stop at that cute diner at the fort town. I'm so hungry from that hike."

"Wow. We're starting off on a trip, and we're going to stop to eat after twenty minutes. I'd forgotten what it's like to travel with a woman."

"I know! Isn't it great?"

"I guess we'll see."

When we approached the RV, Thao went to the passenger side. "Everybody ready?" she asked. "OK, we're back on the saddle."

"It's back *in* the saddle," Duane said.

"What? I don't think so. How can you be *in* a saddle?" She answered her own question: "You *can't*. Right, Ross?"

"I know it's a bit counterintuitive, but the idiom is actually 'in.' "

"Uh, I don't think so. That doesn't make any sense, does it? Think about it. *In* a saddle?" She paused, presumably to give us time to mull it over.

"…Okay, then, let's go. Get *on* the car." She awaited our response to this, but I personally was willing to admit defeat, and Duane seemed to have mentally drifted onward. Having thus won her point, she assumed a triumphant pose, hands on hips.

Frankie and I situated ourselves on a bench behind Duane. We drove into the lot at the Fort Shaw diner around noon. The black pickup with the flag decal was there, but not the white one.

I tied Frankie's long leash to the bumper of the RV, near shade, although the day was plenty cool. As I was doing that, I heard someone yell in an angry voice.

Across the road, the guy with the bushy hair was facing us.

"What did he say?" Thao said.

"I think he said to hurry up," Duane said.

"Hurry up and what?" Thao asked.

The guy took a couple of steps forward. "Get moving! Goddamn it!"

"Jeez," Duane said. "Is this guy a nut or what?"

"I don't think he's talking to us," I said.

The door of the restaurant banged behind us. The scrawny kid staggered out, two big bags of ice on each shoulder.

The bushy-haired guy was unimpressed by his load. "Hurry *up!*"

The kid hurried past, muttering as he went, "C'mon. Relax, willya?"

We watched the kid's progress across the street. When he got halfway, the guy pivoted and headed into the garage.

"That was interesting," Thao said.

As we were entering the diner, Disco Dan came out. He had on his white cap. He eyed us briefly, checked out the RV, and headed to his pickup. I laughed out loud.

"What's so funny?"

"It's one thing after another. One, the kid says, 'Relax' to the mean guy. Two, the man in the *white* cap drives the *black* pickup."

Thao, unamused, turned to Peg behind the counter. Peg showed no sign of remembering me from our encounter in the summer, which actually made me feel a little hurt, which if you thought about it was funnier yet. She gestured to the vacant tables. "Anywhere." After we ordered I called the Maysie Puppy Farm. When May answered I heard dogs yapping.

"I'm feeding," she said cheerfully. She proclaimed that she would love to have Frankie. She had just adopted out his brother and littermate, but there were lots of other dogs to play with.

"I'll bring his food," I said.

"Oh, no need. I have plenty."

"He's used to this food. If that works for you."

When I got back to the table, Thao was already well into a hamburger and an order of fries. She finished before Duane and I were halfway through our sandwiches.

"After lunch I should get some shots of the fort," Duane said.

"I've been there, and there's not much to see. No fort left. The Army abandoned it in the 1890s, and it was turned into a boarding school for Indian kids, so they could be taught how to be white. Whiter, anyway. Now there's just a house and some markers.

"OK. I can shoot the markers."

Thao insisted that they would pay for lunch. "The Herald can afford it," she said.

"I do have cash, you know. I have a card, too."

"You won't need either on this trip. You're helping us with our story."

As we walked out the door, all three of us looked across the street. The man and boy were out of sight.

The Fort Shaw markers sat maybe a hundred yards away. We walked along the gravel road with Frankie tugging at his leash, voraciously sniffing at every weed and dirt clump and dog turd along the way. The house was white, wide, with three gables. A front porch had been added at some point. I thought it projected a comfortable, non-military hominess. The marker in front explained that this had been the quarters of the commanding officers of the fort from 1867 to 1891—including, from '72 to '78, John Gibbon, 7th U.S. Infantry.

I pointed to his name. "Not the most illustrious name in the annals of the Indian Wars," I said.

"No? Why not?"

Duane took a photo of the marker.

"He was part of the 1876 campaign against the Sioux and Cheyenne, and he marched a troop of men from here to the Little Bighorn, but he got there a day late. So he ended up just burying Custer's dead. And then, about one year later, he was sent to cut off Chief Joseph's band at the Big Hole River. A couple hundred miles southwest of here."

Thao, while not exactly rapt, was at least listening, so I pressed on.

"Here's the basic story on how it all got started. The Nez Perce had just kicked ass on General Howard's troops in a fight in Idaho, but they knew there was only more trouble to come, so they decided to head to Montana, and eventually Canada. But Gibbon intercepted them at their camp at a place called the Big Hole, and took them completely by surprise in the early morning. Burned some teepees, killed some people in the camp—including women and children, by the way—but somehow, incredibly, he lost the advantage. It just went upside down on the soldiers, and they were completely routed, and Gibbon was flummoxed. The Indians even took their howitzer. They left that night, heading east, through Yellowstone, then north, eventually ending up around Prague, where we're going. And Gibbon and his troops limped back to Fort Shaw."

"But he captured the Indians after that?"

"No, not Gibbon. Other generals. Miles. Howard eventually caught up, too."

"I think I need to get a book about this."

"We can find you one in Great Falls."

Duane had wandered off in the other direction, and now was taking photos of a metal sign, arching over two steel poles maybe 10 feet high, spaced about 12 feet apart. The arch floated above a chunk of granite, which had a metal replica of a basketball sitting on top. The base of all this was a single square of cracked cement, around which lay an assortment of weeds, discarded snack wrappings and cigarette butts. The inscription on the arch read:

1904 World Champions
Fort Shaw Indian School

Etched on the granite were the names of 12 girls who had traveled from Fort Shaw to the 1904 World's Fair in St. Louis.

Thao read the names out loud. "Wirth. Snell. Roberts. Burton….Not very Indian-like."

"Yeah. It was a time when the noblesse oblige thing to do was to try to wipe away all the vestiges of savagery from the Indians…which, as it turned out, included their entire cultural identity and a sense of how and why they belonged in the world, which had been formed over centuries. But never mind about that, I'm sure the girls looked darling in their little basketball dresses. I bet they were quite the attraction. Right, Duane?"

He had stopped shooting. He was reaching up to put his hand on the basketball, palming it Michael Jordan-style. "I don't know anything about it," he said. "But this was a pretty impressive feat. Basketball champions of the world."

"You don't think it might have been staged, sort of? An exhibition of how America in the new century was generous and sporting, even toward the vanquished savages of the Plains? Just speculating."

"You're pretty cynical," Thao said. She read aloud from the plaque. *The boundless spirit of these extraordinary young women lives on in generations of their descendants.* She copied the words down in her notepad. "I wonder if that's true."

"I would suspect that for every day they spent at this industrial school, their spirits were that much less boundless. And I would also suspect that many or most of their descendants became drunks, victims of abuse, jobless, or dead at an early age. Maybe all of the above."

"Hmph."

"I guess they couldn't fit all that on the plaque," I added.

When we got back to the RV, Thao asked Duane to drive. But just as he started to crank the engine, she said, "Wait, I want to go talk to that guy across the street."

Duane's shoulders sagged. "What guy?"

"That guy we saw, that weightlifter or whatever he is. He might have some historical perspective on this area."

"And you can tell that how?"

"I think he's been here for a while."

"And you know that because he has a beard?"

"I have an instinct about these things. As you should know."

She pulled together her pad and pen, opened her door and jumped down. Duane killed the engine. She marched over and tapped on the door. No one answered. She moved to the front window and tried to peer in.

Duane opened his door and leaned his head out. "No one's there! Come on!"

She poked around another 30 seconds or so before she gave up and came back over.

"What did you see?"

"Nothing." She brushed off some unseen dust and pulled on her seatbelt. "There's nothing in there at all. It's completely empty."

Duane started up the RV again and pulled onto the highway.

6. The Disability

Our so-called stealing of this country from them was just a matter of survival. There were great numbers of people who needed new land, and the Indians were selfishly trying to keep it for themselves.

—John Wayne, *Playboy* interview, May 1971

The Sun River meandered eastward. It seemed unable to summon the focus necessary to stay consistently close to the road. Sometimes we were right up on the water; other times, we could just make out the banks in the distance.

Thao chattered as we went, pointing out sights that she deemed noteworthy or curious, such as a knot of men outside a gas station in Fort Shaw. They all wore black hats and suspenders over striped shirts. A few feet away, there was a complementary group of women, in headscarves and long skirts. "There are *Amish* here?" she asked.

"They're called Hutterites."

"But they dress exactly the same as Amish."

"There are fundamental differences, but I see what you mean."

She duly recorded this in her notebook with a brief scrawl, punctuated— literally—with a sharp jab of the pen.

Just outside of Fort Shaw, Duane slowed. Up ahead, a large bird was in the middle of our lane, picking at something. When we got within 40 feet, I could see it was a red-tailed hawk. It spread its wings and laboriously climbed. A rodent was wriggling in its talons. The hawk flew higher for a few more beats, glided away from us, and lit in the dry grass off the road.

"Oh, how awful," Thao said.

Hearing this brought the usual clang of dissonance in my head. I never was able to fully assimilate this Truism About Me, i.e., one person's awesome is another's awful. "I wasn't thinking of it quite that way," I said. "To me, it almost has the feel of liberation. You're a gopher, you spend your whole life on the ground. But for the last few moments, you get to fly."

"I doubt that the gopher feels that way."

"Who knows? It's in shock. Maybe it's thinking: 'I'm soaring!'"

"More likely, 'I'm dying!'"

"Soaring. Dying. A major difference?"

"Yes, as a matter of fact."

"If you say so."

About 20 minutes down the road, we passed another butte to the south. "Wait," Thao said, "it's the mountain with the top cut off. Is that the same mountain?"

"No, it's a different one. This one is called Square Butte." I affected the deep tones of a travelogue narrator. "Square Butte is often used as a backdrop in the paintings of Charles M. Russell, 'The Cowboy Artist.' Russell, whose log-cabin studio was located right in Great Falls, was fascinated by the shadows and shades of the rugged butte, and featured it as the backdrop in many of his depictions of Montana and its rough-hewn inhabitants."

"Rough-hewn. Is anything ever hewn in a different way?" She continued to gaze at the butte. "What's the name of your mountain?"

"Where I live is Crown Butte."

"It appears to be just the same. And, gee. The sky is very strange over there."

A ragged ink-blue cloud enshrouded the eastern portion of the butte. The fringes of it tore apart, then mended themselves, then tore apart again.

"It's raining there," I said.

"How weird." She maneuvered in her seat to broaden her sight line. "The sky is completely clear except for that one area. But it's a storm? And it's moving."

"Yes. Heading our way."

"I've never seen a place where you could see the storm actually come right at you, all by itself."

It was on us within a matter of minutes, but we got just a little of it. We felt the wind first, as it slightly rocked the RV; the sky suddenly darkened, and the visibility shrank from infinite to a hundred feet. The dull light seemed to emanate from the road rather than the sky. Fat drops of rain, driven by the wind, blasted the windows of the RV. Duane was still groping to find the control for the wipers when we suddenly emerged onto dry pavement and into the bright sunlight.

"My god," he said. "Whew."

"I know. That was almost scary." Thao leaned forward to peer out Duane's window as the squall twisted away. "The sky here is very unusual. It's bigger?"

"Oh, 'The Big Sky.' That is an illusion," I said. "The sky appears to be big here, because the people are so small."

"Is that so? I thought people in the West were supposed to be larger than life."

"No, they are small. That's why John Wayne was invented. When you are in these vast spaces, and you are so puny, people have to make up stories to make themselves seem bigger."

"Like Paul Bunyan?"

"Like the basketball players from the Indian School."

From there I said increasingly little, other than an occasional word to Frankie, whose head was in my lap. When we got close to Vaughn, I directed Duane to the house. It was a manufactured home in the midst of a full acre of lawn, encircled by chain link fence. Six or seven dogs ran to the fence and barked at the RV. A lean woman with her blonde hair in a ponytail waved from the outside of the kennel gate.

"I'll be back in a minute," I said.

"No rush," Thao said. "Take your time. Wow. They have all kinds of dogs here."

Frankie was on full alert at this sudden turn of events, the hair behind his neck bristling to bolster his body mass by a factor discernible only to other dogs, or perhaps just to him.

I grabbed the bag of his food and toys. "C'mon, Braveheart. Let's go meet your new friends."

When I returned 10 minutes later, Duane was either sleeping or faking it. Thao was writing in her notepad.

"Sorry that took so long."

Thao looked up at me, then at the yard, where Frankie was playing—somewhat cautiously—with a pug. "He seems to be getting along. Are you OK?"

"Yeah. I have allergies." In other words, I am pathetic.

"And they seem to come on quickly. Listen, really, you can bring him with us.

"No, he'll actually be a lot happier here. And he needs to get acclimated."

"To what?"

"To other dogs."

"Are you getting more dogs?"

"I don't know. Are we ready?"

Duane was studying me. "We're ready whenever you are, chief," he said.

I climbed in. " 'Chief.' That's good. As in Chief Joseph? Or Perry White?"

"Perry White…the singer?"

"Uh…yeah. Can't Get Enough of Your Love, Chief. Great song."

"What the heck are you two talking about?" Thao asked.

"Americana."

"Hm. Are you sure? They didn't teach us that in my citizenship class."

"I will give you a new perspective on Americana."

"Looking forward to it."

We came into Great Falls on Central Avenue West. The street, with light but steady traffic, ran along an assortment of small buildings and businesses, most of which were vintage 1950s. We were coming up to an intersection with a green light when Duane suddenly veered to the sidewalk.

Thao gasped. "What happened?"

He was already halfway out the door, his camera somehow suddenly in his hand. "I want to make a picture of this."

As he gauged the passing traffic, he went around the RV, sometimes actually stepping out into the road, all the while sizing up a building on our right. It was nondescript—a square frame building with cheap brown siding. Nondescript, except for its roof, which featured a life-sized representation of a stark-white polar bear crouched on an ice floe. Its head hovering above the sidewalk, the bear glowered at the street.

A few feet down, a large sign on the exterior wall, more or less centered beneath the bear, proclaimed the name of the business. The letters were painted in orange, against a black background.

CASH COW
Checks Cashed / Payday Loans
Holy Cow! Come in now!

Thao absorbed this tableau. "That sign is awfully glarish," she said. "Plus, I don't get it. 'Cash Cow.' Is it supposed to be ironic?"

"Ironic? Oh, god, no. When you're in the check-cashing business, you don't do irony. Really, you fart at irony."

"Uh, OK. But why is there a bear on top of the Cash Cow building? It's kitschy?"

"The bear was here first. This used to be a little cafe. The Iceberg Cafe. Now, as you can plainly see, it's a crappy check-cashing joint. Of which, by the way, there are a hundred in this town, along with a hundred pawn shops, because there are a thousand bars with poker machines. Now, they *could* have had a sign that says, 'Can't BEAR to go without cash?' But they obviously preferred the alliteration of Cash Cow. They don't care about ironic or unique or kitsch. This is just a corner building they picked up cheap."

Duane was climbing back into the RV. He balanced himself, one foot on the floorboard, the other on the armrest of the door, and took some shots over the top of the door. Traffic from the other direction slowed. I could see the drivers' pale faces as they went by, gawking at us—a middle-aged woman in a McDonald's uniform, driving a station wagon; a wizened man in a brand-new pickup, wearing a straw cowboy hat, with a large square bandage on his cheek.

"Hiee!" Thao waved at the man in the pickup as he drove by. He

74

somberly raised a finger to his hat as he coasted by. "So, there are casinos? That's legal here?"

"They call themselves casinos, but they really aren't. They're just bars with poker machines. Frequented by drunken chain-smoking zombies."

Duane was re-situating himself behind the wheel. "'Drunken Chain-Smoking Zombies.' That would be a good name for a rock band."

"Ross, I'm detecting some bitterness here," Thao said.

"The casinos ruined this town, that's all. It used to be a typical, picturesque Western town, with a regular downtown, tree-lined streets, clean parks, all that. Except for a few skid-row bars where the Indians hung out, of course. But that was part of the charm. The casinos have just made a mess of it."

"You know this town."

"I grew up around here."

"You did? I just assumed you were from California."

"And what happens when we assume?"

Duane pulled back onto the road. "OK," he said. "So how do we get there again? We go north…"

I started to respond, but Thao interrupted. "I have the directions right here." She was holding a piece of paper. "South on River Road, off of Central Avenue West. That way, I guess." She pointed straight ahead.

He drove along slowly for a few minutes, leaning hopefully forward, as if six inches closer to the windshield might clarify the route. A bridge came into view. "Which side of the water?"

"Wait," Thao said, "you don't cross the river. Or do you? Go right here. Then right again up there." Two blocks later our course bumped into a phalanx of box cars. "Right again," she said hopefully, "then left." This put us exactly back on Central Avenue West, only now we were heading back in the direction from which we'd just come. Up ahead the Cash Cow bear loomed on the left.

"Congratulations," I said. "You've actually managed to turn us completely around. This is just like being with Meriwether Lewis and Sacajawea."

"Well, there are no helpful signs in this town," she said. "OK, Mr. From-around-here. How do we get to this address?"

I guided Duane there in under five minutes. Mike's RVs was on a knoll overlooking the junction of the Sun and Missouri Rivers. It was situated so that the customer parking section, just outside the main building, provided a view of the Sun River, meekly insinuating itself into the brawny brown flow of the Missouri. There was a picnic table on a grassy area in front of the parking under some pine trees. We parked in front of the table, and piled out of the RV.

Thao stretched and sighed. "Isn't this pretty? Duane and I actually almost decided to have a picnic here."

"Why didn't you?"

"We were in kind of a hurry to find you. We didn't know how long it would take."

A tall, broad-shouldered blond man came out of the building. "Hey, how ya doing' there! Oh gosh, the California folks are back!"

"Hi, Mike. The shower in the RV—"

"The shower don't work. I know. My guy gave ya the wrong rig." He was already vigorously shaking Duane's hand, and then Thao's. He extended his hand to me. "Mike Hodges." His grip was strong, but not show-off strong.

"Mike, this is Doug Rossiter," Thao said.

"Pleased t'meet ya, Doug. Are you a reporter, too?"

"Oh, no. I'm just an innocent bystander." I glanced sideways at Thao.

"Ross used to be a reporter," she said. "Ross," she repeated, with the deliberate enunciation of a schoolmarm. "He's helping us with our story. He lives over at—" She stopped.

"Out past Simms," I said.

"Simms, why, sure. My cousin runs some Charolais out that way. Edward Edwards?"

"I don't think I'm acquainted with an Edward Edwards."

"No? He's pretty well-known over in that country. One of his eyelashes is white as snow."

"I'm sure I'd recall Edward Edwards with the white eyelash. Um, which

I don't."

"I meant, the eyelashes all over on one eye."

"Right. Still not ringing a bell."

"Oh, too bad." He waited another half-beat in case a bell might tardily peal, then turned back to Thao. "My guy gave ya the wrong rig. Jerry! As soon as he come back in and told me what rig he gave ya, I thought, 'Oh no, gol-dang it.' I tried to call ya, but the number you gave me was in California at some office, and all's I got was a recording with your voice on it."

"Oh. Guess I should've given you my cell phone number instead." Thao slid her feet to plant herself directly in front of Mike and squared her shoulders, exhibiting her full height of about five-one. "In any case," she said in a flat voice, "I am going to have to insist that you make this right, as we have been inconvenienced."

Mike's head bounced back as if he'd been tapped firmly on the forehead; his mouth formed into an O. "Heck, it's our fault, for sure," he said carefully. "That rig was just parked there waitin' to go over to the shop, and Jerry got in a hurry or somethin.'"

"So, can we get a different one?"

"Sure you can. I won't charge you for these two days, neither. Of course not. But shoot. The only thing is, we might not have anything ready just now. I don't wanna send ya off in somethin' that's not tip-top." Mike squinted out toward the lot at the back of the building, moving his gaze to and fro, suggesting he could ascertain even from that distance what, if anything, was presently tip-top.

"How long is it going to be? As I said, we've already been inconvenienced. My friend here was hoping to get a nice shower in the RV, and we wanted to drive to Prague today."

"Oh, gosh." Mike checked his wristwatch. "I don't think I can get you out right away. I'm real sorry. Tell you what—"

"Let's get a pickup instead," I said.

"What? A pickup?" The tone she employed for *pickup* could just as well have been used for *space shuttle*. "What do we need a pickup for?"

"It's so much easier. We can get to where we want to go easier and faster."

Mike seemed perturbed at this notion. "These RVs, y'know, you can pretty much take 'em anywhere you wanna go now. And they got all the comforts, whereas a pickup...it don't."

"We don't really need a big-ass RV," I said.

"He's right," Duane said. "Plus, when I drive it, I feel like I'm my old man headed to a KOA." This may have been the first time he agreed with anything that came out of my mouth.

"But it's so convenient," she said. "We're driving the back roads and we don't have to worry about finding a motel every night."

"If you are traveling on a road that accommodates an RV, you're never going to be more than an hour from a motel," I said. "This is Montana, not Siberia. And it's probably just as cheap to stay in motels as it is to rent and gas an RV."

"What about all our things?"

"We really don't have that many things," Duane said. He asked Mike: "Do you have one of those pickups with a back seat?"

"A crew cab? Sure. But I can't get one ready any sooner than the RV." Thao sighed in frustration. "I tell ya what I was gonna say, though," he hurriedly added. "It'll only take a couple hours to get it cleaned up and gassed and ready to go. RV or a pickup, either one. And it's our fault for sure that you're in this pickle in the first place. Let me get my guys goin' on this"—he checked his watch again— "and I hafta go home to see about my boy, because his sitter can't stay past 3 today. And Doug—Ross, that is—can take a shower at my place. By the time we do that, have a cup of coffee, the truck'll be ready to go and you're on your way."

At first no one said anything. Finally, Thao asked: "Are you serious?"

"Sure. ...About what?"

"You want us to come to your house? And he's going to use your shower?"

"I'm finding it a little unsettling that everyone is so eager for me to get a shower," I said.

"Aw, it's not that, there, Doug. Haw. And it's no trouble. It's the least I can do."

"We can just wait here," Duane said. "We don't mind."

"No, no, come on over t'my place. You'll be a lot more comfortable there."

"OK," Thao said.

"Wait," Duane said. "What?"

"Why not? Let's go over to Mike's house."

I had to hand it to her, she was quick. She was strategizing how this odd man and his odd offer would constitute color for her travel piece. *Go to Montana, where the businessmen talk funny and invite you to right into their homes. To shower!* You had to travel outside California to encounter such an oddity.

"OK," I said. "Duane?"

"Sure, fine."

"Great!" Mike said. "Ross, grab your bag. I'll be back in a sec, and we'll get the show on the road. Go ahead and pile into my rig. Right in front of the office."

Mike's SUV appeared to have been recently detailed. The only indication that it had not just been driven off of a show lot was the "Town Pump" coffee mug in the beverage holder. I thought Thao might call shotgun, but she and Duane went directly to the back doors. It was a big step up for Thao. I took her arm to help her up.

She squirmed into the seat. "Thanks."

I put an index finger to the brim of an imaginary cowboy hat. "You bet, ma'am."

We had barely just settled when Mike jumped in. When he started the vehicle, the radio came on. He jabbed at it with a thick forefinger, but was having difficulty hitting the off button. The announcer was talking about wheat futures. Something had gone awry with the futures, but Mike squelched the report before we could find out what.

"We all set? Buckle up. These Great Falls drivers are crazy." Mike approached the street from his parking lot, looked both ways with elaborate care, though it was clear that there were no cars approaching for at least a quarter-mile either way. He proceeded, according to the speedometer, at a steady 25-mph pace until he got to the stoplight at 10th Avenue South, Great Falls' main business strip. He drove down 10th for a ways, through a blown-up Rubik's cube of car dealerships, casinos, pawn shops, restaurants and gas stations. But when he turned off, we were almost immediately in a well-tended older neighborhood, with elm tree branches arching over the streets to form a canopy of goldenrod leaves that quivered in the breeze. Many of the houses were Victorians, meticulously painted, their whites and tans in sharp contrast to the deep green lawns around them.

"This is the scenic route," Mike said, in an understated but genuine tone of pride.

"It's so pretty," Thao said. "Where are the great falls?"

"They're down at the other end of town. I'd sure take you there, but the thing is, I gotta get home to the boy."

"That's all right, we can go later. Huh, guys?"

"Yeah, you don't want to miss that," Mike said. "It's somethin,' I tell ya."

Within five minutes we came to a park with a lagoon and dozens of ducks and Canada geese, and two white swans. Mike pulled up to a sandstone two-story house facing the park. He stopped. "Here we are."

"Is *this* your house?" Thao asked.

"Yep. Sorry, haven't had a chance to mow the lawn lately. Me and the boy'll hafta do that this weekend."

"It's so beautiful! How old is this house?"

"It was built way back in 1925."

Thao jumped out of the pickup without assistance. We paused to admire the house. The public sidewalk where we now stood was old and scarred, but the walk leading to the front door must have been poured recently. It was dyed a light rust color. On either side of the walk was a perfect lawn, which ended in two patches of freshly turned earth in front of the house, undoubtedly the site of the summer's flower garden.

"You really keep it up nicely."

"Thanks. It's a runnin' battle, but I've got nothing else to do with myself. C'mon in."

As we neared the front door, a voice became audible. There was a TV blaring, and above the noise, the sound of a kid's voice. "High-sticking! High-STICK-ING!"

Mike opened the door and ushered us into an entryway, which had shiny hardwood floors. The room smelled of floor wax. "Jimmy!" Mike yelled. "Company! Shut that darn thing off."

The play-by-play of a hockey game stopped. The audio switched abruptly to a game show, then to a soap opera, then back to the game show. Then silence. A boy of about 12 came as far as an interior open door frame. He gawked at us.

"Are you watching that same game again?" Mike asked.

Jimmy did not respond.

"He watches a tape of the same hockey game over and over," Mike said. "Canucks and Flames. Over and over. That game was three years ago."

Jimmy paid no attention to Thao and Duane. He was eyeing me. "Who are you?"

"Jimmy. That's not polite."

"Oh, that's OK," I said.

"Hi Jimmy," Thao said. "I'm Thao, and this is Ross, and Duane."

"Who are you?" he repeated to me.

"Jimmy, stop it. Where's Margaret?" Mike turned to me. "Sorry." He tapped his temple. "He has a disability."

"She's downstairs doing the laundry."

"Laundry? She's supposed to be heading out the door. Here, you folks come on into the living room, make yourselves at home." Jimmy backed into a corner, allowing us to pass by, while his dad led us into a sitting room. The furniture was a mixture of antiques, two large Sears-style recliners, a leather couch and a big television with a VCR next to it. "Sit down, make yourselves comfortable, I'll be right back." Mike went through another doorway into the interior of the house. Jimmy reappeared in the entryway.

Thao went to a bookcase that rose nearly to the ceiling, jammed with books. "Someone here likes to read. Jimmy, is it you?"

"No."

She traced her finger along the spines. "*Old Jules...Son of the Morning Star...Young Men and Fire...Undaunted Courage....* Have you read any of these?"

"No." Jimmy was not looking at Thao, but still at me. "What hockey penalties can you name?"

"Not many. I'm not much of a hockey fan."

"Let's see," Duane said. "There's cross-checking, holding, interference.... That's about it, I think...."

Jimmy showed no sign he'd heard this. He asked me: "Do you know?"

I took a stab. "High-sticking?"

"Boarding, charging, cross-checking, elbowing, fighting, high-sticking, holding, hooking, instigating, interference, slashing, spearing, tripping."

"There are a lot, aren't there."

Jimmy pointed to his temple. "I have the disability."

I poked around in my sparse cupboard of responses, and could find only one stale sentence. "Seems like you're doing all right, though."

I walked over to Thao and pointed to a book about Chief Joseph called *Children of Grace.* "I read this," I said.

"Which one?" Mike came bustling in the room, holding a tray with four full cups of coffee, a little white pitcher, four spoons and some sugar packets. "Oh, that's a good one." Trailing behind him was a 50ish plump woman pulling on a jacket.

"Margaret, these folks are from California. There's Thao and Duane and Ross."

Margaret was huffing slightly. "Pleased to meet you. I'm sorry that I have to run right off. I've gotta get my mom to the doctor for her annual. Mike, Jimmy ate, and there's a sandwich in the fridge for Sally if she wants it, and I'll see you tomorrow morning."

"That's fine. See you tomorrow morning. Give my best to your mother."

"I will. Bye, Jimmy."

"Bye."

"Margaret's gotta run off," Mike said. "Usually, she's here until my daughter gets home. But this is workin' out anyway, because we're here now, and Ross can get that shower. Here, have some java." We all obediently took a cup. "Are you history buffs?"

"Not so much as you, it would appear," Thao said.

"Yeah. I love history. That was my major at Montana State, down in Bozeman."

"How interesting."

"Yeah. Big deal. What they say here—the farmers send their daughters to Missoula, and their heifers to Bozeman. Haha."

"I'm sure it's a fine school."

"Sure it is, I'm just teasin' ya. That's where I met my wife. She was the real history buff. She forgot more than I ever knew about history, I tell ya."

"Oh, is that your wife?" Thao pointed to a photo on one of the shelves. A pretty blonde woman with soft features and big hair.

"Yes, ma'am. She was a history teacher over at C.M. Russell High, and I can't tell you how many kids have told me she was the best history teacher they ever had." Mike walked over to the shelf and held out that photo so we could see it better. "I don't want to brag on her, but it's the truth."

"That's great," Thao said. "She's beautiful."

"Yep." Mike carefully set the photo back on the shelf. "We lost her to the cancer in '91."

"Oh. I am so sorry."

"Yeah. This place—" Mike gestured at the walls, the ceiling, the windows— "was her pride and joy, so we try to keep it up." He touched his finger on the photo, a wistful smile on his face. He briefly, vigorously shook his head. "But what are you gonna do? Life goes on."

"You sure do a great job of keeping it up. It's just gorgeous."

"Like I said. Got nothin' better to do. Huh, Jimmy?"

Jimmy remained fixated on me. "Is she your wife?"

"Who? Thao? Oh, no. We're just friends."

Mike made a noise of discomfort; it may have been intended as a chuckle. "It's Thao and Duane here who are together, Jimmy."

Thao sat up. "No we're not!"

"Oh, you're not? I thought...you were. I mean, you got the RV and all...."

"God no. We're just co-workers. Duane is engaged."

"Oh. My mistake. Sorry." Again, the uncomfortable chuckle. "Engaged, huh Duane? Is your girlfriend back in California?"

"No. She's doing an apprenticeship in Delhi this year."

"No kidding. Like at Subway or somethin'? They do that?"

"What?"

"Which deli is she workin' at?"

"No… she's in New Delhi. Her family is there."

"Hm."

"She's Indian," Duane added.

"Oh. She's Indian, too. That's great."

"He means, Asian Indian," Thao said.

"No kidding. *Asian* Indian. That's super. I never met anyone Asian Indian." He looked expectantly at Duane, as if a quick cultural lesson might ensue; but Duane had nothing more to say about it, so he pressed on. "Well. So, Ross, whenever you're ready, you go through this door upstairs, and you'll find the guest bath right at the top. There's a clean towel up there, and you just help yourself to whatever you need."

"Are you sure it's no imposition?"

"None at all. You go right on up."

"It's really kind of you." I placed my half-empty cup on the tray. "Guess I'll just go ahead and jump in."

Jimmy started to follow me.

"Whoops. No, Jimmy, you stay here with us. We'll chew the fat with these folks."

I ascended the stairs, hearing Mike's voice recede until, when I entered the bathroom, it lingered as a bass-level hum. The bathroom—spotless as the rest of the house—was oddly gender-neutral. It had been redone, the tub and shower enclosed in glass, but it still retained a Victorian feel, with a free-standing vanity and the toilet tank mounted on the wall. I stripped and pushed the clothes into a paper grocery sack I'd stuck in my travel bag. I turned on the water, went to the mirror above the vanity and considered my reflection. I had a hand-mirror at the shack for shaving, but this mirror—or this light—revealed an unfamiliar sight. I knew I had lost weight, but was surprised that this was so evident in my face. And there were lines around my eyes and on my forehead that I either did not remember, or were newly acquired in the past year.

When there was steam, I stepped into the shower. The hot water stung me. I wasn't sure if I'd adjusted it too hot, or if it was just that my skin was unaccustomed to such a sensation. Plus, the force of the water was surprising. I twisted the knob to cooler until I finally could stand it, which was at a point only slightly warmer than my solar shower.

The difference, though, was that this showerhead dispensed an infinite and forceful supply of water. I lathered myself from top to bottom, rinsed off, did it all over again. With intense scouring, most of the grime embedded in the cracks in my fingers came out. I worked at the knees and elbows. My arms and hands were deeply tanned; everything else I could see was pale. When I bent over to scrub my white feet, it occurred to me that I could have been witnessing the hands and feet of an entirely different person.

After I finished washing, I resisted the temptation to just stand under the showerhead and let the water pummel me. Instead, I turned the spout off, and grabbed the towel, which seemed as big as a robe. Assessing its soft droopy mass, I wondered: do they make bigger towels for bigger people?

When I returned to the sitting room, there was a teenage girl with the group. She was seated on the couch next to Jimmy, legs crossed underneath her. Her shoes and a backpack lay on the floor. Like her dad, she was long-legged and blonde. But she had none of his broadness and coarseness; she was lithe, and her features were soft like her mother's.

"Here he is. All cleaned up!" Mike said.

"That was great. Thank you so much."

"My. You clean up real pretty," Thao said.

"Thank you, ma'am."

"Ross, this is my daughter, Sally. Sally, this is Ross."

She rose and shook my hand. She was nearly as tall as I. "I'm pleased to meet you," she said. Her eyes were a shade of light blue he'd never seen in anyone's eyes before. I forced myself to release her hand.

"Are you from California, too?"

"Indirectly. I live out by Simms now."

"Oh. Are you a farmer?"

"No, a hermit."

She laughed. "How fun!"

"Fun. Yes. Hasbro is making a board game based on my life."

She laughed again. Her teeth were shockingly white. I almost spoke again, the words hanging suspended in that microsecond between conception and articulation. But I stopped myself. Thao was in one of the recliners, a book in her lap, and I saw she was watching me.

"What would they call the game, I wonder?" she asked.

"I don't know—Help Squirrel Find the Nut."

"A squirrel. Cute!"

"Yeah, that's the thing about squirrels."

"I know. Really, they're irresistible."

"We should go," Duane said.

Thao held up a book. "Mike lent me this. It's all about Chief Joseph."

"That Chief Joseph is quite a story," Mike said. " 'From where the sun now stands, I will fight no more forever.' "

"Yes. It's quite a terrible story."

"Did you know they got within 40 miles of Canada? Just 40 miles to safety. And they stopped to camp, and the cavalry caught up with them."

"Yes."

"Quite a story," Mike said again.

"So, if we're ever going to see the site of this story, we're going to have

86

to get going," Duane said.

"Yep, your rig oughta be ready by now. It'll be dark by the time you get to Prague. Just take it easy on those two-lane roads."

"Shouldn't we grab a bite before we go?" Thao asked. "Are there any good restaurants in Great Falls?"

"Oh, you bet. Great Falls is known for its fine dining."

"Thao, are you serious? We're never going to get out of this town," Duane said.

"I'm hungry. Aren't you hungry, Ross?"

"Now that you mention it…"

"Can't we just pick up some burgers or something?" Duane asked.

"We can't miss out on a Great Falls fine dining experience. Mike, what's good?"

"If you like Mongolian barbecue, there's a place over in Black Eagle—"

I saw Duane smirk, and thought Mike may have seen it, too.

"Or, Sis, what's that sushi restaurant on 10th Avenue South? I guess it's a bar, too…?"

"We were thinking of maybe something with more of a local flavor," Thao said.

"Sure. Yeah, both those places are local."

"Dad, they want steaks or something. They can get their sushi in California any time."

"Oh, I got ya. You want steaks?"

"Yes."

"OK, you want to go to Freddy's, then. Big steaks, I'll tell you what. Yeah, they're real good." He added, while taking a cautious sideways glimpse of Duane: "They have good raviolis, too. Freddy's—it's over there in Black Eagle, on Smelter Avenue. Just across the street from the Mongolian barbecue."

"Dad, forget the Mongolian barbecue."

"Sure, sure. So—Black Eagle. It's a real neat place. You'll have a ball. You just go across the river."

7. Back in the Race

I believe that to have a friend, a man must be one.

—Fran Striker, "The Lone Ranger's Creed" (1933)

Freddy's Supper Club was a windowless white cinderblock building, squatting on the corner like a bulldog resistant to the leash. The cinderblocks had been laid with perfect, flat symmetry, offering no concession to design or even variation. Standing in contrast to this spare white square was a tall sky-blue and pink neon sign that read, in elaborate script, "Freddy's." Beneath that was a black-on-white addendum: "Steaks, Cuisine, Packaged liquor."

We sat three across in the front seat of Mike's SUV: Duane behind the wheel, Thao in the middle. When we'd returned from Mike's house to the RV lot, our pickup was still on the rack getting an oil change, so Mike insisted we take his SUV for the evening. "It'd be kind of dicey for you, gettin' around Great Falls during rush hour in a big ol' RV," he'd said. He'd also suggested that we consider spending the night in the RV on his lot, rather than taking to the road after dark, "especially if you've, you know, had a few."

Thao had unilaterally accepted this invitation, before remembering to say to Duane and me, "OK, guys?" In response, he and I were matching bobblehead dolls.

The sun was just now setting, and the Freddy's sign mimicked the cold blue and pink of the sky.

"Have you ever eaten here before?" Thao asked.

"Sure, I've eaten here. Classiest joint in Great Falls. It's been a while, but I don't imagine it's changed much."

"It looks like a mausoleum," Duane said.

"The design was inspired by the ICBM silos that are all over the prairie out here."

"Really?"

"Uh, no. This building actually predated those. If anything, Freddy's inspired the missile silos, not vice-versa. So are we going in?"

"You guys go ahead," Thao said. "I have to make a call. Have a drink and get us a table. I won't be long. Can you leave the heater on, Duane? It's so cold."

She held the cell phone, the fingers of her right hand resting lightly on the keypad. I hesitated as Duane got out. In the flattening light, her cheeks—contrasted against the white of her coat and teeth, and against the black of her hair and eyes—were brightly flushed, as if she had coated them with rouge. But I was pretty sure she wore no makeup at all.

"Yes?" she said.

"Oh. Sorry." I looked down. The phone. "Your fingers."

"My fingers?" She held them out to examine them. "What's wrong with them?"

"You could be a fingers model. A hand model, I mean."

"Oh, I bet you say that to all the girls." She nudged my leg with her knee.

Duane was at the front of the pickup, his shoulders hunched. "Dude, let's go."

We took the last open table in the bar. The interior of Freddy's probably had not been changed since the place was built in the '40s. Low lighting was absorbed by dark paneling. Candles in red globes glowed at the tables. The seats at the booths were dark red leather. On the wall there were numerous paintings and photographs. One was a huge sepia photograph of a bucking bronco, its hind legs high in the air. A cowboy floated near the bronc, completely and ignominiously upside down, legs akimbo. His hat hovered maybe four feet off the ground; his inverted head was another couple of feet above the hat. In the background other cowboys could be seen standing at the chutes, observing impassively, as if this were an everyday sight.

The place was crowded, and a jukebox in the corner played Perry Como. I didn't see a waitress. "Care for a drink?" I asked Duane. "Or don't you imbibe?"

"Sure, I imbibe. I'm not into wine, though."

"OK. What are you into?"

"I'm more of a brown liquor drinker."

"A brown liquor man. Then brown liquor it will be. Canadian Club?"

He reached into his back pocket. "That sounds good. I've got it."

"Forget it. I know I seem crazy and poor, but I'm not completely destitute. I saved up a few bucks over the years. And my cost of living at present is on the lower end of the scale."

I edged my way into an opening at the bar. There was a handwritten sign taped to the mirror at the back: "Bounced checks DO NOT serve." The list of names under this sentence numbered probably thirty. I had never written a check here, let alone bounced one, but I found myself scanning the list for my own name until I determined, with a vague sense of relief, that there was no sign of me.

When I returned to the table, I saw that Duane had gone to the jukebox, and was feeding coins into it. The twangy ache of country music was on now. I walked over and gave one of the glasses to him. He immediately drank down half of it.

"Bravo," I said. "All right, then." I knocked down the same amount and joined him in reviewing the song list. "Interesting combination. Some country-western, some rat-pack, some...Perry Como."

"They have some great standards in here. Look." He tapped the glass. "When's the last time you saw 'Sing Sing Sing' on a jukebox?"

"I would have to say, never."

"That's right. 'Sing Sing Sing' is maybe the greatest song in the history of the world. But nobody knows it anymore, because you never hear it anywhere. This place is growing on me."

"You're into the big-band sound? What's this that's playing now?"

"How would I know? Some suicidal country shit. 'Sing Sing Sing' is in the queue." He finished his drink and smacked the glass squarely on the console of the jukebox. "Big-band is the apex of American music. Nothing approaches it."

"I agree it's a great song. But nothing approaches it?" I fished in my pockets, but remembered I had no change. "Gershwin? Jimmy Reed? Dylan? Miles Davis?"

"Yeah, OK. But Benny Goodman and Gene Krupa set your brain on fire. Here." He put four quarters on top of the juke box. "Play something."

"I'm on it." I scanned the selections. "What kind of music does Thao like?"

He abruptly turned and headed back to the table. I perused the selections on the jukebox and punched some buttons before I followed him. He was seated, drumming his fingers on the tabletop. His glass was empty.

"You know, Duane." I sat down. "I can't help feeling that maybe we've got off on the wrong foot."

"Really."

"Really. You seem a bit stiff. Like just now. And you can correct me if I'm wrong, but I have the sense that it has to do with Thao."

"What makes you say so?"

A waitress appeared—50ish, stone-faced, eyebrows drawn on. "You boys ready for another one?" Her voice crawled out of her throat through the residue left by fifty thousand cigarettes. Even though customers were smoking throughout the bar, I could smell it on her.

"You bet. Two Canadian Club doubles, with ice. Also, can you put us down for a party of three for dinner?"

She was giving the table a quick swipe. "No reservations? It might be a while."

"We're in no hurry."

"OK. Two Canadian Club doubles. Looks like you could use some water, too." She left before I could tell if she was joking.

"All I'm saying," I said, "is you act a little bit touchy about her. That's all. Maybe a little proprietary? Like I'm horning in?"

"Proprietary! I'm not at all proprietary toward her. There's absolutely nothing between us."

"Of course not. You have a girlfriend in India."

"That's not really relevant."

"It's not? Because…?"

"Because we broke up. Which Thao doesn't need to know. Not that it matters because there's nothing between us."

"That sounds definitive."

"It is."

"So why are you defensive about her?"

"I'm not."

"You are, somewhat."

"I'm not defensive at all. It's just that I find her obsessiveness about you is kind of tiresome."

"You can't be serious. Obsessiveness? In what way?"

"Dude, if you want to go for her, go ahead. I don't care."

"'Go for her'? Brother, take a look at me." I ran my hand along my bristly head. "I'm not in a position to go for anything or anyone, except maybe a tambourine player in a troupe of Hare Krishnas."

"But you're interested in her. It's pretty obvious."

"It is?…OK, sure, it's nice to be around someone who's pretty, and who smells that good, especially when you've spent the past year sleeping with a dog. And yeah, she's kind of funny, and charming in a way. But I have no illusions about the nature of her interest in me. So this notion of obsessiveness…I don't get you."

"You will." He dug out his wallet and put a 10-dollar bill on the table.

The waitress came up from behind me, set down the drinks and snatched up the bill without a word. He immediately took a healthy drink.

"Boy, you weren't kidding about being into the brown liquor."

"So?"

"So nothing."

"I know what you're getting at."

"I'm not getting at anything. But it's true that we're all molded by our pasts, aren't we?"

"Sure, tell me all about your past."

"When you grow up in a town like this, that's how it is. For instance, there was this very common expression we used: 'Drunk as an Indian.' It meant, you know, really drunk."

"I get it. Sorry to disappoint you, but I don't intend to get drunk. Can you keep up?"

"No, but I'll try to maintain a reasonable pace behind you." I raised my glass and tipped it toward him; after a moment, he raised his. "So, just for the sake of argument," I said, "let's say you're not interested in her, and for whatever ridiculous, hopeless reason, I am. You're not helping."

"I'm supposed to help you?"

"Of course. You're my wingman."

"Since when?"

"Only since about the 18th century. Haven't you ever heard of Manifest Destiny? You should be Tonto to my Lone Ranger. Or the Last Mohican to my Hawkeye. Mingo to my Dan'l Boone. Pick any helpful, noble, doomed Indian you want, fiction or non."

"OK, so that's another thing. You keep making these cracks about Native Americans."

"I'm only joking around. No offense."

"You keep saying 'no offense,' which is a bullshit trick to avoid taking responsibility for saying offensive things."

"It's just a feeble stab at irony. I actually believe that this country's treatment of Indians has been as bad as its treatment of black people. In some ways, worse. I want you to know, if it's not clear yet, that that's the main reason I'm on this trip with you. If there's a story that comes out of this trip that's remindful of how America has fucked over the Indians, I'll consider it time well-spent. But I'm not going to go around pretending that, through their struggles, they have somehow achieved equality or assimilation or adjustment. All that does is belie the actual state of affairs. Which is, since before this country was even born, that the lives of American Indians have gotten steadily worse instead of better."

"I disagree. They have achieved equality and assimilation, to a large degree."

"'They'?"

"I am only one-quarter Native American. I don't know why you're so eager to lump me in with them. But fine. 'We.'"

"Lump yourself with whomever. I was just asking. Anyway…When I say 'assimilation' I don't mean getting a monthly stipend from the reservation casino fund."

"Neither do I, but what do you mean, then?"

"I mean, nearing the point where Indians have a family income comparable to the U.S. average. I mean, reaching the point where their average rate of alcoholism, divorce, suicide, life expectancy, pick any of those, comes within shouting distance of the U.S. average. And if that's too statistically minded, how about just being able to point to a few exceptions who have achieved prominence in American life? Comparable to, say, George Washington Carver or, I don't know, Thurgood Marshall. Or Louis Armstrong. All of whom achieved their successes in spite of Jim Crow, mind you. Name me any Indians who achieved success as journalists, or politicians. Or judges or actors. Musicians. Who's the Indian Benny Goodman?"

He drained his drink. "Politician: Ben Nighthorse Campbell. Actor: Burt Reynolds."

"OK, you just named an extremely obscure senator, and the guy who starred in 'Smokey and the Bandit.' Who I don't even think is an Indian."

"Jim Thorpe."

"Not a member of any of the occupations I listed, but an excellent example of an American Indian whose life ended up a complete mess, and who died destitute and drunk. My point is that Indians were kicked into a deep pit by greedy, vicious and racist Americans, to such a degree that it's been over 100 fucking years since the Bear Paw, and they still have not gotten a toehold out."

"Some have."

"And every Pine Ridge or Alcatraz that supposedly galvanized a movement was just a circle-jerk that ended up gaining absolutely nothing."

"Some have, I said."

"OK, sure. Present company excepted, of course."

"I don't mean myself. You're making these broad characterizations, which, by the way, are racist themselves, and ignoring the accomplishments of millions of well-adjusted people."

"Racist, or realist? Look, I'm just trying to make a point here. I grew up around Indians, went to grade school with them, saw them bullied and beaten until it made me sick, and it made me sicker yet that I didn't do a goddamn thing about it. Is it better now? OK, kind of, a little. But you can't all of a sudden concoct a new world in which everyone is 'well-adjusted.' The reservations are a great example. You still can't set foot on them without having your watch, eyeglasses and socks stolen. I knew a guy once whose kid was on a state road crew out at Rocky Boy. One day the kid's pickup gets stolen. A couple of days later his buddy tells him he's spotted it out behind some Indian's shack. So the two of them go find it, and he has a spare key, so he figures what the hell, he'll just drive it back home. But it turns out the Indian had left some cassettes on the front seat. So what does the Indian do? He calls the reservation police to file a complaint, saying this white guy has stolen his cassettes. Now I ask you: is that a lifestyle that's well-adjusted?"

"You can find examples of people acting crazy anywhere, anytime. What about the nuts in Waco? They were all white."

"Yes, but 'crazy' connotes aberrational. Among the Indians, crazy is the norm."

"Didn't anyone ever tell you that stereotyping is a form of racism? Not to mention, the whole notion of assimilation is overrated. What's the virtue of assimilating into a corrupt society and culture?"

"None, of course. The problem for Indians is that they are eternally drifting in limbo between a bygone and dead culture, and another that now surrounds them. The only choices I see are to assimilate or drift. For now, the choice seems to be to drift."

"I'll show you."

He faced the entrance and raised his hand in a beckoning motion.

"Ah. So you've surreptitiously assembled and hidden a group of highly adjusted Indians, and you're now summoning them to prove your point. Well-played, sir. By all means, bring them forth."

He continued to gesture. "I'll show you."

I turned, half-expecting to see something like the Ames Brothers in tuxes, but no, it was Thao. She was up and down on her toes, scanning the room.

"Oh." I stood and waved.

Even from this distance, I could see that her cheeks were as red as before. She spotted me and began to maneuver through the tables toward us. I sat back down. "Show me what?"

"Just wait." The waitress brushed by, and he reached toward her, but too late.

"Hey! Hey!" he said to her back. "Over here, lady!"

"Whoa," I said, "no need to shout. Man, I'm still working on my first one. You are way ahead of me...And 'lady'?"

"I wasn't shouting."

The waitress and Thao got to the table at the same time. The waitress glared at Duane. "Two more, please," I said. "And a glass of red wine for her."

The waitress did not seem to hear me. Her expression suggested she was on the verge of removing her white soft-soled shoe to use as a club. But Duane was unflappable, or at least unaware. Slowly, she said to Thao, "We have burgundy."

"That will be fine. Thank you."

The span between the waitress' painted eyebrows narrowed. She walked off.

"I see you guys have been making friends," Thao said.

"She doesn't like to be called 'lady,'" Duane said. "So what did Ed have to say?"

"He's thrilled that Ross is coming with us. He's glad to hear he's doing well, and sends his regards. And he's jealous that we're eating at Freddy's. I guess you guys ate here once? He came up here to go fishing or something?"

"Yeah, we came up here one summer for a few days. He wanted to rough it, so we stayed at the shack. One night, I think. After which he didn't want to rough it anymore. So the report is that I'm doing well?"

"Sure. Aren't you?"

"Insofar as I'm not howling at the moon yet."

She reached for my untouched second drink, took a sip and made a face. "How can you drink that?"

"We've transitioned to brown liquor. Duane has declared himself a brown liquor man. So what's the word from San Jose? They're on board with this?"

"Oh, sure." She pushed the drink back toward me. "Ed said the Wood piece is perfect for the Travel section. He'll tell Sherry. Full speed ahead."

"Full s'eed ahead!" Duane said. "Awright!"

"Oh, no. Are you getting tipsy?"

"I resemble that remark."

"Ross, you'll be driving." She handed me the SUV keys.

"Oh, c'mon," Duane said. "You're not going to go all schoolmarm now, are you?"

"We need to be extra, one-hundred-percent careful with Mike's car. After all he's done for us? I told Ed about him. He couldn't believe it. I still can't believe it. Ross, can you? The man is like a saint from heaven."

"I don't know."

"You don't know what?"

"'Saint' seems kind of strong. As does 'heaven.' Is he from heaven or hell?"

"What!"

"Saint, or devil?"

"Are you drunk, too?"

"Seriously. He's a tempter, like the devil."

"He tempts you to do what? Borrow his car?"

"Tempts you with the illusion of redemption."

"You're insane." She reached over and smartly slapped the back of my hand. For a half-second, her hand rested atop mine, as if to atone for the slap.

Her model's fingers were still cold. "He let you use his shower, for god's sake. He lost his wife, and he has those two kids to raise. That poor little boy. But Mike is like, hey, everything is fine!"

"That's what I'm talking about. He acts like everything is fine."

"And my god, his daughter. Gorgeous. It was pretty obvious that she turned your eye."

"That sounds painful, but I think I get your drift. And yes, both of us noticed—right, Duane?"

Duane's head was cocked, and he was leaning away from the table. "Listen," he said. "Hear that, Dougie?"

It was the syncopated tom-tom that starts "Sing Sing Sing." Duane began to drum his fingers on the table. Somewhere in my gut, I felt the same sense of excitement that had surfaced the night before inside the RV. Krupa's pulsating tom-tom led into the trombones, who laid down a patchwork of fuel that ignited the trumpets. This was followed by the jostling call-and-response between the reeds and the brass. I found that my head was bobbing, keeping time of its own accord. Duane was deeper into it, eyes half-closed, swaying and banging on the table.

Thao appraised the two of us. "It seems I'm late to the party."

The waitress appeared again. "Your table's ready."

She led the way, Duane directly behind her. I could hear the first short drum break by Krupa, then more tinder laid by the trombones, followed by the sound of the trumpets, rising up like flames from squirts of gasoline. Duane began to move in rhythm. Then he went all out, pretending to do an Indian war dance.

I heard Thao behind me. "Oh my god." There was some muttering among the diners. I heard the words, *Some drunk Ki-Yi.*

Just as we got to the table, the waitress did an abrupt 180, went around Duane, and came within about 8 inches of my face. I had a clear view of her taut cracked lips below a set of bleached mustache hairs. "You're gonna hafta control him. This is a restaurant, not a pow-wow."

Duane was grinning.

"Sure, no problem. Now that we've got our table, we'll get him under control. We'll tie him up if necessary."

The volume of the jukebox abruptly dropped. All I could hear now was the faint thump of the tom-tom. Duane raised his hand like a witness taking the stand. "How," he solemnly said.

"Duane, sit down," I said. "Sorry," I added to the waitress. "Don't worry. If he starts to get loud we'll sit on him."

She laid our menus in front of us, contorted her lips into an approximation of a smile and left us with this perfunctory declaration: "The prime rib is very good tonight."

"Now that was embarrassing," Thao said. She turned to the diners at the adjacent table, and mouthed, "Sorry."

"Just having a little fun," Duane said. "Giving the tourists a little local color."

"Hello, you're the one who's the tourist. You don't really have any local color to provide."

"Sure, I do. It's red."

"We need to get some food in you."

"C'mon, take a joke. I'm not drunk. I'm just making a point."

"Really? Which is?"

"Sammy knows. I mean, Dougie. Dougie knows."

"I'm not sure that I do," I said, "but let's just assume so."

A teen appeared with water, a basket of breadsticks with butter pats, three plates of iceberg lettuce with tomato wedges, and a salad dressing holder supporting four aluminum bowls, into which four different-colored dressings with the consistency of mayonnaise had been ladled to the very top.

Thao poked at the lettuce with her fork. "This appears to be very fresh lettuce."

"It's the quintessential lettuce for the Northern plains palate," I said. "I really wouldn't recommend eating any of this, as it has the nutritional value of cardboard. Save your appetite."

But Duane had already appropriated the Thousand Island dressing. He spooned several dollops onto his salad.

"Unless, of course, you're really hungry," I added.

"Maybe we should have done the Mongolian barbecue," Thao said.

"Just have a nice ribeye steak and some ravioli, and you can thank me later."

She picked up the menu and started to scan it. "I'm all for steak, but ravioli?"

"Yes. In the '20s and '30s a lot of Italians immigrated here to work at the copper smelter. This place has been using the same recipe for ravioli for probably 50 years. You've never tasted sauce like this, I bet. It's Northern Italian cuisine. Trust me."

"I do trust you."

"That's heart-warming," Duane said. He had a buttered breadstick in one hand, which he jabbed in Thao's direction. "You trust him. And he trusts you, too. Huh, Sammy? I mean, Dougie."

"You are really obnoxious," Thao said. "Let's order, I'm starving."

"Hey, 'That's Life.'"

"Ross, will you order for me?"

"Sure."

"'That's Life,'" Duane repeated.

"Duane, please stop it."

"It's your song, isn't it?" he said to me. "It just started over again. You played it twice."

Whoever had lowered the volume on the jukebox must have turned it partway back up. I could hear the organ introduction, which gave way to Sinatra's insouciant declaration: *That's life! That's what all the people say....*

"Oh. Yes."

"It's a great song," he said. "Good job, Sammy."

"It's a pretty great song," I said.

"I've never heard of it," Thao said.

"OK, listen."

She dropped her fork, folded her hands and sat quietly while it played. I could see it did not make much of an impression. Maybe because the chatter in the restaurant overpowered the nuances of the song, like the key change two-thirds of the way—when Sinatra's voice leaps up, powerfully and effortlessly, like a gymnast hopping onto the balance beam.-

"That was nice," she said when it ended. "I think I *have* heard it before."

"Give it one more try."

The song started again. Organ, drums, bass sauntering along, then Sinatra.

"Jeez, how many times did you play it?" Duane asked.

"How many quarters did you give me?"

A new waitress came to the table. Apparently management was rotating them through so as not to wear them out. This one was the opposite of the first—naturally blonde, fresh-faced, soft high voice, perky. If she knew we'd been trouble, she didn't show it.

"So you want me to order for you?" I asked Thao.

"Please."

"Order for me, too," Duane said.

"You make it so easy. Three ribeyes, medium, three sides of ravioli. No potatoes."

"Anything to drink?"

Duane's glass was empty again. I drained mine. "Two Canadian Club doubles, please. And I believe she has a burgundy on the way."

"You guys are crazy," Thao said. "Am I going to have to end up driving?"

"Don't worry. These ravs will soak up any alcohol in our system. OK, listen to this key change coming up here." I spoke the lyrics in synch with the music.

I been a puppet, a pauper, a pirate, a poet, a pawn and a king.
I been up, and down, and over and out, and I know one thing.
Each time I find myself laying flat on my face
I just pick myself up and get...
"Right here:"
...back in the ra-ace.

That's life! That's life! and I can't deny it.

Duane joined in, and we both croaked the words all the way to the end: *"My! Myyyyyyyyyyyyyyyy......"*

When we stopped, she quietly said, "Yes, it's a nice song."

"Do you really think so? You don't seem to be feeling it."

"Maybe not to the extent you are. I actually *have* heard this song before. I always thought the ending's kind of odd, though, isn't it?"

"How's that?"

"The whole song is all about how he picks himself up after every hardship or misfortune. But at the end, if nothing's shaken in July, he's going to curl up in a big ball and die."

"He's doesn't mean it," Duane said.

"He doesn't?" she asked me.

"Of course not," I said. "Sinatra don't curl up for nobody."

It was the kid who brought out the dinner. The steaks were so large they covered the plates, and the ravioli was served on side dishes.

"That is a lot of meat," Thao said.

"It really is excessive," I admitted. "God. I haven't eaten a steak in a year, and suddenly I have an entire cow in front of me."

"Why are you eating a steak now, all of a sudden?" Duane asked.

I poked at it with my fork; juices seeped out. "Road trip. All the usual rules have been suspended."

I gamely struggled through half the steak and two-thirds of the ravioli. Duane accomplished about the same. Thao ate all of hers, making the same sounds of satisfaction I'd first heard that morning, in the RV at breakfast. "This is the best meal I ever ate," she said. "I'm absolutely serious."

"I'm glad you like it. Your appetite continues to impress."

She beamed in genuine pride. "Thank you."

When we left the restaurant, the crescent moon was dangling in the sky. We exhaled thin white puffs of vapor. I got in the driver's seat. Thao scooted in the middle, but Duane got in the back seat.

"Duane, why are you in the back?" Thao asked. "Come up here and get warm with us."

"No, the wingman goes in the back seat."

"The what?"

"That right, Kemosabe?"

I felt her thigh solidly against mine. "Sorry if I'm crowding," she said. "But I'm freezing to death."

The light from the Freddy's sign seemed to suffuse everything in the cab with a pink glow, except her black irises. "Me too."

She stayed in that spot as I drove back to Mike's, keeping at the speed limit, stopping completely at stop signs.

The RV was parked in the picnic area. Mike had left the lights on inside; it glowed in the cold dark like a lantern floating on the water. When we stepped in, I immediately shed my jacket. After a minute, Thao and Duane got rid of theirs.

"Toasty in here," I said.

"Mike. He put the heat on. I bet the shower is fixed, too. He thinks of everything," Thao said.

"Yes. Frightening, isn't it?"

Thao was stretching her arms. She half-stifled a yawn. "Huh?"

"Are you played out? I am, too. What about you, Duane?"

"This day has seemed like about three days," he said. "I'll take the bed over the cab. You can have this one." He gestured to the made-up bed, which had been pulled out from the table area.

"Whatever works. I can sleep anywhere. And I guess her highness gets the big bed in the back."

"Yes," Thao said. "And I hope Mike removed any peas from underneath the mattress." She stretched again, hands behind her ears. "Since you boys have had it for the day, I'll just retire. If you're going to use the bathroom, you'll have to do so now." She went to an opening behind the refrigerator, and pulled an accordion door out a foot or so. "Once this door closes, it stays closed for the night."

"That's good, because I wouldn't want you interrupting my sleep with a refrigerator raid at 3 in the morning."

"Oh, the rules apply only to you," she said. "Not to me." She headed toward the back.

Duane was already moving toward the bathroom. As he passed, we stood shoulder to shoulder in the narrow space. Our faces were just inches apart.

"So now you know," he said, his voice a soft grunt. "Heap tough fight. Man's heart snaps—" He snapped his fingers. "—like twig. Kemosabe."

Jack McMahon

February 1995

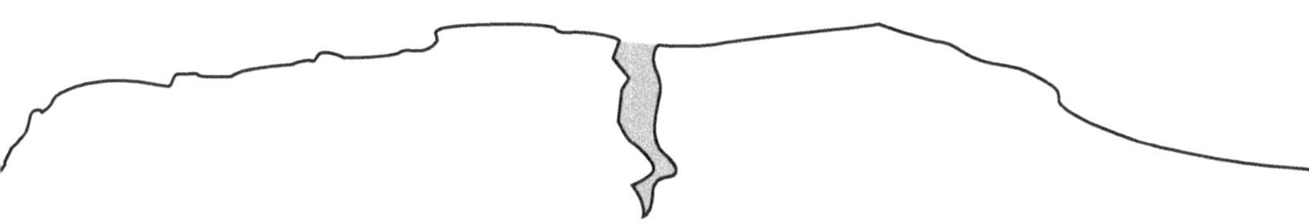

With the thoughtless resignation of an ox under the yoke, Rossiter sat down at his desk on a Thursday morning and began to plod through his daily routine when Blasingame called.

"Just wanted to give you a heads-up," he said. "Jack McMahon is being paroled. Two weeks."

"Really. That time went by fast."

"Five years probably didn't go that fast for him. But yeah, he had a very good P.D. Good counsel from start to finish. What are the odds."

"He seems to be a lucky guy in general, strangely enough."

"That's what living wrong will do for you."

"An inspiring thought. So, what are the conditions?"

"I haven't seen the papers, but it's the usual, I suppose. No booze. Can't contact his ex. Don't think she's around anyway. Stay away from schools. That kind of stuff. His arresting officer told me they got him a job at some greasy spoon."

"Just easing his way back to become a productive member of society, sounds like?"

"I could have told you 10 years ago that that wasn't going to happen. And five years in the pen on a child abuse conviction decreases the odds to about nil. He'll be in another mess in no time. I just hope some innocent person isn't the victim again."

"There's a resounding endorsement of the justice system."

"I would prefer more justice, and less system."

"Right. Anyway. Thanks for the heads-up. I'll send over the Ballantine's."

"No need."

"Even so. Just my way of saying thanks for your years of public service."

"Just 'job well done' is all the thanks I need."

"Sorry. Can't go that far."

He got lost at first trying to find the McMahon house. He'd forgotten the name of the street. All he could recall was that it was off of White Road, and you bore right where there was a little neighborhood market. But sometime during the past 10 years the market had disappeared. It must have given way to a Jack in the Box or a 7-Eleven or whatever. So he drove up and down streets, and in and out of cul de sacs jammed with cars but absent of people. After a half-hour of driving around, he saw the big palm tree. The numbers had faded to nearly nothing, but he recognized the house.

He backed up until he found a spot into which he could manipulate his car and survey the neighborhood. The houses were smaller than he remembered, and so was the street. But there certainly were a lot of cars. Several had spilled over from the curbs onto what, at one time, were front lawns. Most of them were situated at random angles, the owners apparently lacking the wherewithal or will to park them straight.

From his vantage point he could see the front door of the house. Two vehicles sat in the driveway: a mid-70s Dodge sedan, which was cream-colored but which might once have been white, and a forlorn green Datsun pickup of about the same vintage. He was there maybe twenty minutes when a woman came out. She was about 50, heavy-set, pale lifeless hair, wearing a blue sweatshirt and blue sweatpants. She waddled gingerly to the Dodge and folded herself in. As she drove down the street toward him, her eyes were focused straight ahead. A half-hour later she returned to the house with a single paper bag.

He came back on several different days, at different times, before he saw McMahon. It was on a Tuesday morning, a little after 11. McMahon came out of the front door, a cigarette in his mouth. Rossiter recognized him—the same shuffling gait, same scrawny build, same long blond hair. Before, he'd worn it carelessly, hanging all around his face. Now it was in a ponytail. He might have been an inch or two taller than he was 10 years ago, but maybe only 10 pounds heavier, if that.

He drove off in the pickup. Rossiter followed, staying about a block back. They wended out of the neighborhood, back onto White Road, onto Alum Rock Avenue, and onto the freeway toward downtown. The late-morning traffic was light, and following him was easy.

McMahon took the downtown exit and drove about a half-mile to a business district commonly known as D-town. He pulled into a small parking lot at a brick building with a sign featuring the Miller Beer logo at the bottom, and in bold letters above that, BUD'S BAR AND GRILL. Rossiter drove by the lot entry slowly enough to read the hand-painted sign at the entry: "Bud's parking ONLY Others WILL be TOWED."

No matter, at least to anyone not named Bud; there was plenty of street parking. Rossiter drove halfway down the block and pulled in. He knew the neighborhood. Most people thought D-town was a reference to the adjoining downtown, but it actually was a remnant of its old nickname: Dago Town. That's how the city's more prominent and influential elements had referred to the shops and apartments where western European immigrants settled in the early '20s. Today, D-town was close enough to the actual downtown to evoke a bygone prosperity, and far enough away to quell any aspiration of regaining it. The brick storefronts now housed a couple of Viet pho cafes, along with some thrift shops, used bookstores and coffee houses, the latter of which somehow stayed in business while their few, morose patrons pored over the local alternative weekly and slowly sipped their seventy-five-cent coffees. And Bud's place, of course. The bus station was one block to the north. One block beyond that was the soup kitchen.

There were maybe 10 diners inside Bud's, which was more than he expected. He took one of the half-dozen seats at the counter, at the opposite end from a corpulent man in a city transit uniform. Rossiter allowed himself a glimpse of the man; he was dipping a roast beef sandwich in a bowl. Dark hair, jowly. Ralph Kramden, teleported from the '50s.

From his perch Rossiter could see into the kitchen. A scowling cook in a white T-shirt was working the grill—Rossiter presumed this was Bud. To Bud's left, against the wall, McMahon was removing dishes from a battered tub and scraping them into a sink. Rossiter observed this procedure for a while. There were a lot of dishes to scrape, but McMahon's approach to the task was not alacritous. In fact, his pace seemed to slow with each passing moment, and Rossiter wondered whether he might eventually reach an entropic tipping point, curl up and sink into the tub.

The diners were being served by just one harried waitress. While she must have attended to Mr. Kramden at one point, she now showed no inclination to circle back to the counter. Rossiter sat there for another 10 minutes, watching McMahon, waiting to see if they might make eye contact, but McMahon showed no interest in the dining area. Rossiter left the counter, and went back to the 4-Runner. He waited there for several hours, until McMahon came out of Bud's, got in his pickup and drove off.

Rossiter spent his mid-days over the next two weeks parked across from Bud's, learning McMahon's mundane workday routine, which was: arrive at Bud's parking lot at 11, take a smoke break outside in his apron at 1, exit the building at 3:30, get in his truck and head back toward the freeway.

It wasn't until the end of the second week that the routine changed. At 3:30 McMahon came out of Bud's through the side door and got into his pickup, as usual. But instead of immediately driving off, McMahon rooted around in the cab for a while and then exited holding a white object the size and shape of a book. He started walking up the street, toward downtown.

When he was almost a block away, Rossiter got out and walked in the same direction, remaining on the opposite side of the street, keeping about 20 yards behind. After another block McMahon crossed onto Rossiter's side, walked another half-block, and stopped at a doorway. A tall gaunt man stood at the doorway next to a couple of kids, one in his mid-teens, the other younger. Rossiter stopped, too, and edged toward the building side of the street. The sign painted on the window read, "Lalo's Shoe Repair."

At first the tall man ignored McMahon, who was shifting his weight and putting his free hand in and out of his jacket pocket. It wasn't until the two kids went inside the building that McMahon's presence was acknowledged. McMahon proffered the white object to the tall man, who raised his hand in a "stop" gesture. He barked something at McMahon, and pointed his thumb toward the door. McMahon went inside. The tall man seemed to scan the area.

Rossiter faced the store window. A row of dusty cowboy boots was displayed, decorated elaborately in various colored stitching, arranged from kids' size to giant. A dozen pair, at least.

He counted to 60, then chanced a look back up the street. The tall man was gone, but more kids were milling about outside. Was it a school holiday? He couldn't think of one. A teacher's day or whatever. Were kids even required to attend school anymore? Was there still such a creature as a truant officer?

Pondering this, he headed on toward the building, and directly through a knot of kids. All boys. They were jabbering, typical boyish nonsense: *I jumped off the roof to the sidewalk / So what I already did that / I did it twice / I could but I don't want to / So what.* The only signage was a paper printout taped to the window that read, "Video Arcade." The door was open. He peeked inside, and saw a dozen or so boys around three or four video games. No adults in sight. He felt the curious stares of a couple of the outside boys. He wheeled around and walked back as far as the shoe repair shop. Within a minute he saw McMahon, empty-handed, exit the arcade.

Rossiter walked as fast as he could back toward Bud's. He crossed against a light and dodged a couple of cars until he neared Bud's, jaywalked to the parking lot and headed straight to McMahon's pickup. Three more of the white boxes lay on the front seat. He could see now that they we were videocassette boxes—the cutouts of the cardboard revealed the black cassettes. He glanced up the street and spotted McMahon, still a half block away on the other side of the street. He tried the door; it was unlocked. The interior smelled of cigarette smoke and marijuana and old vinyl and decaying foam rubber. The gearshift knob had been replaced with a white knob in the shape of a skull. He grabbed one of the videocassette boxes and pressed it against his outside thigh as he got out and started crossing the street. McMahon was just stepping off the opposite curb. Their eyes met briefly, blankly.

When he got home, he watched one full hour of the cassette. It was all child pornography. There were several segments, all filmed in one room with a backdrop of unfinished drywall. Maybe a basement room. The filming must have been done on a tripod, because the angle never changed. There were three segments, each with an adult, probably the same guy, although his face was never seen. He had dark hair on his belly and thighs. He abused a boy of about eight, another who couldn't have been more than four, and a girl who was just a tot.

About five minutes into the last segment Rossiter went to the bathroom and splashed cold water on his face. He came back and watched the rest. The last segment abruptly ended and the screen dissolved to video snow.

He fast-forwarded to the end to see if there was anything else, but there was nothing.

He sat in his chair, in front of the dark TV screen. At one point he pulled Blasingame's crinkled card out of his wallet and went to the phone. But he left it untouched, and went back to his chair.

After another ten minutes, he removed the cassette from the VCR and grabbed the white box, went to the garage and got a hammer. The back door of the garage entered into the backyard. He walked out the door to an old Weber barbecue. He yanked the tape from the cassette, letting it unravel on the cement patio. He took the matches he kept inside the barbecue, and set the tape and white box afire. Then he took the hammer, methodically smashed apart the cassette, and put the pieces in the garbage.

8. Believe It or Not

below this fall at a little distance a beatifull little Island well timbered is situated about the middle of the river. in this Island on a Cottonwood tree an Eagle has placed her nest; a more inaccessable spot I beleive she could not have found; for neither man nor beast dare pass those gulphs which seperate her little domain from the shores.

    – Meriwether Lewis, *The Journals of Lewis and Clark*
    (entered June 14, 1805)

The RV bed apparently consisted no more than a thin layer of foam on a sheet of plywood. I got up while it was still dark. As I quietly dressed, the rhythm of Duane's soft snoring did not change. I grabbed my jacket and eased out the door. The eastern sky was just beginning to show the suggestion of light. For a few moments I accepted the dry cold like a blanket, letting it settle over every part of me. Then I shivered, shook my arms vigorously, and pulled on my jacket. I headed toward the picnic area, stopping a respectful distance away to pee against a tree.

Lights were already on inside the office, and a car was parked outside, but I walked away, toward the river. At first I couldn't make out much more than its dark mass, and it made no sound other than a deep, faint grumble. I stood there not really seeing it, but listening to its inexorable motion. As I peered into the blackness, a bit of light seemed to catch something on the surface, maybe 40 feet out. If I fixed my gaze on it, I saw nothing; but if I focused just to the side, I thought I detected an object floating there, not moving with the current. The sky and water transformed in slow syncopation from black to dark gray to gray. Finally the object soaked in enough light to transform from gray to a dull orange. Hung up on a branch, which itself was hung up on a rock, it revealed itself to be just a rag—maybe one of those orange vests that a highway worker would use, but with its reflectiveness now all washed away. The current pushed either hapless end of it, so that it wrapped around the branch into a V. After maybe five minutes, for no apparent reason, it broke free and started to float downriver. I watched until its shape and color were absorbed again by the water.

The RV was still dark, so I went to the office. I could see Mike inside behind a counter. A bell tinkled when I opened the door.

"Ah! Early bird, eh?" The office was warm, and suffused with the aroma of coffee. Mike held his Town Pump mug.

"Compared to some. You, too."

"I gotta get Darren to his school early in the a.m. He goes for a half-day. How'd you sleep? Looks like you already had your walk."

"I slept fine. Thanks for arranging all that."

"Sure. I felt bad about renting her that rig with the bad pipes."

"You've more than made up for it. All that you've done...it's really been too much, I have to say."

"It's nothin.' How 'bout some java? I picked up some doughnuts, too." He gestured toward a pink box on the counter, next to a folded Great Falls Tribune.

"Coffee sounds great."

"Help yourself. Over there by the magazines."

A gleaming, full pot of coffee sat atop an end table, beside several magazines. Neatly displayed, each magazine featured a different model RV. I took a foam cup from the holder mounted on the wall, filled it up, and walked over to Mike, who was leafing through some papers.

"Got the paperwork for the pickup rental here. I guess she'll....?"

"Yep. She's got the plastic."

Mike gathered up the papers and inserted them into a folder, closed the folder and patted it. "Okey-doke, then."

"Man," I said. "I truly admire you. I don't know how you do it."

"What's that?"

"How do you do all this."

"All what?"

"All of it. The doughnuts, the coffee, this spotless office with the fanned-out magazines, the paperwork all ready to go in the folder. The kid with, uh, the disability, the perfect house, the perfect daughter."

"Oh-ho. They're not perfect, I'll tell you that."

I walked back to the counter, and said quietly, "No, it's all perfect. How do you manage?"

"Well." Mike shifted his weight. "Same as anybody else. Just put one foot in front of the other."

"But how do you keep going?"

"That's what we all do, right? Play the hand you're dealt. What's the alternative?" Mike lifted the lid and rotated the box. "What's your pleasure?"

I chose a gaudy one—white frosting, green and pink sprinkles. "You fold," I said.

Mike had already picked up his own doughnut. "Ha." He took a bite. "Can't do that."

"And why not, exactly?"

"Hm." This grunt, despite its inarticulation, economically conveyed two thoughts: *I hear ya,* and at the same time, *We both know that folding is not an option.* "So how was dinner last night? Good?"

OK. Change of subject. "Great. Although we may have drunk slightly to excess, so it's possible we won't be invited back."

"Oh, heck, they expect that in Great Falls. They'd wonder what's wrong if you didn't. Uh-oh. Looks like someone else is up."

I followed Mike's gaze to the door. Thao was heading briskly toward it, her arms folded. She was wearing her down jacket and sweatpants, and her feet, in bright white socks, were in a pair of floppy sandals. She saw us, beamed and unfolded her arms long enough to wave. Mike waved back. "She's pretty cute."

"She is."

"Kind of like a little doll."

"Yeah."

The bell tinkled and she quickly ducked inside. Her hair was wet. "Oh my god it is so *cold* out there!"

"Good mornin', sunshine. Have some coffee, that'll warm you up. And there's doughnuts, too."

"Doughnuts! Mike! We were going to buy *you* breakfast."

"Oh, that's all right. I've gotta stay here at the shop."

She headed straight to the pink box. "What kind of doughnuts? Ooh! Old-fashioned. My favorite. Mike, how did you ever know?"

Mike blushed the approximate color of my pink sprinkles. "Here," he said, "let me get you some coffee."

"You stay right there. I can get my own coffee." Thao set down her doughnut on a napkin and headed to the coffee.

Mike, as he chewed on his doughnut, seemed eager to speak, while uncertain as to the necessary content. "So," he finally managed. "How'd you sleep last night?

"Like a stone. That bed is so comfortable."

"That RV sleeps four, no problem. I showed you that accordion door, didn't I? It kind of privatizes the one side, but the sound..."

"Yes, you did show me, and it worked just as advertised. And I can deal with snoring on the other side of the door."

"Speaking of which," I said, "how's Duane?"

"Still conked out."

"Is he alive?"

"Yes, I could hear him making noises. We can let him sleep for a while. We have time."

"It's a good thing you ended up staying till this morning," Mike said. "You can sightsee on the way up. Stop off at Fort Benton."

"I've been there," I said. "There's really nothing to see."

"Oh, you say that about everything," Thao said. "What's in Fort Benton, Mike? It's another fort? I hope there's more fort than Fort Shaw has."

"Oh, yeah, they've got the old fort there, and the museum. And I saw where they've got a new statue put up of Old Shep."

"Who's Old Shep?"

"You never heard of Old Shep? It's quite a story."

I may have slightly groaned.

"Ross! I want to hear Mike tell about Old Shep."

Mike hesitated, but on hearing no further objection, started. "Yeah, back in the '30s, there was this sheepherder up in Fort Benton, had a dog, of course, they all had dogs. So, the sheepherder gets sick and they take him to the hospital in Fort Benton, and his dog somehow follows him to the hospital and stays right there at the door of the hospital waiting for him."

Mike took another bite of doughnut, a sip of coffee. I assumed this was for dramatic effect.

"Then what? Did the man die?"

"Yep. He dies, and they load his coffin onto the train, and the dog is right there when the train heads back east. And darned if every day, when the trains came in, that dog would be right back there, waiting to see if his master was coming."

"No way."

"It's true. He did it for five years. Met every single train."

"Five years! That is amazing!"

"Yeah, he became kinda famous. They wrote him up in Ripley's Believe It or Not and so on. Anyhow, one day Old Shep was waiting to meet the train, and I guess he'd got kinda old and deaf, and darned if the train didn't hit him and kill him right there on the tracks."

"Oh, no! That's awful!"

"Yep. So they had a big funeral, and of course people came from all over the whole country, and they buried Old Shep on a hill up above the train station, so that he could watch over every train that came in. There's a little marker up there on the hill where he's buried. But now they put up a nice statue downtown by the river, too. Just did."

"We've got to go see this. Duane will love it. We can do a sidebar on it. There's lots of interesting history in Montana, isn't there?"

"Oh, yeah," Mike said.

"Is it history, or myth?" I asked.

"Oh, sure, who knows what really happens, eh? But Old Shep, that really happened. There are pictures of him right there at the station. And like I said, it was in Ripley's Believe It or Not."

"Yeah!" Thao said. "Doesn't sound like a myth to me."

"I'm sure he really existed. I'm not so sure he really was meeting every train every day with the hope of greeting his returning master. Maybe at first. But he was getting fed and getting attention, and I suspect that he adapted to the new world order and just took up residence. So of course he was there when the trains came in."

"I don't know," Mike said. "They say he actually came out and met each train, every day, and looked over every passenger who came off."

Thao had somehow produced a notebook and pen, and was jotting notes. "Old Shep met all the trains," she said aloud. "Looked at every passenger."

When we returned to the RV, Duane, cleaned up and fully dressed, was sitting at the converted table, eating a bowl of cold cereal.

Thao and I paused just inside the door. She gave me a quick poke in the thigh with her thumb.

"Good morning, sunshine," she said to him.

"Morning."

"How are we today?

"I don't know about you. I'm fine."

"Why didn't you come in? Mike had coffee and doughnuts."

"Just felt like a nice quiet bowl of Cheerios." He pointed with his spoon at the box. "They have Frosted Cheerios now. More nutritious than doughnuts. So, are we ready to hit the road?"

"Just as soon as you finish your Frosted Cheerios. We're stopping at Fort Benton on the way. Mike told us this great story about Old Shep the dog."

She related the tale as Mike told it, nearly verbatim.

"I remember going there once when I was a kid," Duane said. "OK. Cool. More pictures for Sherry."

"You are an obliging guy," I said.

"Hey, it's my vocation and my avocation. I like to make pictures."

I went into the bathroom, which was about the size of a closet in the second bedroom of a small house. When I bent over in the sink, I felt as if I were inserting my head into a helmet.

Our pickup was spotless inside and out, and the interior smelled like a new vehicle on the car lot. By some tacit agreement, I was now the official driver. Thao hoisted herself up into the passenger seat, and Duane stayed in the back. Mike had walked us to the pickup, and now lingered at the driver's window.

"If you've got some extra time, you might want to stop at the Russell museum," he said. "Pretty interesting. He was quite a character, Charley Russell. The Cowboy Artist."

"We might have to do that on the way back," Thao said. "I think this morning we want to stop at the great falls. And we want to see the Old Shep statue."

"Yeah, don't miss that," Mike said.

I pulled slowly out of the lot. Mike waved.

"I *love* him," Thao said. When Duane and I did not reply, she added, "And you guys do, too. Now. Ross, you know where the Great Falls are, right?"

"Sure. We'll swing by Black Eagle Falls. It's not too far out of the way."

"But we want to see the Great Falls."

"Yeah. 'Great Falls' actually is named after a series of five different waterfalls. Black Eagle Falls is right here in town. I have to warn you, though, it's probably not all that impressive this time of year."

She made the "pff" sound. "Nothing's impressive to you."

"That's not true. Quite the opposite, in fact."

I put us on a road that followed the river all the way to the falls. Initially, the road ran level and just a few feet above the high-water level before it made a gradual steady climb to a high bluff where there was a turnout. When we got out, we could hear the steady *whoom* of the waterfall. We walked to the edge of the bluff, and the falls were revealed about a quarter-mile below. The dam's floodgates were wide open; the river poured steadily through and plummeted downward, breaking up into a chaos of foam on the rocks below…then slowly regathered into river water and resumed course. A ways down, it hesitated at the tip of a small island before it split in two, like a sheet tearing apart. It rejoined itself on the other side of the island and headed east.

"See? It *is* impressive," Thao said.

Duane took a couple of shots, posing Thao and me here and there in the foreground for perspective, but he expressed dissatisfaction with the angles and distance from us to the falls. He squinted into the distance. "Hey, there's a guy walking across there."

"What? I don't see anything…. Oh wait, I see him."

A solitary figure, no more than a vertical line, a pencil-tip, was visible making slow, steady progress along the skeletal structure that stretched across the crest of the falls. A white smudge, probably his safety helmet, inched along just above the rails of the catwalk.

"Gosh. Everything is so big here. The river, the prairie, the sky. I see what you meant. When you can see so far, it makes the people seem so small."

"You've just distilled the essence of Montana."

"I did? I amaze myself! And I've only been here a couple of days. Duane, you should take a picture of me, distilling the essence of Montana." She struck a pose, one hand on her hip, the other cocked at her side.

"That doesn't really say 'distilling,'" Duane said. "It says, more like 'teapot.'"

"That's exactly the kind of remark I'd expect from someone who can't distill the essence of Montana himself. Now, come on, Mr. DeMille. I'm ready for my close-up."

He took some shots of her. "OK, you're distilling like a teapot. Ooh. You're steaming. Now, hiss." She hissed. "No, that's a cat. Whistle instead." She tried to whistle, but could only muster a breathy *fwwt.* "That's a really weak whistle. Try pouring the tea."

Thao began to sing, her voice thin but confident, about a half-step out of tune: "I'm a little tea-POT, short and STOUT." Duane made a sound of pain, which prompted her to just sing more loudly. "Here is my HANDLE, here is my SPOUT. When I get all STEAMED up…" As Thao started to bend sideways from the waist, I moved a few feet away from them to alter my viewpoint. In the distance, in the water, just above the white smudge, which had now stopped, I thought I saw something. Tiny, a dot, but something moving in the current. An orange molecule. It was bobbing along toward the dam. I calculated: If the current flowed at, say, five miles per hour, and we were a good five miles, maybe a little more, from Mike's RVs, and I had seen the orange vest hung up in the river about an hour and a half ago…it seemed a bit tardy, but of course it could have gotten hung up again somewhere along the way. I watched until it disappeared behind the catwalk structure.

"…Hear me SHOUT! Tip me over and pour me out!"

Thao finished her song with a giggle. She walked over and followed the direction of my gaze. "What do you see now?"

"Oh!" Incredibly, the orange dot came back into my sight, under the catwalk, riding the water downward into the pool of foam. It came up to the island and lingered, as if trying to decide which way to go, then drifted to the far side, and disappeared.

"What is it?" Thao asked.

"Nothing. Tell me—why is it that people who are tone deaf like to sing?"

"That's an odd question to ask of me. But I would conjecture that it's not the *tone* they enjoy…so much as the *singing*."

The highway going out of town took us up a steep hill, with all of Great Falls spread out behind us, sitting in the large bowl that had been carved out by the Missouri. In the rearview mirror I could see segments of silver water river reflecting the sun. We crested the hill, and the town and the river disappeared, and we were on the prairie again, two-lane cutting a straight line on Highway 87 through the dun hills and fields of wheat stubble.

"How far is it to Fort Benton?" Thao asked.

"About 45 minutes."

She dug out the book that Mike had loaned her about Chief Joseph, and read aloud from the jacket. *The amazing story of the journey of the Nez Perce and 'Red Napoleon'...the incredible tale of 800 warriors, women and children, displaced from their homeland, traveling 1,200 miles through the mountains and across rivers, keeping the might of the U.S. Army at bay... the memorable, haunting words of Chief Joseph: 'From where the sun now stands, I will fight no more, forever.'*

She opened the book and flipped through pages. "It really *is* an incredible story," she said to Duane. "They were given a huge reservation to live on in Washington, but a bunch of settlers and gold-diggers came in. So the U.S. told them they had to move to a smaller reservation, but some of them didn't want to. So this General Howard gave them a deadline to get off, and meanwhile, some braves got angry and killed some white people. So they got into a fight, and the Indians beat the cavalry. Then they took off on this unbelievable journey to try to meet up with another tribe in Canada before the cavalry caught them. Eight hundred men, women and children, on foot and horseback, traveling over a thousand miles in four months. Can you imagine?"

She returned to the back cover, which had a portrait of Joseph. "How moving. And what a handsome man. It's so sad. But now he's part of American…what's that word? Galore."

"Galore?"

"Yeah, the legends, you know, of the great people. American galore. I know that doesn't sound right…"

"I'm not sure, but I think you just made up a word by combining "glory" and "lore.""

"I did, didn't I?" Thao confirmed her satisfaction at this accomplishment with an emphatic, "Mm-hm!"

We drove in silence for 15 minutes, until we came up over a hill, and I took my foot off the gas. Ahead of us to the right, a car was pulling up to the highway from off of a dirt road in the stubble. Although it was not moving fast, when it came to a stop, the whole car sagged on its shocks; and then, as if mustering all its weary energy, it slowly rose up again. There was something on the hood, a tawny blanket, part of it drooping over the side.

"What's that?" Thao asked.

"A deer."

"Oh, no…"

I throttled down to 20 miles an hour as we went by. The carcass lay belly down on the hood, as if a pooped-out deer had just decided to jump atop it and lie down there. Its front legs extended over the fender. They were trussed together, the rope a taut line to the undercarriage of the car. It was a young buck; the spikes of its new antlers pointed at us. Its tongue protruded from its mouth, and there were spots of blood around it on the white hood. In the front seat of the car, a man and a boy, both pale, both wearing orange caps and orange vests, viewed us blankly.

"That poor thing," Thao said.

Duane was rustling around behind us. "Wait, stop. I've got to make a picture of that."

"No."

"Really. Stop for a minute. Just pull over."

"No." I accelerated, and checked the rearview mirror. The car crept onto the highway, turning in the opposite direction. After it wobbled onto the road it gathered up some speed, black smoke billowing from the tailpipe.

"C'mon. That would have been a great picture."

"Let's leave them alone."

"How do you know they *don't* want their picture made?"

"I don't. All I know is that *I* don't. And you can't just park on a two-lane highway."

"Yeah, because there's all this traffic zooming by."

"It's disgusting," Thao said. "Why would anybody want to shoot a deer?"

"To eat it."

"That is so gross. Just go to the store to buy your meat, instead of killing a deer and displaying it like it's a hood ornament."

"I'm sure if they could afford a pickup, they'd be driving one, and the deer would be in the bed and hidden from the sight of sensitive tourists from California. I don't know if you noticed, but that was about a 1982 Oldsmobile they were driving. That deer is going to end up as a few meals on their dinner table, and it'll be a hell of a lot cheaper than going to the store."

"It's still gross."

"And I'll tell you something else. I'll bet you anything that just before that buck was shot, he was grazing somewhere with the wind in his nose and the sun on his back. Compare that to the three of us eating a steak at Freddy's from cows that spent their last days on some godforsaken feedlot and then jammed into a truck and herded into a slaughterhouse. If you want to talk about gross."

"I don't like to think about that."

"You have that choice. I envy you."

We were silent for a while. Duane finally said, "You used to hunt?"

"Sure. Kids who grow up in Montana go hunting."

"But you don't anymore, do you?" Thao asked.

"Road trips aside, I pretty much don't eat any meat anymore, period. When I was a kid, my dad and I went hunting, and killed your basic variety of game, and it all ended up on the table, and I didn't think anything of it. But anyway, no, I don't hunt anymore. I've gone soft."

"Soft? I would say enlightened instead."

"'Enlightened.' Is that the word for it? When you're so soft you're completely at odds with the world?"

"That's not at odds with the world."

"Of course it is. The world is a fucking cartoon. Animals eat other animals. One animal chases down another and catches it and kills it and devours its flesh, for Christ's sake. It happens millions of times every single day. And humans, some of them, a lot of them, somehow find that gross. I don't know which is more ridiculous, the world or the humans who live in it."

We drove along on the straight-north road, the pickup gently rocking with the bumps. Nobody spoke for a while, until Thao said, "All the kids in Montana go hunting. I guess they all have guns, too."

"Hard to hunt without one. Unless you're a bow-and-arrow nut."

"Do you still have yours?"

"I don't have any need for a hunting rifle. Like I said."

"Just a pistol? For the snakes?"

"Why?"

"Just curious. I guess it's a Montana thing, huh?"

"It's a bigger thing than that."

"Bigger, how?"

"Just bigger."

She must have seen that I was the pace car in a conversational oval. Rather than push on, she picked her book up and examined the portrait of Joseph. "What a handsome man," she said again.

Like Great Falls, Fort Benton sat in a large basin, the river in its lap. The town, though, was considerably smaller, and creakier than Great Falls. The grasses of the prairie were pushing in from every side. At some of the houses, which were in their prime maybe 40 years past, the prairie had tipped the battle in its favor. Two minutes after exiting the highway, I was steering onto the main street. The town center lay on one side of a three-block street; on the other side was a walkway along the west bank of the Missouri. I drove slowly although there were only a couple of other cars on the street. Most of the buildings were brick. A few had tacked on incongruous wood or stone facades. Bar, antique shop, museum, closed-down bar, saddlery, Stockman's Bar, cafe.

"Hey!" Thao leaned forward and pointed toward the river. "There's Old Shep!"

I pulled into a parking spot, and we crossed the street to the bronze statue. It sat atop a rough block of stone, maybe four feet off the ground. The work depicted the dog as alert and strong, full-chested, standing with his two front paws on a section of railroad track, ears up, tail curled, gazing hopefully in the distance at the imagined train. There was a simple inscription at the base, which Thao read aloud in a reverent tone: "Forever Faithful."

"OK, it's kind of corny," she said, "but you have to admit—" She glanced at me. "—it's also kind of...oh."

I shifted so I wasn't facing her.

"—kind of touching." She took a step forward and sideways, to get in front of me. "More allergies?"

More pathetic. "Up here we call it hay fever."

"Even this time of year?"

"Any time of year except winter…Look, I don't know what to say. Honestly? I disgust myself."

"Disgust? How?" She sounded genuinely surprised. Duane was occupied with taking photos of the statue, or maybe of me. I frowned at the camera. "Fuck that," I said.

He lowered it. "OK. Anyway, this light's not great, and I need a kid."

"A kid?" I cleared my throat, and gave my eyes a quick swipe with my sleeve.

"To stand over by the dog. That would make a picture."

There were a few pedestrians here and there: a man in a cowboy hat walking into the cafe, two teenagers beside the raised hood of a pickup, a couple of young women, jet black hair, bright red jackets, peering into the antique shop across the street. A tall man with equally black hair stood behind them, arms folded across his denim shirt. But no kids.

"I'm hungry," Thao said.

"No way," Duane said. "Really?"

"All I had this morning was one doughnut. Let's go to that cafe."

"Fine. I'm going to hang here for a while. Someone will come along who I can shoot."

I could hear the two women across the street. They wanted to go in the store, but the man was heading off. They called after him: "C'mon, let's go in." He gave a dismissive wave. The women looked at each other and entered the antique shop.

"Ross?"

"Sure. Let's eat."

There were a few people in the cafe, mostly older. Counter spots were open, but Thao steered me to a booth at a window. From there we could see the statue and Duane.

I picked up the salt shaker, rotated it in my hand, put it down.

"So, what do you think of Fort Benton?" I asked.

She scrutinized the scene outside the window. "It's nice. A pretty little town. I love how it's right on the river."

"What do you think of it in terms of your story about towns in the West?"

She was still taking in the view. "It's a little run-down, for sure, but it doesn't seem exactly dried up. It's kind of cute, actually. It's more of a tourist town, isn't it?"

"Yeah, there's some tourism, I'm sure. But I think it's more of an agricultural center. County seat. They're not in their heyday here, but I think they're doing OK. You'll find more of what you want up on the Hi-Line, probably. Those little towns—Prague, Zurich, Harlem. They're bleeding people."

She produced her notebook, and scribbled down the names. "It's like visiting Europe."

"Yes. Maybe not quite as Continental."

The waitress—slender, young, surely not long out of high school— brought menus, water and a pot of coffee. "Hi, folks," she said cheerily. Her name was sewn in script on her white blouse: Lori. "The special today is meatloaf, and it's really good."

"Did you eat any of it?"

"Ee-yep." From her emphatic assent, it could have been inferred that she ate quite a lot.

"OK, the meatloaf," Thao said.

"Think I'll just have a PB and J."

"You bet," the waitress said. As she poured her coffee, I saw her wink at Thao. After she walked off, Thao looked at me quizzically.

"Some people here tend to wink a lot," I explained.

"Because you ordered a peanut-butter-and-jelly sandwich?"

"Maybe. Or maybe because of nothing. It's just a friendly gesture. Doesn't really mean anything."

"Ohhh-kayyy," she said. She jotted down a few words. I read the fragment upside down: *waitress winks, just friendly.* She attempted a wink of her own, but instead of one eye closing all the way, one went down most of the way, and the other about a third of the way.

"I'm intuiting that you haven't had much winking experience."

"Which shows how much you know. This is called the Vietnamese Wink, at which I'm quite proficient."

"OK." I picked up the salt shaker again. "So," I said. "Thanks for not giving me a hard time about the statue."

"Why would I do that? That would just be mean."

"I guess it would be, a little. But I had it coming."

"I did tease you, a little."

"You gave me just a tiny nudge, instead of knocking my ass off my cynical, world-weary, history-or-myth little perch."

"I'm not interested in knocking your ass off of anything. I was glad to see that side of you. There was a little hint when we dropped off Frankie yesterday, too. I'd like to see more of the real you."

"There is no real me."

"That makes no sense. You just don't want to show who you are, for whatever reason. For example, it's interesting, your reaction to the Shep statue, versus your reaction to the dead deer."

I turned my gaze to the window. "Hm. Wonder where Duane went off to." Rather than follow my gaze, she flipped her notebook to a fresh page. She reached her hand over and lightly tapped my wrist with the pen. "Can we have a little talk?"

"I suppose this was inevitable."

"If you'd rather not…."

"Actually, I'd rather."

9. The Extreme Opposite

Thao quickly set down her glass of water, and pushed aside her place setting. She set her notebook down flat where her plate had been, rummaged in her bag and came out with a small tape recorder. I could see the red indicator light start to blink. She poised her pen over the page. "OK?"

"I guess I'd better be. All right—what can I tell you that's not already in that binder of yours?"

She didn't say anything.

"Go ahead. It's all right."

"Right. So…I'm starting to think you might be part of the story here."

"You're just starting?"

"People back in San Jose remember you, you know. They might be interested to hear what happened to you."

"And what is it that happened to me?"

"I was hoping you'd tell me. You know: something like, 'Reporter from a major metro leaves civilization to seek meaning on the empty plains of Montana.'"

"Really? That's it?…OK, you got the 'leaves civilization' part right. And 'empty plains.' The rest is wrong."

"Help me understand what's wrong about it."

I sighed. "You're still going to do the story on Joseph, right?"

"Sure."

"I'm serious."

"So am I."

"Because I don't want anything written about me that is going to get in the way of a story that reminds people yet again of how the United States subjugated, without care or mercy, an entire tribe of people, savaged their persons and the significance of their lives, humiliated and tortured them… and then just forgot about them, and continues to forget about them, and continues to fuck them over. While it nurtures a few ennobling myths designed to salve everybody's consciences and enable them to walk away saying, 'Hey, we've done all we can.'"

"I'll do the story. I promise."

Her dark eyes did not blink.

"So one more thing before we start. Take out a piece of paper."

She opened to a blank sheet and tore it out.

"Now: Write down what you think the most important thing in life is. Don't show me."

"Seriously?"

"Yes."

"In my life? Or in life in general?"

"In your life. In anyone's life."

"But different things are important to different people."

"Just generally, the single most important thing in life."

She put her pen to her mouth and pursed her lips. The tip of the pen pointed to the rounded upturn of her nose. She held this pose for maybe 10 seconds before putting the pen to the paper, using her forearm to block my sight line.

"I won't peek." I closed my eyes. "When you're done fold the paper in half, and hand it to me."

I heard the scrape of her pen, followed by the sound of her sharply creasing the paper. I felt it against my hand. I opened my eyes and put the paper in my breast pocket.

"Thank you. Now. Go ahead. Ask me your questions."

"My first question is, why are you all of a sudden willing to answer my questions? At first you wouldn't even admit you were you."

"It just seems to me that our relationship has reached that point. I think I know a little more about what's in your heart."

"I'm glad you think so. I appreciate the vote of trust."

"I didn't say I trusted you."

"Ah. So…why did you just drop everything and leave? Your job, your home. Your whole career."

"Same reason anybody leaves anything. You don't like where you are anymore. Or it doesn't like you. Or some combination of the two."

She scribbled on the page: *It doesn't like you.*

"It's not all that common, you know. To drop everything, leave an established job and just move out to the middle of nowhere. You were married, right?"

"I didn't really drop everything. I had nothing to drop. I was divorced, as you probably already know. My son was gone. I didn't want to write at the newspaper anymore. There was no reason to stay."

"You still had friends, there, though. Ed is worried about you. He asked me how you are doing."

"So you said. I would love to have heard the answer to that."

"I said you seem to be doing very well, under the circumstances."

"Which circumstances are those?"

"Living by yourself in the middle of nowhere, in a tiny little cabin. Isolated from human contact."

"Okay, when you put it that way it sounds a little bleak."

"I would get so lonely. Don't you miss your friends? People in general?"

"Sure. I do get lonely. Every day. Which, as you probably have figured out, is one of the reasons I'm here right now."

"I do have the impression that you have a bit of a social streak. Which is odd for a hermit…Did you ever think of remarrying?"

I laughed. "No."

"Why is that funny?"

"I like women too much to subject one to that kind of misery."

She took the time to carefully write this word for word. From my seat I could see the statue of Shep gazing hopefully into the distance.

"What happened to your ex-wife? Are you still in contact?"

"No. She moved to San Francisco. Got married to a dance instructor."

"A dance instructor. Not a very common occupation."

"No. You know how it is sometimes in situations like that—a person tends to swing from one extreme to the other."

"So…you are the extreme opposite of a dance instructor?"

"Ha."

"And your son?"

"You know about that."

"Yes, I read the story and the obituary."

"Are they in your binder, too?"

She paused. "Hit by a car. That's so sad. I'm sorry."

"Yes."

"What exactly happened? I know a lady hit him by the school. He ran into the street…"

"Oh…It was a stupid amalgam of circumstances. It was not the lady's fault. Just a stupid…"

A couple with two kids were at the statue. The man was lining up the three for a snapshot. Where was Duane now?

"Jesus," I said. "They sculpted it so that dog has to stand there and keep looking down those goddamn tracks for the next five hundred years. Why couldn't they have given him a break and let him lie down?"

"How was it stupid? The circumstances."

"Oh, I don't mean stupid," I said to the window. "It wasn't stupid—it was just life."

I turned back to her.

"OK. So. We lived just a few blocks from the school. So we let him walk back and forth a lot of the time. The neighbors had two older girls—sweet girls, twins, they really loved him—and he walked with them. Then—you

132

know about the tortoise."

"Yes. That sick story about the vandals."

"After a week or so, the kids in the class were still upset about it. Or maybe it was the teacher who couldn't let it go. That whole episode was so nasty. Anyway, she decided they needed to have a little ceremony to—I don't know what. Mark his passing, say goodbye. The janitor had buried him out under a tree by the ball field, so they were going to just go out there this one day and, you know, say a few words or do whatever you do at a tortoise funeral. Commend his spirit unto heaven.

"She'd told the kids they could bring flowers, and Jay was convinced that was the thing to do, so he got his mom to pick up a little bunch at the store for him. But of course he forgot them that morning, and didn't remember till they'd got all the way to the school. So he wanted to go back to get them, but the girls told him no, they'd be late for the bell. But he started to run home, and they took after him telling him no, and he ran right into the street and the lady hit him."

"Oh, no."

"She stopped and tried to tend to him. The girls just kept running to our house. Just before they got there, I remember I was standing at the counter in my robe, drinking coffee and thinking…you know what I was thinking?"

"What?"

"I was thinking, 'Oh, Christ, he was bound and determined to bring those fucking flowers, and wouldn't you know it, he totally forgot about it. And now I have to take them down there, which means I have to get dressed.' I wish I hadn't been thinking that."

"Why? It's only natural to think that."

"Okay. So I'm standing there pissed off with these flowers in my face and all of a sudden the girls were banging on the door. I ran down the street wearing just a bathrobe. Barefoot. When I got there the ambulance was just arriving. He was breathing. His eyes were half-open. He was barely even bleeding. Just a little from his nose and ear. At first I thought, it's just a bruise, is all. But he went into a coma, and he never woke up. He died four weeks to the day afterward."

"I'm so sorry."

"Thanks."

"That must have been so hard. And to go through a divorce so soon after that…"

I answered the question before she articulated it. "She left me. When you lose a child, it tears open a hole in you. Suddenly all the joy and energy are sucked out of your life, and what's left is this gaping hole. She needed me to help her fill it, and instead of helping, I was another gaping hole. She wanted to find happiness again. I certainly can't blame her."

"I'm so sorry," she said again. "It must have been very difficult."

"It wasn't difficult; it was impossible. The person that I was before—he was gone. He's someone else. Not that he was any good at it in the first place."

"At…?"

"Being that person. A husband."

"Your son's death—did you ever write anything about it?"

"If I had, I'm sure you would know."

"I know you didn't write anything in the paper. But anywhere? A journal? That might be cathartic for a writer."

"It wouldn't have meant anything to write about it. Sometimes you simply can't enhance or alter or make sense of something that has occurred by writing about it or talking about it. You can't define it. You can't even describe it. Writing about something like that adds nothing. It just makes it worse. You end up placing this layer of unreality over it. It's like writing, 'The tiger is beautiful' on a sign, and draping it over the tiger."

"'Beautiful?'"

"Whatever. A gazelle that's half-eaten by the tiger. A sign that reads, 'The ravaged gazelle is awful.' There's no point in writing anything, or saying anything. It's just this futile thing that humans do because they can't think of anything else."

"But you did keep writing after that. Another five or six years. All sorts of columns. Vignettes, character studies, humorous pieces. Indignant."

"Sure. That's what I did for a living…What an odd expression that is. But I didn't write about Jay."

"And then you did quit. In '95. That last kind of abrupt column."

"Yeah. At that point, as you could see, I had nothing left."

"I disagree. But it seemed awfully sudden. I didn't see anything leading up to that in the preceding columns. In fact, that second one I brought was typical. And that was only a few weeks before you quit."

I started to speak, but Lori approached with our food. Thao made a slight noise of impatience, but manufactured a smile.

"OK," Lori said. "One special…" With a flourish, she set down two plates in front of Thao. The first had two large slices of meatloaf, mashed potatoes and gravy, and string beans. The second held two buns and pats of butter. She hesitated for a moment before she set my plate down. No flourish. Just the sandwich with a bag of potato chips.

"Can I get you anything else?"

Thao maintained the smile for one more second before her face went blank. "Nope, that's it; we are all set, and thank you."

"More coffee?"

"No."

"If you need anything, just give me a holler."

"OK."

But Lori decided to linger. "You're going to like that meatloaf," she said. "It's got the secret ingredient."

"Please leave us alone now," Thao said. She spoke in the same flat tone that had caught Mike by surprise and transformed his mouth into an O.

"Why, sure. Sorry. I didn't mean—"

"No problem at all. Thank you."

Thao waited until Lori had edged away. "The second column," she said.

"You mean the one about the person of interest."

"Right. It was kind of funny. You were rather flip about it."

"Yeah. In retrospect, I'd have to say that that was inappropriate."

"Because…"

"Because there was a murder investigation going on, after all. Anyway. You want to know why the sudden change in tone from the second to the third. The change of heart."

"Yes. Was there something…?"

I let the question dangle in the air. Then I took Thao's folded paper from my pocket, and without unfolding it, I held it to my head and pretended to absorb it, ala Carson-as-Carnac-the-Magnificent.

"Family," I pronounced.

I put it on the table and unfolded it. I read aloud what she had written: "Family/loved ones."

"Very impressive."

"Works every time."

"So I'm predictable."

"It's not you. It's everyone. Everyone says the same thing. The minister, the president, the football player. Maybe they'll add God, or their health, but 'family' is never omitted. Take care of your tribe, especially your closest tribe."

"I don't know if *everyone*…"

"Everyone. If you asked a drunk who's living in an abandoned car in an alley in the Tenderloin, who deserted his wife and three kids 10 years earlier, and he hadn't seen them since, and he couldn't even bring to his mind's eye anymore what his kids looked like, if you asked him what the most important thing in life is, he'd say family."

"Let's say for the sake of argument you're right. What's that got to do with your big change?"

"And family is really just a code word for self-propagation, isn't it? Preserve yourself to the extent you can. That's the primary objective, right? Like, all the wellness advice you see—be positive, exercise, reduce stress, surround yourself with friends and family—is mainly designed toward one ultimate goal, which is to extend your life. Exploit others, even your so-called loved ones, to whatever extent is necessary to keep living. You may even have to make friends of certain people because that makes you live longer. Also, you'll have to mate with at least one of them in order to reproduce your DNA.

There's this wiring inside most of us that allows us—actually it impels us—to press on, keep going, keep living. And more important, to protect those who carry your genes. Because you can't live forever, but your genes can. It's the most basic and most powerful of biological urges. Survive. Propagate...So that the shells of flesh that carry your DNA can keep repeating the same stupid fucking mistakes over and over again."

"Gosh." She held up a finger to stop me. She picked up the recorder, checked the tape inside, and set it back down. She put down her pen and cut a sizable piece of the meatloaf, dipped it in the pile of potatoes, stabbed one of the beans while not losing a morsel of anything, and inserted the entire ensemble in her mouth. She slowly chewed it and studied me with open contemplation. I did not touch my sandwich. I felt myself begin to salivate.

"This is all most interesting," she said, her mouth not entirely empty of food. "It's a little weird, to tell you the truth. But I'm still not getting what it has to do with—"

"There's no fighting it, is my point. It's pointless to try to counter human nature. That's just a human trying not to be human. You can't change people."

"Sure you can. It happens all the time."

"How. When?"

"Didn't you read your own newspaper? People quit drugs, take up the ministry. Gangsters quit gangs and volunteer at elementary schools. Ruthless businessmen give away their fortunes to charity."

"They change only to the extent that they've changed their perception of what's best for them. 'I used to be happy taking drugs. Now I realize I'm happier if I don't, because I don't have to eat out of Dumpsters anymore, and people like me better.' It's just a superficial change. I am talking fundamentally. People don't change fundamentally. And included in that inability to change is the inability to accept the notion that we can't change."

Again, she held up a finger. I stopped. "I need to sort out all these negatives here…" She jotted some more notes, took a bite off the plate, jotted more notes. She read the last phrase aloud. "'…*The inability to accept the notion that we can't change.*' Again, for the sake of argument, let's say that's so. Why not just accept it, then? Get over it."

"And that's where I'm deficient. I don't have the get-over-it gene. I dwell on things that normal people learn to overlook. Or maybe they don't have to learn it at all. I'm sure it's an in-born survival mechanism that normal people have."

"What kinds of things do you dwell on?"

"This is starting to sound like a therapy session."

"Mm-hmm. And how does that make you feel?"

"Like I'm being had."

"Nonsense. So what kinds of things do you dwell on? You can't mean your son's death. Anybody in your situation would dwell on that."

"Maybe not to the extent I do, but I'm not talking about that. It's other stuff, which has nothing to do with me personally. For example: the kind of stuff you encounter all the time when you work at a newspaper. Things that normal people in the newsroom—if there's such a beast as a normal person in a newsroom—learn to block out of their minds. Or at least put in a closed-off place in their minds where they can open and close the door as needed."

"Tragedies? Crime?"

"Well, sure. Like there was this story we followed a few years ago that happened down in San Martin. I wasn't even involved in the reporting. You probably heard about it. This woman starved her grandson to death. Emmett Wilson was his name. Emmett. What kind of name is that for a six-year-old? The old woman thought it wasn't really her son's son. That the mother of the kid had cheated on him. The son and his wife were out of the picture, probably in some drug rehab program, and grandma was taking care of Emmett. She kept him in a dog kennel most of the time. He died at the age of six, and he weighed 20 pounds. I wrote a column about it."

"I kind of remember the story. I don't think I saw the column, though."

"Here's his picture."

I took out my wallet and pulled out several folded-up bits of paper. I extracted one, unfolded it and pushed it across to her. It was a newspaper clipping with a photo. It showed a little boy, about 3 years old, close-cropped hair. He wore a wide, impish grin and a Ninja Turtles T-shirt.

Thao wiped her hands on her napkin before she picked up the clipping. "I do remember this. It was awful."

I returned it to the little deck of papers, and extracted another.

"I'm just picking randomly here." I unfolded the paper. Another clipping, this one with a blurry black-and-white photo of a little girl holding something fuzzy. She was smiling and squinting into sunlight. "Farther from home. A wire story. Do you remember a story out of Florida about a little girl who was kidnapped? Her name was Jessica Landon. The guy took her from her front yard. She had a stuffed toy her mom had just bought her—a blue dolphin. He did whatever to her, and then buried her alive in a plastic bag. When they found her body she was still grasping that toy blue dolphin. I had dreams about her, suffocating inside that bag, hugging her toy dolphin. I still have dreams about it."

Thao had stopped eating. She continued to write in her notepad. *Carries clips. Dreams.* Pointing to the little stack in my hand, she singled out the one on the bottom—a studio photo of a little blond boy with a slight scar next to his left eye. "What's that one?"

I placed the stack back inside my wallet. "It's another one of an endless series. And these are just the individual, isolated cases. A person here, a person there. Then there's the big-scale horrors, the purges, the pogroms, the ethnic cleansing. And with a new century staring us in the face, it's still going on. You think humanity learned a lesson with the Holocaust? Post-Holocaust, we have, just to name a few, the Khmer Rouge, Bosnia, Zimbabwe. The crazy-ass, unimaginably awful shit people do to each other. But here's the thing. Here's the big pitch after all this windup. As concerned and activist and peace-loving as anybody might be, they can't live their life obsessing about the bad. And normal people don't. They somehow deal with it, make sense of it in whatever way they can, skip to the conclusion that good eventually triumphs over evil, that God eventually will make sense of it all for them. And then they maybe go to the movies. Play ball, have lunch. Sing. Live."

"So maybe you are just unusually empathetic. You're a very sensitive man."

"It's not empathy, it's insanity. The miserable aspects of life attach themselves to me like ticks."

"If you're that depressed, maybe you should be on meds."

"Even if they worked, I'd still know all this shit is out there. It would just be like pulling a blanket over my head. The sounds might be muffled, but I'd still hear them grinding and groaning."

"What about therapy? Someone qualified, as opposed to me."

"You're saying find a cure, but I really don't feel there's anything wrong with me. There's nothing to cure. It's just the way I see the world. But you can't see the world that way and work in a newsroom at the same time and still maintain your sanity."

She picked up one of the buns, broke it in half, and applied the butter neatly and evenly to each exposed side. She took one and slid it across the plate, sopping up most of what was left.

"You really enjoyed that," I said. "In spite of the conversation. Or the conversationalist."

"Mm-hmm, I did. Why aren't you eating?"

"I will."

"You should've had the meatloaf." She used the second half of the bun to clean up the remaining gravy, and popped it neatly into her mouth. She tapped her notebook. "So tell me. Do you really believe all this? Were you always like this?"

"Nuts, you mean? Oh...I think I used to be something nearer to normal. At least I pretended I was, which I was able to pull off as long as I didn't think about it too much. But once I got started, it was difficult to extricate myself. And at some point I stopped trying. It was like trying to extricate myself from gravity...But do I really believe all this? Sometimes yes. Other times I'm not so sure. For some reason—like right now."

She cast her eyes down and seemed to redden.

Another party entered the diner. "Hey, there's Duane," I said. "He's made some new friends."

140

She followed my gaze, toward the entrance. Duane was at the counter, facing away from us. He was with the two women in red jackets. On the back of the jackets there was an emblem of an Indian chief's head, framed by "Browning" above and "Indians" below.

He half-turned to us and gave one brief nod.

"What is he doing?" Thao asked.

"I have no idea. He doesn't appear as though he's going to join us."

Duane said something, and the two women laughed. He said something else and gestured toward the booths. "Nope," one said, and the two laughed again. With their hands over their mouths, they sat down at the counter, leaving one stool next to them at the end. He eased onto that stool.

"My," Thao said. "It seems he's very amusing." Lori poured coffee for all three and handed them menus. "We shouldn't stare."

"No? Oh. Right."

"Let's not lose track of your wind-up pitching. You explained—actually, I'm not really sure that you explained anything, per se." I started to speak, but she went on. "Aside from the fact that you consider yourself to be…" She flipped back through some pages in her notebook. "…deficient…insane… nuts…You haven't explained the timing. Which I think was the original question. Why the sudden departure?"

I was in the process of taking a bite from half of my sandwich. It took some time for me to swallow the mouthful.

"That's hard to say. Literally, with this peanut butter. But it was the cumulative effect of everything, you might say."

"That's it? There wasn't one particular incident…?"

"There never is. It's all bound together in a very non-linear way. Like a big ball of string."

"Hmph." This sound conveyed both disappointment and skepticism. I took another, larger, bite of the sandwich. The peanut butter pushed up against my palate; the feel of it in my mouth evoked setting cement. Thao went all the way back to the first page of her notes, and started going through them page by page. At some point—she was holding the notebook up, so I could not see where—she stopped.

"What about God?" she asked.

It took some effort, but I swallowed. "Unfathomable."

"But you believe he exists."

"If he does, not in any way that would affect you or me."

"Hm. That doesn't really sound like the definition of 'God.'"

"That's because you want to define him in the human way, instead of the God way."

"How nice for you, that you know the God-way definition."

"It is, isn't it? So, here's my theory on how God made the world. He was doing whatever he does, you know, architecting the infinity of the universe, and his kid was hanging around him, like kids do—"

"You mean Jesus."

"No, no. Just his kid. So while God is preoccupied with his heavy lifting, the kid is messing around, and he picks up a little bit of clay and molds it into a ball. And he's kind of rolling it around in his hands, and he forms the earth and everything on it in the space of about 15 seconds. So it's pretty crude. And God notices what the kid is doing, and snaps at him, 'Quit fucking around and throw that goddamn thing away.' So the kid shrugs and kind of flips it away, and they both immediately forget about it, and get back to the business of the vast universe, and never give another thought to tiny earth and its evolution and humankind."

"I must have been absent from catechism the day they taught that one."

I picked up the remainder of the half-sandwich, but did not take another bite.

"It's an odd concept," Thao continued. "There's really no consolation in that, is there? The concept of a just God at least provides the consolation that there's justice in the world. Ultimately."

"I'm fine with the idea that there's no justice in the world. Ultimately."

"Still, it's only natural to want to believe in justice of—"

"Thao." I reached over and put my hand on hers. She seemed startled. "I'm going to be frank with you. I like you. Obviously. Right?" She did not move.

"But I like you less when you are coy. Let's stop playing this game. If you want to ask me something, just ask it."

"I'm trying," she whispered. Her eyes started to moisten. "I've been asking, but your answers don't all make sense to me."

"You're not asking all the right questions."

"I don't know how. Help me."

I took my hand away. She reached into a bag, took out a tissue and dabbed her eyes.

"Really. You don't know how. How long did you do cops and courts?"

"A couple of years. Why?"

"And how old are you?"

"I'm 32." Her voice was at its normal pitch now. "Why?"

"Oh, I'm just wondering what you really do know and what you don't. And what you are pretending you don't."

"Clearly, I don't know enough." Her tone was suddenly defiant. "But how much do *you* know? I think there are more things in heaven and earth than your philosophy ever dreamed about."

"Sure, stipulated. Oh, hell. Never mind."

Her dark eyes were still moist.

"Well then." I shifted in my seat. "Go on." I tried a smile. "I don't know enough, either, so it appears we're in the same club."

She didn't smile back.

"OK, OK." I pushed my plate to the side of the table. The chips were unopened. "You have to remember that I have not had a conversation this long in probably a year."

"You keep using that as an excuse. Maybe you're just rude."

"I would say 'spontaneous' instead."

"I wouldn't."

"I don't mind dancing with you a little. I'm just out of practice."

"I thought you were the extreme opposite of a dancer."

"I think those are your words, not mine. But I take your point. I'm not so much a non-dancer as I am the drunk older guy dancing at a wedding."

She was showing just a hint of conceding an almost-smile. "I think you may be exaggerating your abilities."

"Wait just a minute. I think I'm not being immodest when I say that, when the funk starts—when the funk starts, I can—"

There was an argument going on at the counter. I had to speak a little more loudly. "Let's just say that people have been known to clear the dance floor. Have you seen this Michael Jackson video where—"

A sudden loud voice cut through the diner.

"'Chief'!? You don't call me 'chief'! Who the fuck is this breed?"

Duane was standing by the counter, his hands up and palms raised in a whoa-take-it-easy position, and facing the man in the denim shirt we'd seen earlier with the two women outside the antique shop. He was tall, made taller by a pair of gray ostrich cowboy boots. His black ponytail came down like a stake between his broad shoulders.

He was facing the two women in the red jackets, but pointing at Duane. The index finger emanating from his thick fist was long and a little crooked. Duane's hands remained up, as if to ward off the energy of this assaultive pointing, which was aimed approximately between his eyes.

The women were not responding to the question. Not-Chief was not moving. Duane was not moving, either.

"I said: Who the FUCK is this?"

Every head in the café—in the booths, at the counter, behind the counter—had twisted to witness this spectacle.

"Relax!" the taller woman finally said. "He's just gonna take our picture. For the newspaper."

"Take your picture!" His tone made it sound as though this were about as probable as Duane's levitating the two of them side by side, and passing a hoop over the length of their bodies. "The newspaper!"

"C'mon," Duane said. At least, that's what it sounded like. His voice was low.

Not-Chief pivoted to Duane, exposing his impassive face. He was a young man, and his brown skin was taut over his cheekbones. Prominent nose, prominent chin. He looked Duane up and down, once. He was easily six inches taller, and about twice as wide. His expression seemed more uninterested than threatening, which somehow made him all the more threatening. "Walk away," he said. He had lowered his tone, but it was still audible across the room. "You better walk away." He picked up the camera on the counter, his hand carelessly on the lens, and shoved it into Duane's mid-section. This caused Duane to take a step back. He held up his hands—one grasping the camera, the other still with the palm open.

"Man, what's your problem?

Not-Chief slowly shifted his weight back onto his back leg, and tucked his left shoulder in. This prompted Duane to back up another step. "I don't want any trouble."

"Then you better walk away, breed."

Duane glanced at the two women, but they quickly turned their heads.

Thao stage-whispered his name. "Duane! Come on!"

Not-Chief sat at the stool where Duane had been. He picked up the hamburger off the plate and held it up, examining its partially eaten asymmetry, and took a large bite of it.

Duane made a loud noise of disdain—maybe he said *Dick!*—and walked toward our booth.

"God! What are you doing?" Thao scooted over to give him room. "We don't need you locking heads with anybody."

"I'm doing my job...Dick!" he said again, louder.

"Will you let it go? Ross, tell him!"

"Yeah, she's right, man. No point in getting into it with a guy like that."

"I'm not afraid of him."

"A little fear might be the better part of valor in this case."

Lori came over. "He took your hamburger," she said. "Do you want me to call the sheriff?"

"What? No. He can choke on it. Don't worry, I'll pay for it."

"You don't have to."

Duane started to extract his wallet. "No. I ordered it; I'll pay for it."

"Just put it on our tab," Thao said. "And can you bring us another hamburger?"

"I don't want another fucking hamburger."

"Duane!"

"What a *dick*!"

At the counter, Not-Chief slowly looked our way. Duane maintained his gaze straight ahead, across the table, somewhere around the top of the seatback by me. Not-Chief put a French fry in his mouth, and chewed it slowly.

Lori was still standing at our table. "Are you sure? You shouldn't have to pay for it."

"We're sure," Thao said. "We don't want any problems. We're just tourists. Just bring the check, please."

Lori silently accepted this notion that, thankfully, we were tourists, and therefore not inclined to want problems.

"I'm going to make a photo of those girls tomorrow," Duane said. "They're going to be at the football game in Havre. Their brother is going to play."

"Make it or take it, it might not be the soundest plan."

"I'm going to make a photo of them. I create the shot. I don't 'take' it."

"Why are you so determined to take their picture?" Thao asked. "I mean, make it?"

"Because it's visually interesting. Those bright red jackets, the black hair. That Indian-head emblem on their jackets. And I find their features visually very interesting. I'll shoot the brother, too, if I can, in his uniform. The three of them together, that would make a great shot."

"Speaking of tomorrow…" I said.

"And it's a football game, for Chrissake. It's a public event."

"Speaking of tomorrow…"

"Ross is right," Thao said, "we should make a plan for tomorrow. We have to go to the battlefield, remember?"

"Maybe we can wrap that up today," Duane said.

"Ross, we don't have time, do we?"

146

"I doubt it, but it all depends on how much time you need there. We can be there in an hour and a half, probably."

"Yeah, but I want to spend some time. I can't just do a 15-minute drive-by of some battleground before I write about it. Isn't there a museum? Or at least a visitor's center? What time is the game?"

Duane removed a notebook from his back pocket and flipped through a few pages. "One o'clock."

"That'll work," I said. "Havre's only a half-hour from Prague. Let's go to Prague now. And yes, there's a museum in Prague. If you need more time, we have plenty of time in the morning."

Lori brought our check. "Thank you!" Thao said brightly. She wrote a note on the receipt and stuck it in her purse, and left cash on the table.

We had to walk past Not-Chief and the women on our way out. Duane led the way. "See you later," he said as he passed.

Bringing up the rear, I could see them in my peripheral vision. The two women had gone expressionless. Not-Chief was taking a last bite of the burger.

Thao stood on her tiptoes and whispered to me: "I am not done with you."

10. Ain't Dead Yet

The Whites, by law of conquest, by justice of civilization, are masters of the American continent, and the best safety of the frontier settlements will be secured by the total annihilation of the few remaining Indians. Why not annihilation? Their glory has fled, their spirit broken, their manhood effaced; better that they die than live the miserable wretches that they are.

—L. Frank Baum, *Aberdeen Saturday Pioneer*,
Dec. 20, 1890

The sign painted on the door read, "Prague Museum of Local History and Battle of the Bear Paw." Taped below that was a sheet of paper, with the scrawled message: *Have to run to Havre, sorry. Back at 3 p.m.*

"Oh. It's closed! At 3:30 in the afternoon?" Thao tried the door, maybe figuring that the sign on the glass was out of date, or there was some other mistake. "How can you close a museum in the middle of a weekday? Are you not expecting visitors at that time?"

"Sometimes you just have to run to Havre," I said. "These places can't afford a lot of staff. It's not Hearst Castle."

"We can come back in the morning," Duane said.

The only other people around were a 60ish couple in matching blue windbreakers, who on our approach had stationed themselves a polite 10 feet from any of us. Thao breached the distance without hesitation. "Is this typical?" she asked them.

"I don't know honey," the woman said. "We're from out of town. We been waiting since 2." The windbreakers bore a golden script across the chest: "Mustangs."

Her partner snorted. He wore a blue ball cap with an "M" insignia. "Typical is about right," he said. "Typical government worker. Loaf half a day, take the rest of the day off."

"I don't think the folks who work at the museum are government workers," the woman said.

"Sure they are. Who do you think pays 'em? The Indians? It's you and me who pays 'em. So they can go shopping at the Kmart in Havre in the middle of the day."

"Do you think they'll be here tomorrow?" Thao asked. She pointed to the sign. "'Open at 9 a.m.'"

"I'm sure they will be," the woman said.

"Don't do you no good if you're headin' back to Malta first thing in the morning," the man said.

"We don't have to leave first thing, Gerald," the woman said.

"Malta," Thao said. "Is that far?"

"Far enough," Gerald said. "But you ain't missin' nothin' anyway, if you come all the way from China or wherever to see this. We been here once before. They got some old farm machinery and a movie and that's about it."

"...'Come all the way'...I beg your pardon?"

"I say, they got some old farm implements and a movie about the battle and that's about it."

"Don't pay any attention," the woman said to Thao. "Gerald, she didn't come all the way from China, for god's sake."

"And how'm I sposed to know that?"

"Can't you hear her speak English?"

"Well, she come from somewhere." He cocked his head toward Thao and narrowed his eyes, as if to intuit whether she was fully comprehending this exchange. "Anyhow, like I say: You ain't missin' nothin.' You can't have a real museum about Indians because all they did was use sticks. Threw sticks, had bows and sticks, carried stuff behind their horses on sticks. They couldn't even make a wheel. How many sticks can you put in one museum?"

"Jeez," Duane said. "Are you for real?"

"You bet. Read up on it, son," he suggested. "Don't take my word for it." He sized Duane up, and added, "Course, you folks were real good horsemen. That's true."

"If there's nothing but sticks inside, why have you been waiting here since 2 to get in?"

"Oh…" He pointed with his thumb. "The wife's interested."

"There's a lot more than sticks in there," the woman said to Duane. "A lot. You could spend a whole day just looking at the beadwork."

Thao sighed, gave a quick peek through the window at the dark interior, then pivoted to survey the scene. Across the street from the museum was a bar and café. A large and somewhat decrepit neon sign loomed above the entrance, depicting a cowgirl lounging in a martini glass, one leg stuck jauntily in the air, the tip of the cowboy boot demurely pointed.

"Stockman's Bar," Thao read. "Is that the same company as the one in Fort Benton?"

"There's a Stockman's Bar in every single town in Montana, but alas, it's not a franchise," I said. "It's just the only name anybody seems to be able to think of."

"It looks like fun. Let's go over there and plot our next move." She addressed the couple: "It was nice to meet you."

"Nice to meet you, too, hon," the woman said. Gerald tilted his head and touched the bill of his ball cap.

Duane started to shoot some photos of the neon sign. "Climb up there and drape your leg over the martini glass," he suggested to Thao. "I'll take your photograph with this stick."

"I would, but I need cowgirl boots and a hat." She posed for a couple of shots at the entrance, with Duane crouching low to include the sign in the frame.

"Too bad they don't sell them in China."

He aimed the camera at me. "Stand right there," he said. "I want to get those two in the background of this shot."

"They're just going to keep standing there," Thao whispered.

I stood in the middle of the street, arms folded, while Duane snapped off some shots. "Crack a smile?" he said. "No?"

When he finished we walked three abreast through the wide door of

Stockman's, and stopped just inside, waiting for our eyes to adjust to the darkness. Numerous posters and advertisements were posted on the wall of the entry. Firewood for sale; Karl Jorgenson Farm and Ranch Realty; Missing Blue Heeler. The largest was a poster for a Battle of the Bear Paw Reenactment from two weeks before. *See actors reenact famous battle! / Genuine period dress and native garb / Authentic period firearms! / See and hear surrender / 'From Where The Sun Now Stands.'*

"Oh no," Thao said. "I can't believe we missed the reenactment! By two weeks!"

She removed the poster, folded it and stuck it in her purse.

We took a few tentative steps inside, then wavered before the shady figures and forms. Unmatched stools and chairs were arranged haphazardly. Here and there, decorations sprang incongruously from the tables: a stuffed pheasant, a chipped cookie jar in the shape of Fred Flintstone, a vase of plastic flowers. A half-empty bowl of Chex mix sat beside a large jug of murky fluid. I shifted my gaze to the grimy, pressed tin ceiling.

"I bet that ceiling is a hundred years old," I said.

"Really? Wow," Thao said.

"Wow!" a man's voice repeated.

I peered deeper into the dark interior. There were several elderly ladies at one table. A haze of wispy gray cigarette smoke was tangled in their wispy gray hair. They were staring at Thao. I stared back at them until they turned back to one another, murmuring. Two tables over, two men in cowboy hats were seated across from each other in a booth, with four cans of Lucky beer between them. They were deep in conversation.

Two more men roosted at the bar. They were facing the mirror behind the bar. I met the reflected gaze of one. "Wow," the man said into the mirror. He grinned, showing a silver front tooth. He wore a striped snap-button western shirt. Two or three days' beard growth. Next to him was a broad-shouldered dark-haired man in a flannel shirt.

"Let's sit at that table over there," Thao said. "The light's a little better. I want to read."

I was still looking at the reflected face of the man with the silver tooth. With Thao's statement the man's mouth opened, and his eyes went round and big. "Wow," he said again, loudly. "I believe this will be the first time anyone has ever read anything in this bar. Oh, maybe one time somebody in the can read what it says on the rubber machine."

After maybe five seconds, his partner said, "What about the newspaper." It was a statement, not a question. His voice was both deep and tremulous. A novice tuba player might create such a tone.

"The newspaper! It's too dark in here to read the newspaper. All them little words?"

Again, a five-second pause. "I've read the Prague Opinion in here. A hundred times."

"I never seen that."

Pause. "Plenty you never seen."

As this conversation lurched along, Thao and Duane were heading toward a booth. I stepped up to the bar, standing next to the jug, and several stools down from the two. The jug had a hand-written label written thickly in black marker: *Home-made pig knuckles.*

The bartender came over.

"A double Canadian Club, and a pitcher of whatever you sell the most," I said.

"Olympia."

"OK." I pulled a five from my wallet and set it on the bar. As I waited, I glanced into the mirror. Silver-tooth met my gaze.

"That's smart. Oly's the fresh beer." When I didn't respond, he tried another tack. "…So. …Ya think we'll be gettin' snow some of these days?"

"Kind of early, isn't it?"

"Oh, yeah. It's way too early." The tone of this response seemed to dismiss the notion of snow as ridiculous, even though he was the one who suggested it in the first place.

"Seen it snow a lot earlier than this," his partner said. The delay of his responses evoked a TV report in which the far-flung correspondent has to wait several seconds for the anchor's words to wend their way to a satellite, and then bounce down to earth and into his ear. "September. A lot."

"Oh, sure. Hell, I seen it snow in August."

The bartender loaded up a tray: the bourbon, the pitcher, with the head of the beer trembling just over the lip of it, and three frosted, weighty mugs. I checked out the mirror one more time. The silver-toothed man was still looking at me; the other man was looking at nothing.

Thao had extracted her book again, and was expounding to Duane as he fiddled with his camera. I set down the bourbon, but Duane slid it aside and pointed to the pitcher. I poured three beers.

"…so after this amazing military campaign, waged against generals who were educated at West Point and veterans of the Civil War, they stopped short of the Canada border because they knew they were way ahead of General Howard. But they *didn't* know this other general, General Miles, was coming from the other direction. He did a surprise attack and the cavalry got most of their horses. So the Indians were kind of stuck, and then it started snowing. But they fought some more. Then most of them gave up. And all that happened right down here by Prague."

She stopped and raised her full mug. I sat next to Duane. He and I tapped her mug with ours and we all took a sip.

"Ooh," Thao said. "That's cold."

Duane gave an exaggerated *Ahh* of satisfaction.

"How did you all of a sudden soak in all this knowledge?" I asked.

"I was busy researching last night while you two were snoring. It's such a fascinating story. I couldn't stop reading about it."

"How far did you get?"

"All the way to the speech."

"So you got as far as the middle."

"I know. It's like a Shakespeare play. There's still Act Four and Act Five. But the speech is a pretty amazing climax."

"Yes, white people in this country have climaxed over it for years. Or over Wood's version of it."

"Whoever's version it is, it's quite impressive, you have to admit." She opened to a page she'd marked with her business card. "Listen to this—"

"Oh my god. Are you actually going to read it?" Duane asked.

"Ahem. Please hold your questions and comments until the end." She put her index finger on the page. "Here it is. Now, one thing you have to know is that Joseph was not the only chief. For example, some of the other chiefs who were more of the warrior chiefs, they got killed. That's who he's referring to." She began to read in a clear, earnest tone.

Tell General Howard I know his heart. What he told me before, I have it in my heart. I am tired of fighting. Our chiefs are killed. Looking Glass is dead. Too-hoo-hool-zote is dead. The old men are all dead. It is the young men who say, "Yes" or "No." He who led the young men is dead. It is cold, and we have no blankets. The little children are freezing to death. My people, some of them, have run away to the hills, and have no blankets, no food. No one knows where they are — perhaps freezing to death. I want to have time to look for my children, and see how many of them I can find. Maybe I shall find them among the dead. Hear me, my chiefs! I am tired. My heart is sick and sad. From where the sun now stands I will fight no more forever.

Silver-tooth echoed the last line from his seat at the bar. "I will fight no more…forever."

I could hear the old ladies cackle at their table. "Oh, brother," one said.

This seemed to throw Thao. She squinted at the smoky table, then shrugged.

"Anyway," she said to us, "it's practically poetry, speaking of Shakespeare. It gives me chills."

"Yes. Quite a coincidence, because Wood was a poet, too. He obviously had a strong sense of the rhythm and power of words."

"So you think Wood wrote all that?"

"I think he thought of Joseph's words as dynamic rather than static, and it's very likely he embellished, at the least. His heart was in the right place, and he did all he could to shame America by depicting this scene, with Joseph as the noble warrior. Which of course is just how America likes its Indians. Noble in defeat."

"He would've been nobler if he'd won the battle and made it to Canada," Duane said.

"It could not have played out any better for Joseph, in terms of the myth. He surrenders. They promise him reasonable terms, and promptly ship him and his people to some godforsaken, freezing reservation. He begs the U.S. to make good on its promise—what he thought was Miles' and Howard's promise—to let them return to their homeland. He even does kind of a tour, making speeches, pleading his case, winning the admiration of polite society. The noble red man. He's like one of those inflatable punching toys that keeps getting up after you knock it down. And it can't punch you back. What more could the Army and the U.S. government and the mythmakers ask for?"

"Stop being so cynical," Thao said. "He was inspiring. And brilliant, too. And handsome." She displayed the photo on the book jacket. "I wonder if the curator is back yet. Maybe we should just go to the battleground. How far is it from here?"

"I don't remember for sure. Just 10 or 15 minutes. But there's not a lot there."

"What about the museum?"

"I don't remember much about it. I don't remember any movie."

"I can't believe we missed the reenactment."

"I bet the outcome was predictable."

"That's not the point. You were so determined to have this story written. That would've been the perfect angle to get into the story."

Suddenly Silver-tooth was standing five feet from our table. "Yep, you missed quite the reactment," he said. "I was in it. Joe was, too." He nodded toward his immobile partner at the bar.

"You?" Thao asked. "You were in the reenactment?"

"Sure." He stood uncertainly, his gaze going from him to Duane to Thao. "Just about every able-bodied man, woman and child in Prague was. 'Course, I been in it several years now, so I know quite a little about it. And Joe there, he's actually a descendant of Chief Joseph himself."

"He is?"

"Oh, you bet. You can see, he's Indian."

"I can't believe we missed this! Practically everyone in Prague was there. It would've been perfect. See, I told you, Ross."

"Tell us," I said, "Whom did you portray in the reenactment? General Miles? Howard?"

"Oh, gosh, no. Mr. Kershaw plays the general every year."

"Which one?"

"Ben. The one who has the funeral home. Bob Kershaw don't do it no more, since he froze his feet. You know the Kershaws?"

"No. I meant, which general?"

"Oh. Uh, the main one."

Silver-tooth had a mug in his hand. There was barely enough thin liquid in it to cover the bottom. He eyed the pitcher on our table.

"Would you like a beer?" Thao asked. "Please join us."

"Oh, that's OK. I was just goin' to the can…"

"No, really. Have a seat. Fill your glass."

"Well…" He approached slowly and gingerly set down his mug. Duane poured it full. "Thanks," Silver-tooth said. With sudden quickness he eased into the seat next to Thao, taking a drink from the beer while still in motion. This resulted in a bit of foam attaching to his nose. He wiped that off, and pronounced, "Yep. That's the fresh stuff."

"You were telling us about the generals," I reminded him.

"Can you really tell it's fresh?" Thao asked. She took a small sip. "Mm. It does taste fresh. So, I'm Thao. This is Ross and Duane."

"Pleased to meet you…Tay-ow." From the elaborate caution with which he pronounced her name, there ensued some collateral damage to ours. "And… Russ, and Dane. I'm Harold."

"It's Duane," Duane said. "Ross and Duane."

"You bet. Duane." He reached his hand across to shake. "Harold. Pleased to meet you." With these niceties accomplished, he took another healthy swallow of the beer, peering over the brim as Thao took notes.

"Duane and I are from a newspaper in California," she said. "We're writing a story about the battle. Ross here is our local expert."

"No kiddin'!"

"Yes. It's quite fascinating. So, who did you play in the reenactment?"

"Oh, I'm just one of the calvary."

"Do you ride, then?"

"Oh, sure. We all do in the calvary. Ride and shoot. Shoot the Indians, you know. Joe's an Indian, but he don't get shot, just kinda herded around there towards the end. Hey, Joe!"

Joe slowly circled on his stool.

"Come on over here! They're from the news in California! Writin' all about the battle." Harold lowered his voice. "I used to be an Indian, too," he said to Thao. "I can do either. My gramma was half."

Thao was writing this down. "Half…?"

"Indian. Probly like Duane here. You the cameraman?"

He directed a wink at Duane, but Duane's only reaction was an impassive assessment of the approaching Joe. Harold maneuvered closer to Thao, leaving space for Joe, who wordlessly placed his mug—even emptier than Harold's had been—on the table. Duane gave him a pour, which filled it halfway. "I guess we need another pitcher," Duane said.

Harold reached into one back pocket, mumbled something inaudible, reached into the other pocket.

"Oh, we've got it," Thao said.

"No, that's OK, lessee here…Not sure if I left that twenty in my other shirt…"

"No, really. We'll get it." Thao, who was obscured from the bartender's point of view, raised her hand and waved. "Sir? " She projected her voice confidently. "Can we have another pitcher, please? We'll settle on our way out?"

"That's mighty white. I mean, nice," Harold said. "Nice of you." After a moment, he added, in a lower tone: "We don't say 'white' no more."

Since I was closest, and Joe displayed no inclination to budge from his spot at the table, I went over to the bar. The bartender was already filling the pitcher. "Old Harold is full of shit," he said. He didn't lower his voice.

"Thanks, we're taking that into consideration."

When I got back to the table, Harold was speaking animatedly. If he'd heard the bartender's remark, it made no discernible impression. "…then the horses come up all at once, and we start shootin' over toward the camp." Thao was writing. Harold pointed to the notebook. "Not real bullets, of course."

"Right," she said. "'Not real bullets.'"

"So we shoot back and forth for a while, and a couple of soldiers fall over like they're shot, and we shoot some Indians. I don't get shot. Joe don't get shot, neither, right? Just captured."

Joe had pushed his now empty mug forward. I filled that one first, then Harold's—which was suddenly as empty as Joe's.

Joe took a deep drink, and set his mug down on the table. "I ain't dead yet," he said.

"Ha. That's for sure."

"Is your role that of any particular Indian?" I asked.

"Huh?"

"The character you play, is he a named member of the tribe? For example, Looking Glass?"

Joe turned to Harold for guidance.

"No, he's just an Indian," Harold said. "He can be any of 'em."

"I understand you are a descendant of Chief Joseph," Thao said.

"That's what my momma used to say. On her side. Her grandpa's uncle or something. Cousin."

"How interesting. Do you have any possessions of his? Or photos?"

"Nope. Just what my momma said, is all. She don't know, though."

"Yes, she does," Harold said. "Why wouldn't she?"

"You must be very proud," Thao said. "You should play Chief Joseph in the reenactment."

"I know!" Harold said. "He shoulda been it this year! But it was that Jesse One Bull over at the sheriff's office. Jesse… One… Bull." He drew the name out contemptuously. "Thinks he's so big with his new three-quarter-ton Chevy pickup. It's all just politics, who plays Joseph."

"I can imagine," Thao said. "But it must be quite the spectacle all the same. I'm sorry we missed it."

"We could do it for you again," Harold said.

"What?"

"We could do the reactment again."

"How would you manage that?" I asked.

"Well, it wouldn't be the whole shebang, of course, but we could get a few fellers to do it, just to show you how it went. And Joe here could be Joseph."

"Oh, we couldn't ask you to go to that much trouble," Thao said.

"Wouldn't be much to it. Just get a few horses and some guys. Just to show you how it goes, ya know. How the battle really went and so on. And the speech. That's the main thing."

"That's nice of you, but we're only going to be here until the morning."

"We could do it in the morning."

She made eye contact with Duane.

"It might be worth taking a few shots," Duane said. "Couldn't hurt, right? Just as long as we get to the game by 1."

"Ross?" Her pen hovered over her notebook.

"What exactly would you do?" I asked Harold.

"Hmm…I don't know how many of the fellers I can gather on such short notice, but I think the main thing you're interested in is the surrender, right? So we could just shorten it up, do kind of the final battle there, and then have the speech."

"You're not suggesting that you're going to just show up there at the site itself, and start traipsing around with horses?"

"No. We'll be nearby, though. You can't tell one hill from another out there anyway."

"We'll just have to do our best in that regard. So, how much?"

"What's that?"

"How much do you intend to charge for this spectacle?"

"Hm. Lessee." Harold began to tick off tasks on his fingers, starting with the thumb. "I'd hafta get the stock trailer from Nelson… gas up the truck…. get some extra feed for the horses…." He paused, concentrating on his extended fourth finger. "…Maybe pick up some of that fake blood at Woolworth's?"

"Woolworth been closed 10 years," Joe said.

"Oh, yeah. The Dollar Store, I meant. I think they got some in the Halloween section."

"Anyway, all told," I said. "How much?"

The complexity of his computation did not allow for rushing. "'Course, the real reactment charged 10 bucks a head. But that had your economics of scale."

"Economics of scale?"

"Yeah, that means that if you have a lot of—"

"Right, right. I just wasn't quite sure how you were envisioning how economies of scale would apply to a battle reenactment. But you're quite right. Go on."

"Yeah. Anyhow, I'm thinking probably sixty apiece would be about right. So….that'd be one-eighty. Or if you rounded it up…."

"We can give you 50 dollars, total," Thao said.

"Ooh." The tone commingled surprise with pain. He rubbed his chin as if he'd been struck there. "How 'bout we split the difference," he finally said. "Make it a hunderd."

"I think we have a flaw in the ointment," Thao said.

"Mm…we do?"

"Yes. I didn't mean to suggest that I was bargaining with you. We can give you 50 total. That's all."

"Mmm," Harold said.

"OK," Joe said.

"Boy, I dunno…"

"OK," Joe said again. "Half tonight, half tomorrow."

"I'll give you ten tonight, and the rest after the reenactment."

"OK."

"Gosh, Joe…we've never done it for that much before. And we usually get 50 percent down. But…I guess it's OK, since they're from the news."

Thao laid a ten on the table. "Can you get us a receipt tomorrow?"

"Oh, sure. We can gin somethin' up."

She wrote down Harold's phone number, and had each of them print his name in her notebook. They wrote in similar blocky letters: Harold Eklund and Joe Tanish. She closed her notebook. "Great. So we'll see you in the morning at the battlefield? The parking lot? What time?"

"Oh…you gotta run? What time tomorrow? Ten-, eleven-ish?

"Earlier would be better," Thao said.

"We could maybe get there at 9. We gotta round up the horses and so on."

"Certainly, do what you need to do. But no later than 9, please." She took one more sip of beer. "Mm. Ready?"

"They gotta go," Harold said to Joe.

Joe grasped the pitcher, his mug and the untouched whisky, and without a word, got up and headed back toward the bar.

Harold shook our hands again. "See you bright and early!"

Outside it was nearly dark, and the wind had died down to just a breeze, but it was cool. Thao was the only one who had brought a jacket, and she pulled it close around her. We crossed the street back to the museum. The handwritten sign on the door was gone, but now it was after 5.

"Dang," Thao said.

"It's just sticks, anyway," Duane said. "Sticks and beads."

"Fine, I want to see the sticks and beads," Thao said. "We'll get in here sooner or later."

"They're closed for the weekend now."

"There's always next week."

We headed to the pickup in the small museum lot. I opened her door first, and helped her to climb in. "That's quite a duo," I said. "You did hear the bartender in there, didn't you?"

"Yes. And I wouldn't trust those two with a ten-foot pole."

"So exactly what kind of *reactment* are you anticipating from them?"

"One worth fifty dollars. Or less."

"I see. From a news standpoint, they make up color. Make up, in more ways than one."

"A travel feature needs color."

I headed the pickup south to the battlefield. The darkness had seeped into the terrain by now. Just 15 miles down the road, the site of the battlefield was marked with a single small sign on the highway: Bear Paw Battlefield National Historic Park. There was no gate. I parked in the empty gravel lot, facing south, near a naked flagpole. The crescent moon provided just enough light to outline the hills, rounded across the black sky. Near one side of the parking lot a large stone jutted from the ground. No other object stood out. Inside the cab, with the windows rolled up, we could hear nothing. The stolid hills seemed to soak up the sound and the light.

We sat for a while in the quiet. I could hear her breathing. I wasn't sure if she was now facing me. I thought I felt her soft exhalation, just the faintest suggestion of it, waft against my cheek.

"Hey!"

I flinched.

"God, Duane, you scared me!" Thao said. "What?"

"The sky!" He pointed out the back window.

A luminous light danced on the glass, or just behind it. It shimmered in the air, pulsing with blue and purple beams that quivered and melted into one another.

"Whoa. What—?"

"Oh. A wonderment," I said.

" 'Wonder'…?"

"The northern lights. A wonderment."

"My god. It's beautiful. Let's get out and see."

The breeze had died, but it was colder now.

"Gosh, the way they move," Thao said. "It's like it's alive." She reached her hand out as if to touch the sight.

Lacking a tripod, Duane set the camera on the rail of the pickup bed and aimed it at the lights. While he was adjusting it, Thao took a sideways step toward me. "It's funny, that word you used." Her arms were crossed against the cold. She was still facing the sky. I edged toward her, until our arms barely touched. She came closer, firmly against me. "Brr." She looked up at me. "A wonderment?"

"Yeah. Yeah, there are a few of them in the world."

"There are? What are the other ones?"

"That depends."

"On?"

"On who you are. Where you are, what you are." I could smell the fragrance of her hair, her skin. "There's a whole range of things, isn't there? Just pick…just point at random."

"But what do you pick? That's my question."

"OK. Let's see. How about: A warm olallieberry pie from Gizdich Ranch in Watsonville. Nina Simone singing 'I Loves You, Porgy.' Um…the way a flock of blackbirds scatters in the sky, like grain flung from someone's hand. Or…what it feels like, the smell and warmth you feel when a person is standing right by you."

I felt her staring at me; I felt, or imagined I felt, the hair on my arms rise against my sleeve.

We viewed the dancing lights for a few more minutes, until Thao went back to the pickup. We got in, saying nothing. I started the engine and headed it back to Prague.

When we got into town, Thao picked out a motel with a restaurant. "You and Duane don't mind sharing a room, do you?"

"I don't. After last night, it's like we're frat brothers."

"As long as there's two beds," Duane said. "I don't want to get too brotherly."

He and Thao had chicken-fried steak for dinner. It came with mashed potatoes and gravy, and peas. I ordered a dinner salad, which proved to be a large bowl of iceberg lettuce, a half-tomato that had the consistency, color and smell of a traffic cone, and Cap'n Crunch-like croutons.

We retired to our rooms immediately after dinner. Duane turned on the TV. "Matlock" was on. After watching for a few, I caught myself dozing. I forced myself to get up off the bed, take a leak and brush my teeth in the stale-smelling bathroom. When I lay on the bed, I closed my eyes and immediately saw the dark ridgelines of the battlefield. I had a groggy sensation that I was lying atop them, bent as they were bent. And all night I churned and squirmed, seeking any position of comfort on their obdurate shapes.

11. No More, Ever

I have carried a heavy load on my back ever since I was a boy. I learned then that we were but few, while the white men were many, and that we could not hold our own with them. We were like deer. They were like grizzly bears.

—Chief Joseph of the Nez Perce, speech at
Lincoln Hall in Washington, D.C. (1879)

Harold and Joe pulled into the parking lot at the battlefield just before 9:30 in a GMC pickup, of which the various sections—hood, driver's side door, roof—were painted in shades of black and primer gray. Except for the tailgate, which was egg-yolk yellow. A gun rack was visible in the back window. Ours were the only two vehicles in the lot, but Harold pulled up and lurched to a halt just about 18 inches away from us, pointed in the opposite direction. As he squeezed out he kept one hand mashed down on his hat while the wind grasped at it.

He grinned as I brought my window down. "Mornin', Russ! Kinda breezy today!" He had to raise his voice; the wind seemed to swat the words away from his mouth.

"Where are your horses?"

"So, it turns out Nelson is movin' his cows this weekend with his good horses. His boy had some two-year-olds all summer, but not a one got broke. Dang Nelson—why the heck would he be movin' his cows this time of year?"

"That would be hard for me to say. What about the cast? When are they coming?"

Harold switched hands on his hat. It was a blue flat-brimmed hat, with a yellow crossed-swords insignia at the front. The rest of his ensemble was also blue: denim jacket, denim pants. No blood was evident, fake or otherwise. "What, now?"

"Where is the reenactment cast? The cavalry? The Indians?"

"Oh." He gave a dismissive wave of his free hand. "They couldn't come, neither. We really don't need 'em. Joe there'll give the speech, and I'm the general." He bent slightly to peer inside the cab. "Miss Tayow said she was just interested in the surrender, anyhow, right?" Harold's cheeks were growing redder by the second.

"Seriously?" Thao said. "The battle reenactment consists of just you and Joe? On foot?"

"Yeah, but Joe's gonna do the speech. He practiced almost all night. He's still practicin' now." Harold pointed at the GMC, and we obligingly looked that way. Joe was facing downward. He wore a broad red headband, which contrasted starkly with his black hair. His lips were moving. "We can do it right here," Harold added. "Makes it more authentic, anyhow. You all were right. Makes no sense to do it somewhere else."

"Fine. Shall we get going?"

"You bet. Let's get the show on the road." He scanned the area. "Good thing nobody else is here. We can do it right over by the rock." He pointed to the large stone we had seen the night before. "Same exact spot as where it really happened. You folks gather up over there. Joe and me'll get ready." He pulled the hat down almost to his eyebrows, hopped to Joe's side of the pickup and tapped on the window.

"This is going to be even worse than I thought it," Duane said. "I wouldn't give them any forty dollars."

"What can you do?" Thao said. "Nelson is moving the cows."

We got out of the cab and into the wind. Thao was blown a half-step sideways. She put her head down. "My…god!"

"We'll be right over!" Harold called out. He tapped again at Joe's window.

We pulled up our jackets tightly and walked the 20 yards to the stone. Affixed to it was a bas relief tableau depicting the moment of surrender, with Joseph facing a bearded Miles, his hand raised. The iconic proclamation floated over their heads: *From where the sun now stands I will fight no more forever.* Next to the monument, mounted on a post, there was a wooden box with pamphlets inside. Thao pulled one out, and shoved it into her jacket pocket.

Other than the gravel parking lot, a flapping flag on a tall flagpole, and the monument, there wasn't much to distinguish the battlefield area from the surrounding rangeland. Whoever had raised the flag was not around now. The terrain revealed itself in the daylight to be middling hills with gentle grassy slopes, which descended here and there into gullies and draws. A narrow trail formed a rough oval that corresponded with the boundaries of the battlefield. An enclosed picnic shelter stood about a hundred feet from us. None of the slopes rose into anything that would qualify as a hill. In fact, the sightlines were such that the modest Bears Paw Mountains were clearly visible in the distance.

Thao produced an elastic band and pulled her hair, which had been whipping wildly across her face, into a ponytail. Her cheeks were also growing red. She cupped her hands around her mouth and yelled, "Can you please hurry?"

As each word came from her mouth, the wind obliterated it. Harold put his free hand up to his ear. She made a beckoning gesture. He held up a finger, indicating, presumably, one minute, although it potentially could mean one hour, or any other unit in his space/time continuum. But no, he soon bustled over to the driver's side of the pickup, crawled into the cab, and emerged hatless, carrying a shotgun.

"I see why he's glad nobody else is here."

Joe emerged from the pickup. He wore a buckskin blouse that hung to mid-thigh, jeans, and a pair of moccasins. He had something in his hand—a piece of paper, which he was cramming into a breast pocket. Harold held out the shotgun to him. Joe accepted it and they started walking, Harold talking as they approached. Joe somehow had grown overnight. Dwarfing Harold, he moved in a slow, stately gait, the butt of the shotgun tucked under and behind his armpit, the barrel pointed downward. Harold would get two or three steps ahead of him, and have to wait for him to catch up. But when they got within about 10 yards of the monument, Harold stopped talking, and his pace also slowed. He pointed to their left; Joe headed that way, descending down a path into a draw. Soon all we could see of him was the fluttering black hair with the red headband. Then that was gone, too.

Harold approached us.

"So, what exactly—"

Harold held up his hand. He was glaring at the spot where Joe had disappeared.

"Oh, he's already in character," Duane said. "I'd better start making pictures."

Thao had her pad and pen out. She manipulated them in her gloved hands with some difficulty. Duane photographed Harold frowning, putting his hands behind his back, pacing back and forth. At one point he stopped and faced the spot in the draw. And back to pacing. A full minute passed before he stopped again.

"Come out of there, Joseph," he yelled. "You are surrounded by the United States Calvary!"

There was no movement, other than the dry grass shuddering in the wind.

Harold cupped his hands to his mouth, as Thao had done. "Come out of there, Joseph!"

Nothing.

He walked a few steps forward. "Hey! Come on up now!" He walked on, nearly to the lip of the slope, stopped, and waved. Then he trotted back to us. He wheeled around, wheezing, and pointed back toward the draw.

Slowly, Joe's black hair and red headband became visible, followed gradually by the buckskin blouse, his jeans and moccasins. He was walking even more deliberately now. He held the shotgun cradled across his chest. He looked not at us, but off to the southwest. His face was grim; each step seemed slower than the last.

When he got within five paces, he stopped. Still, he did not look at us.

"You better give me that gun, Joseph," Harold said.

Instead, Joe put the butt on the ground and held it by the top end of the barrel. Harold stepped forward, his hand reaching toward the gun. Joe raised his chin defiantly and shook his head.

"Oh," Harold said.

Everyone was still but Duane, who was moving around, clicking off shots from different angles.

Harold licked his lips. "Well," he said. "Do you have anything to say?"

Joe gave a slight shake of his head.

"You're surrenderin,'" Harold said. "Right?"

Joe stared at him for a good eight or 10 seconds before he pulled out the paper. He unfolded it and held it with both hands in front of his face, letting the barrel of the shotgun balance against his hip, and began to read.

"Tell Howard that I know..." He cleared his throat and started again, much more loudly this time. His deep voice cut into the wind. "Tell... Howard…that I know…his heart."

After completing the sentence, he put one hand on his heart. The paper flapped smartly in the wind. He viewed it numbly, then took hold of it again with both hands.

"What he told me before…I have in my heart." This time he just glanced downward, in the general area of his heart. "I am tired of fighting… Our chiefs are killed…Looking Glass is dead. Tu-hoo-too...Tu-hil-hoo...Tu. Hul. Hil. Sote. Is Dead." Pause. "He is dead," he added somberly. "The old men are ALL dead."

He spread his arms wide. The snapping of the paper sounded like firecrackers. Harold started to say something—"Oop"—just as the wind snatched the paper cleanly from Joe's hand and shot it away, several feet off the ground, for a good fifty feet, until it dived to the earth and caught up against some scrub brush. Joe took one step in that direction, but before he could take another, the paper jerked upward as if it were pulled by a string, and flew off, toward Prague, and probably by day's end, somewhere in Canada.

"Uh-oh," Harold said. He started to add something, but Joe interrupted him.

"Now the young men make the decisions!" he said. "It's cold. We don't have nothing to eat. Where is everybody?" He looked around. Harold looked around, too. "Probably out there freezing! I don't know where my kids are, neither!" His face had taken on almost a ferocious expression. "Do you?"

"Why…no," Harold said.

"Hear me my chiefs! I'm sick of this! Where the sun now stands, I will fight no more. EVER."

He picked up the shotgun and abruptly extended it away from his chest. Harold took it. "Thanks, Joseph," he said loudly. "That was a fine speech."

Without a word, Joe started walking back toward the GMC.

"Gol-dang," Harold said. "He memorized the whole thing word-for-word. How 'bout that?"

"Yes. Commendable," Thao said.

"'From where the sun now stands.' How 'bout that?"

"Yes," Thao repeated. "So, the program is over?"

"Pretty much…" Harold surveyed the empty lot. "Nobody's around. I guess we could shoot off the shotgun a time or two…"

"Please, no, thank you." She pulled an envelope from the same jacket pocket where she'd put the map, and offered it to him. He took it, started to open it, changed his mind and held it up in a sort of salute.

Duane had switched to a longer lens. He was still photographing Joe— or more accurately, Joe's back.

"You maybe want a picture of me with the gun?" Harold asked. He held it up to his chest.

"That won't be necessary."

"Oh."

Joe finally reached the pickup. Instead of getting in, he walked on a few paces. Facing the southwest, he paused, arms folded, motionless. He took off the headband, turned around and got in the pickup.

"OK," Harold said. "Guess we'll hit the road. Hope you enjoyed our show."

"Yes, thanks," Thao said.

Harold shook hands all around. "Real pleasure," he said. "Real pleasure." He then scurried back to the pickup. When he crawled into the cab, he did not take the time to put the shotgun back in the gun rack. The pickup pulled out immediately, tires spinning on the gravel.

Duane replaced the long lens on his camera. He ambled off, taking photos along the trail. Thao wrote a few more notes in her notebook. She pointed toward where Joe had been staring. "Canada?"

"No. You're turned around. That's southwest, more or less where they came from."

"The Wallowa?"

"What?

"The Wallowa." She pronounced it WALL-oh-wuh.

"It's Wal-LAU-wa. Let's get out of the wind."

We made our way to the picnic shelter. Barn swallows darted here and there. The shelter was walled on three sides, with protection against the west wind. Thao leaned against a picnic tabletop. "Whew. What a relief. I've never ever felt wind like that."

One wall held a map of the battlefield. She pointed to its southwest corner. "So this is the direction they came from. Howard, too." She pointed back toward the coulee where Joe had disappeared. "And the Nez Perce were there."

"Right. But Howard was always hopelessly behind them."

"So it was Miles who surprised them. And he came from there?" She pointed to the southeast.

"Right."

"And he had 500 soldiers."

"He did? Plus there were Indians with them, too. Crow."

"Yeah, I read that, too. I don't get that. Why were there Indians helping to chase the Indians? The Nez Perce had hoped to join up with the Crows, but instead the Crows helped the soldiers."

"It's like I said before. Tribes are inclined to take care of themselves and fight other tribes. They decide on who's their worst enemy at a given time, then ally themselves with anybody else to fight them. Crow scouts supported the 7th Cavalry against the Sioux and Cheyenne at the Little Bighorn, too.

Some of them got killed right next to the soldiers. And Miles had Cheyenne scouts with him at the Bear Paw. The Indians switched allegiances from year to year. The fact that they were all 'Indians' didn't make them part of one homogeneous group. Some of these tribes hated each other as much as the Hutus hate the Tutsis."

Thao pointed to the top of the map. "If only they'd gone a little farther. Just 40 more miles to Canada. How disappointing. But they must have been exhausted, coming all that way."

"Yeah. To have Miles' cavalry suddenly descend on them, catch them by surprise. Take their horses. Really, without the horses, they had no chance. And then it started to snow, and the wind was blowing, of course. And it was a wet snow. I don't know if you've ever been wet and cold like that. I mean, wet through and through, every piece of cloth, your hair, your eyelids, your shoes and your feet. Out here, if it's just cold—and even if it's just cold and the wind is blowing—people can usually find a way to deal with it because the air is dry. It's miserable, but you can deal with it. But if you are wet on top of that, you can't. At some point, you just can't convince your body to keep trying. So here you are, exhausted and freezing, and a bunch of men are trying to kill you, and your lifelong friends and your brothers and the women and children you're responsible for are dying all around you. It's hard to imagine how hopeless they must have felt. All he could do was give up."

"But the Army tricked him, didn't they," Thao said. "They shipped his tribe off to Kansas and Oklahoma, even though Joseph thought they had a deal to go back to the … Wallowa. They had to live in this terrible swampland and they were overcome by disease. More of them died in Oklahoma than all the battles they had."

"Really? I didn't know that. I guess you did some more reading last night. Well. They had to be taught a lesson."

"My point is, maybe he shouldn't have given up."

"And what…let them kill every member of the band who was too young or old or slow to run off? Miles had the 7th Cavalry with him, with its proud record of slaughtering Indians of any age and sex. No, sometimes you just have to admit you are defeated."

"He must have been devastated."

"More like relieved, I would think."

"Maybe a little. But mostly, I bet he was really sad. If only he could have known that he'd end up being this revered figure."

"Revered. That's the white person's version. Or, in your case, not to put too fine a racial line on it, the yellow white person's version."

"Most people don't really refer to Asians as 'yellow' anymore. Maybe you haven't heard…"

"OK. The point is, it's the western—or again in your case, the eastern-western—fixation on narrative redemption. The fact is, the true story of the plains Indians is one without redemption. That's why no one wants to hear it."

She tapped the notebook that peeked outside her breast pocket. "Oh, they'll want to hear it, all right. They're not going to be able to resist the Yellow-White Eastern-Western redemptive version." She pulled out the pamphlet and unfolded it. It was the same map and diagram that was on the wall. "So let's get going. A little breeze isn't going to stop us. Let's go see—" She peered closely at it—"markers A-Z or whatever."

We first went to the ravine from which Joe had appeared. Duane was there now, at the bottom, which was somewhat protected. We came onto a marker, where visitors had deposited items around it—whole cigarettes, some dimes and quarters, a beaded bracelet.

Thao read aloud from the description of the marker in her pamphlet. *Ollokot fell here.* "Do you think this is really that spot?"

"Oh, who knows. I'm sure everything here is just a best guess. But at least there were eyewitnesses on both sides—as opposed to, say, the Little Bighorn—so they probably were able to put together a pretty good idea of what happened where. You'd think they would be at least close on where Joseph came out. Miles and Howard were both there, and Wood, of course. Taking notes and undoubtedly embellishing them at the same time."

We walked the path around the site, moving slowly and stiffly. Thao stopped at each marker and read the description aloud. *This rock…Looking*

Glass was shot…he stood hoping…to their aid. About half of what she read was audible. The wind swallowed the rest.

Maybe 40 minutes later we were back at the surrender spot. Thao ran her gloved fingers over the tableau. It was pocked with dings and dents; its coppery symmetry undoubtedly made for prime target practice. The artwork depicted Joseph—a single feather sticking out of his head, one hand balancing a rifle with its butt on the ground, as Joe had done—standing before the bearded Miles and pointing straight up to the sky.

"From where the sun now stands," Thao said. "See? He's pointing to the sun."

"I don't think so. He's just pointing to his destination. 'Ready to go there!'"

"Stop it." She placed her index finger against Joseph's raised hand. "No," she said firmly. "The sun."

Jack McMahon

February 1995

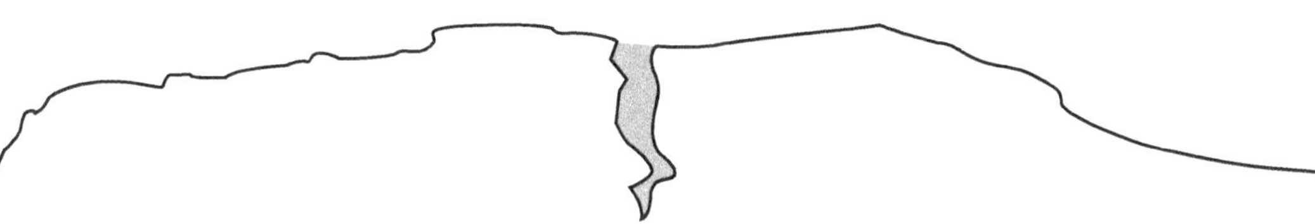

Moved by some nameless impulse that transmitted from his medulla to his extremities, Rossiter drove back to the house with the palm tree that Friday evening. He had no reason to think McMahon would come out, other than that it was Friday night.

He scrunched down in the seat a little. It was twilight. He would be easily visible in this light. You never know when someone has appointed himself Neighborhood Watchman, just to keep an eye on things. Stay vigilant. Like this house right here where he was parked. One of the rooms had curtains designed with a series of two concentric circles, like floating eyeballs. Whoever would buy such a curtain?

Someone who fancied himself the Neighborhood Watchman, that's who.

Rossiter pictured the Watchman peering out from behind this crazy curtain, digesting the sight of an out-of-place-vehicle with a suspicious man inside. Maybe he would call the cops. And a cop might come.

The cop would flash a light inside his car.

Rossiter reflexively reached over and felt the lump under the jacket on the passenger seat.

"Sir, can I see what's under that jacket?" the cop would ask.

"There's nothing," he would say.

"Would you mind lifting up the jacket, sir?"

They always made it a point to call you "sir" in such situations. Feigning respect. It was almost comical. Cops' idea of irony.

"As a matter of fact, I do mind. I don't have anything to hide, but I don't have to show you anything."

"Please step out of the car, sir."

"Why, am I under arrest?"

"You're not under arrest. However, I have probable cause to search your car. Please step out."

"You don't have cause to search me or my car. I am a newspaper reporter at the Herald. I'm aware of my rights."

"Sir, I'm asking you for the last time: Please step out of the car."

Eh. He shook his head vigorously, to dislodge this stupid fantasy that was devolving into disaster. He scrutinized the eyeballs curtain and the other houses on this side of the street. There were no signs of life. Nobody was watching, he told himself; nobody cared.

Two hours passed without any sign of McMahon. Stars flicked on in the moonless sky. Rossiter found that he was content to wait. He wasn't hungry or cold or bored. He felt like he could sit there literally all night. The minutes, purposeful as ants, would march by, uniformly and mindlessly. Five hundred could pass by before you knew it, and any one of them could be any other.

McMahon came out of the house, alone, at about 10:30. He was in a shapeless hooded sweatshirt, baggy jeans and sneakers. He got into the Datsun pickup in the driveway, pulled quickly into the street and sped off. Rossiter had planned to wait until he got to the corner before following, but he could see now he didn't have time to wait. He started his car and drove ahead, squealing his tires a little. "Relax," he muttered.

He didn't turn on his headlights until he made the corner. By that time the pickup already was two blocks off, and gaining distance between them. He was going to lose the guy within the first half-minute of tailing him. Even in the annals of complete-amateur tailers, he thought, that might be a record.

But a half-block farther, the Datsun's brake lights suddenly came on, and the vehicle veered right, at a bright sign advertising a mini-mart. Larry's Liquors. Rossiter slowed down, pulling into the parking lot in time to see the shuffling figure go through the door.

He backed into a stall on the street side of the lot and turned off his lights, but left the engine running. His hand kept wanting to reach toward the jacket.

"Relax," he said again. "It's not going to crawl off."

McMahon came in and out of view inside the store. Rossiter could discern the blond crown of his head moving from aisle to aisle. When he made it to the cashier, he set a six-pack on the counter and pointed to cigarettes. The clerk—a dark-haired woman—pulled out a pack. McMahon's shoulders dropped. He pointed again. She replaced the first pack and picked out another. He made an impatient "give them here" gesture. She handed the pack to him. He tossed it onto the counter next to the six-pack and fished into his pocket. This took some time. Rossiter was surprised that he seemed to be counting out the exact change, fastidiously, slowly, like an old man paying for a book of stamps at the post office.

When he was done counting, he gazed at a spot above the woman's head while she sorted through the coins. She did this twice, then said something. He worked his hand into a pants pocket, drew it out, and opened it to spill more coins onto the counter for her to count.

When McMahon finally came out, he paused at the front of the Datsun, a brown bag under his arm, and he started to peel open the cigarette pack. He balled up the wrapper and dropped it on the sidewalk, put a cigarette in his mouth, lit it and flicked away the still-burning match. He glanced at the 4-Runner, then took another, more direct look. He cocked his head slightly, as if he were trying to identify who was inside.

Rossiter looked down at the dashboard, reached to fiddle with the knobs. "Am I imagining this?" he said to the radio. "You don't see me. No you don't see me, ha ha hee hee."

He didn't raise his eyes until a half-minute later when he heard the Datsun start up. It was already turning out of the lot onto the street. Rossiter went right behind, his headlights on. If McMahon figured out he was being followed, oh well. Ten minutes later, just south of the city limits, the Datsun pulled into the parking lot of a tavern. Rossiter had never seen it before, but he recognized the name: Mendoza's. He drove on a quarter mile, turned around and came back.

The lot was not crowded. He parked a few spaces away from the Datsun, where he had a clear view of the door. Mendoza's was always on the police blotter. Fights, robberies. The cops would fax out a news release involving Mendoza's about every other night, it seemed. One of the copy clerks on the night shift used to pick up the faxes and call out, "Mendoza-gram!"

One night a fat burglar had tried to break into the tavern during the early morning, and he got stuck in the window. When Mendoza himself arrived, he called the cops, but not until after he had beaten the backs of the guy's legs with a pool cue. After that, the guys on the city desk referred to the place as "Mensa's."

Rossiter sat there for a while, just gazing at the door to Mensa's. Occasionally someone would enter; someone else would exit. Not a lot of business for a Friday night. He pulled his flashlight out from underneath the seat, got out of the 4-Runner, and walked around the perimeter of the lot. At the north end of the lot he saw there was a grassy drop-off onto a slope that ran about 40 feet. The slope bottomed out onto a flat area around an old oak tree.

He went to McMahon's pickup. It was unlocked. Nobody was around. He got inside, pushed in the clutch and put the transmission in neutral. It didn't take much exertion to move the truck forward. He pushed it along, steering it toward the other end of the lot. He went all the way to the end, and just before the slope started, he jumped in and turned on the headlights. The Datsun bucked a bit from unseen bumps, but he was able to steer it all the way down, next to the oak tree. He stopped there and turned off the headlights, got out and walked up the slope.

Back to the 4-Runner. A few people, guys mostly, went in and out of the building. After about 45 minutes, the door opened and stayed open, and a thin figure hesitated in the door frame. The opening was suffused with a subdued reddish light, dimmed by a haze of smoke. The figure—he was no more than a silhouette—tilted his head back and took a long drink from a can. He straightened and flung the can away. His legs were obscured by the darkness and the smoke; he was suspended in that rectangle of light, seeming to float in the light and the smoke like an angel. When the door closed, the only light left was from a wan yellow bulb above the entrance.

Rossiter took his keys out of the ignition. He reached over, flipped his jacket to the floor, and picked up the revolver. He got out and delicately inserted it in his waistband, at the small of his back. He looked to the doorway. "Come here," he whispered.

McMahon floated outside the door frame, into the darkness of the parking lot.

12. These Parts

Give me snuff, whiskey and Swedes,
and I will build a railroad to hell.

—Attributed to James J. Hill (b. 1838-d. 1916)

Twixt Hill and Hell there's just one letter.
Were Hill in Hell, we'd feel much better.

—Early 20th century Northern Plains
schoolyard rhyme

We drove along Highway 2 from Prague to Havre, parallel to the railroad tracks. About halfway there, a passenger train came rocking in our direction.

"Is that the Empire Builder?" Thao asked. "The Amtrak train?"

"Yeah. It goes from Seattle to Chicago. You know it?"

"Named after James J. Hill, railroad magnate and namesake of this county, right? He built the railroad, right? Then he conducted a giant P.R. campaign to attract thousands of homesteaders, bringing commerce to support his investments. Unfortunately, there was a drought, the land could not yield much in the way of milk and honey, and many people who came seeking the promised land ended up struggling just to feed themselves."

"You did your homework."

"Duh. That *is* the premise of my story, after all. These vast expanses of land have proven to be unconducive to human settlement. Their hopes and dreams notwithstanding."

"But some of them did make a living here. They stayed, and their kids stayed, and their kids' kids. People, once you get them somewhere, and they put down stakes, they tend to call a place theirs. And stay put."

"Fewer and fewer do, it would seem. Stay put in a county named after Mr. Hill. Where they watch the Empire Builder go to Chicago every day."

I followed her gaze out the window at the empty tracks, and at the prairie rolling out beyond the tracks in a yellow smear, rolling and rolling until it faded into the void of the horizon. She took out her notebook and started to write.

We pulled over for gas and got directions to the high school. The route took us through a residential neighborhood, the street lined with elms. On the road, hundreds of golden leaves skittered and whirled along the road in small packs, blown first one way, then the other, as if they had been just escaped captivity but now couldn't choose which way to flee.

Havre High School was an imposing old red brick building, typical of many schools built in the West in the 1920s—designed to be sturdy enough to withstand the brutalities of the climate and an endless progression of careless teenagers, but also with a Gothic Revival grandeur. From the front it probably did not appear much different than it had 20 or 40 or 60 years before, except for an LED sign on a tall pole that flashed, "Home of the Havre Blue Ponies," and "Go Ponies Beat Indians." The football field was behind the school, surrounded on three sides by houses. We walked through an open gate directly onto a cinder track circumscribing the field. At one end of the field behind the goal posts there was a small wooden structure where refreshments were sold.

Thao stopped to read the handwritten sign in front of it. "Ohh, sloppy joes," she said. "What do you think, guys?"

Duane held up his camera. "I can't make pictures and eat sloppy joes at the same time."

"Yeah," I said, "I'll try some."

"Really? I never know what you're going to eat, or not eat," Thao said.

"Sometimes neither do I."

Duane hung a press ID around his neck and headed to the opposite end zone, where the Havre team was gathering. We dawdled on the grass behind the goal posts and ate sandwiches, which had been served on paper plates and augmented with spoons. Thao eschewed her spoon. "I say, if you are going sloppy, go all the way."

"A hearty if indelicate approach."

"That's me."

The Havre team, dressed in blue uniforms that matched the sky, had started going through a brisk series of choreographed calisthenics, punctuated by the occasional collective grunt: "Huah!"

"They are going to wear themselves out before they even start," Thao said.

As we were finishing our sandwiches, and cleaning up with the complimentary Wet-Naps, a yellow school bus nosed slowly onto the track and headed onto a gravel area near the snack building. The doors opened and the Browning team spilled out, dressed in white uniforms with red numerals. Their red helmets were decorated on one side with a single feather. The coaches gathered the players just a few yards away and immediately started them on jumping jacks.

"They come already dressed up?" Thao asked.

"They must dress out somewhere else. Maybe another school."

"Dress out? Not up?"

"Yeah. Change into uniforms."

"They're just children!"

"Yeah. Just high school kids. As you get older, they seem younger every year."

"But the blue team seems so much bigger. Also, why are there so many more of the blues?"

"Maybe the visiting teams are limited in how many can travel. Or maybe Havre just has more kids turn out for football."

"That doesn't seem fair."

"I think they try to match up schools that have similar enrollment. Anyway, you can only play 11 at a time."

"Really? It isn't more?"

"Just 11 to a side. Have you ever actually seen a football game?"

"Only about a thousand times. *The quarterback has to pass. But watch out! Now he's in a sack! Did you see that player from the other team rushing away?*"

"OK, Frank Gifford, I stand corrected."

"And I suppose you think I don't know who Frank Gifford is."

"Do you?"

"No."

We strolled on the track that encircled the field. At one point a gaggle of diminutive, pink-cheeked Havre cheerleaders trotted past us, giggling and shrieking.

"They are so cute," Thao said. "Everyone here is blond and blue-eyed. Does everybody in Havre resemble Barbie and Ken?"

"Pretty much, except for the Indians and the meth addicts."

"All these people seem pretty healthy to me."

"There's lots of Scandinavian heritage up here. Tough people. They settled in these parts in the homestead days."

"These parts?"

"Yes. This area."

"'These parts.' That's another funny expression."

"I suppose it is."

Duane caught up with us at about the 30-yard line.

"This sky is perfect," he said.

The cumulus billowed out beneath the blue. The wind was taking a rest, exhaling steadily but softly. The sun already tilted to the west, and across the field in the eastern stands, the caps and jackets and pale flesh of the gathering spectators glowed. Everyone from old folks to tots was dressed in blue, except for one end of the stands where there was a pocket of people in red.

"I see that your friends from Fort Benton are here," I said to Duane.

"They are? Where? I didn't see them."

"No way you can see them from here," Thao said.

"Yeah, you can." I pointed. "Third row up. See them? One is standing up with her back to us. The other one is talking to a guy wearing a tan vest."

"Hey, you're right," Duane said. "I was just down there. They must have just shown up."

"Are you still going to take their picture?" I asked. "I don't see the dude."

"I don't care about any dude."

"Duane, you're not going to do anything dumb," Thao said.

"You are right. I'm not going to do anything dumb. I'm going to make some pictures of them. I'll grab them at halftime."

"You don't want to do it now?" I asked. "The game doesn't start for another half-hour."

"No…The sun will be lower then. Better light. Anyway, I want to shoot down at the Havre end for a while. And I want to be in the right spot for the kickoff."

The Blue Ponies had broken off their calisthenics, and now gathered around a coach. "Right now! Right now!" the coach yelled. Duane jogged toward them as if he were being summoned himself.

"I should do some work, too," Thao said. She pulled out her notebook and pen. "I'll meet you?"

I picked out a spot in the western stands, just below an enclosed section at the top. "I'll be up there, right below that booth. Right at the 50."

"OK. Fifty."

"The 50-yard line. It's the center of the field."

"As if I didn't know that fifty is centerfield."

"Right. I'm wearing a gray sweatshirt. See? I'll keep an eye out for you."

"Sir, I made it from Vietnam to the Philippines in a fishing boat. I think I can navigate from the field to the stands in Havre, Montana."

I walked up the aluminum steps to the top row, which afforded an excellent sight line of the entire field and surroundings. Beyond the field, people carrying blankets and bags were still making their way toward the stadium, except at one spot—at a red pickup where five or six guys in red jackets congregated, leaning against the bed. Appeared to be drinking beer. Judging from his size and posture, I was pretty sure one of them was Not-Chief. They showed no inclination to head to the stadium. Duane was still down at the Havre end of the field.

Thao was now on the track. She was not much bigger than many of the kids milling about, but she circulated with an easy confidence. She was targeting couples with kids. I could imagine the routine. Smiling approach; apology

186

about being a bother; polite boilerplate introduction with name, affiliation and intention; offering of a business card, followed by a few questions. I observed her as she did her interviews. At the conclusion of each, she handed her notebook and pen to the subjects. They all wrote in the notebook, undoubtedly fulfilling a request for the correct spelling of their names, and phone contact information. The conversations seemed very earnest. Most of the interviewees, including the women, bent over slightly while talking to her, as if she were a child.

"Oh, she's good," I said aloud.

After the fifth interview, she put away her notebook and faced the stands. She had gone halfway around the track by that time, so she was looking up at the wrong side. With one hand shielding her eyes, she scanned the seats. At one point she put the other hand on her hip. *I'm a little teapot.* Finally she did a 180 to face in my direction. I waved, kept waving; she pointed at me and waved back.

She wended her way back across the track, and—after some additional searching—found the steps leading to the stands. She bounded up, arriving just a bit out of breath.

"Why did you move to the other side of the field?" she asked.

"Just tell me if I'm right about something. You made it all the way from Vietnam to the Philippines, but your intended destination was actually Australia instead—right?"

"Ha-ha. Very funny. I'm just a little bit challenged when it comes to directions."

"A little bit, yes. So, did you find anybody good?"

"People here are so nice."

"Can you use them in your story?"

"One for sure. This lady's brothers and sisters all moved to Washington and Oregon. But she doesn't want to move because she likes the schools here. But her husband just got laid off from the Napa store, and she wishes her kids could see their cousins more. She invited me over to her house tomorrow to talk some more, and Duane can take her picture."

By now most of the spectators were seated. Outside the stadium the red pickup was gone. A van was parallel parking in the vacated space.

Havre scored three touchdowns in the first two minutes of the game: kickoff return for a touchdown, interception for a touchdown, fumble recovery followed by a three-play drive for a touchdown. Browning got one first down on the ensuing series, then had to punt. A Havre player ran into the punter, giving Browning another first down, but the punter stayed down for several minutes. When he got up, wobbly, and limped off the field, the Havre fans gave an enthusiastic round of applause. On the next play Browning lost the ball with another fumble.

Browning ran a complicated offense, with backs always in motion before the snap. Sometimes the deep back took the snap directly, zipping toward either flank, or pitching to a trailing back, or to a flanker on a reverse, or faking any of those options. On three consecutive plays, Thao asked, "Which one has the ball?"

Little of this resulted in forward progress, however. The Havre linemen were so much bigger than Browning's that they simply bulled their way into the backfield on every play and chased down the ball carrier before he had a chance to turn upfield.

After scoring one more touchdown, Havre began to substitute freely, and the scrimmage lines remained between the 30-yard lines until the half ended. When the whistle blew, the two teams trooped to their sidelines, the Havre players trotting and high-fiving one another, and the Browning players pacing slowly, their heads down.

"I feel sorry for Browning," Thao said.

"I guess it's not their day."

"How long is the intermission? Have you seen Duane?"

"Yeah. He's down there at the Browning end."

"Where? I don't see him."

"He's on the track, right at the stands. See? He's got two women standing there on the bleachers, and he's taking their picture. It's those women from Fort Benton."

"We should go get him," Thao said. "Surely he's shot enough by now."

The red truck was back, near the same spot as before. But it was perpendicular to the other parked cars, as if the driver had just pulled straight onto the sidewalk. *Drunk as an Indian.* There was nobody around it.

"Maybe we should leave that to him. He's the professional."

"What? No, come on. We don't want to be late."

"For what?"

"Hm?"

"Late for what?"

"I want to take a tour of Havre. See what this Kmart is all about."

By the time we negotiated the steps to field level, skirted the Havre pep band and walked almost all the way to the Browning section, Duane apparently had indeed shot enough. He was leaning casually on a railing that ran above a waist-high cement barrier, the top of which was level with the floor of the bleachers. His camera slung behind him, he was chatting with one of the two women from Fort Benton. The other woman was talking to some people a few aisles up.

"Hey, Duane," Thao said.

He held up a finger. "Hey. Just a sec." He turned back to the woman. "I promise, Jean. If it doesn't run with the story, I can still send you some prints. If you give me your address."

"It's Jeanine," she said. "Not Jean."

"Jeanine, right."

"You better write it down. And my address."

He extracted a small spiral notebook and pen from his breast pocket, and began to write. "Jeanine. Jeanine Spotted Bird. That's a very pretty name."

"Thank you." She gave him a number on a Browning street that sounded like "Grampa Road."

He underlined what he had written, and put the notebook back. "Great. OK, guess I'd better get back to work. Thanks for letting me take your picture."

He extended his hand over the railing. She took it, and held it.

"You ought to come to Browning," she said. "It's pretty there."

To my right, Not-Chief emerged out of a knot of people in red jackets, maybe 20 paces away, and started walking quickly toward us.

"Uh-oh."

"What?" Thao asked.

"Trouble approaching." I pointed.

"Oh, god. Duane, come on," Thao said.

He was still facing Jeanine. "I think I was there once…It's by Glacier, right?"

Jeanine noticed the approaching Not-Chief. "Whoops," she said. She let go of Duane's hand.

"Duane, come on!" Thao put her hand out, toward Not-Chief, who was suddenly just a step away. "…No, wait!"

Just as Duane opened his mouth to say something, Not-Chief grabbed him from behind by his collar, and shook him hard two or three times. "You don't learn, do you, breed?"

Duane slapped the arm and jerked away with a reflexive quickness. "Keep your hands off me, motherfucker."

When Not-Chief's fist hit Duane's face, it made a sound like an uncooked pot roast dropped onto a tile floor. Duane wobbled but didn't go down. Not-Chief quickly hit him again. There was a pop, and I wondered if it was Duane's nose that broke, or a bone in Not-Chief's hand.

Duane staggered two steps backward against the concrete barrier, rebounded a foot forward and fell, first to his knees, then all the way down on his belly. His camera bounced once on his back.

"Omigod," Thao said. "Ross!"

We bent to help him, but he was already clambering up on his own. Little black pebbles from the track clung to his cheeks and speckled the blood that was beginning to pulse from his nose. He jerked his arms free and put his hands up in something resembling a combative stance, but his eyes were glazed, and he seemed to be gazing off to the left of Not-Chief, who uttered a derisive grunt. "Huh."

Duane took a half-step before his knees buckled again and he sagged to the ground. He leaned forward, palms down, and vomited.

When he was done, we slowly helped him to his feet, edging away from the vomit. He gazed blearily at Thao, who was dabbing at his face with a tissue.

"Is he all right?" Jeanine asked. "Billy, you asshole."

"Huh."

"I'm OK," Duane said. His voice was muffled and nasally; he was now holding the tissue against his nose.

Two men in blue hooded sweatshirts came trotting at a quick pace around the end of the track and toward us. When they came up Not-Chief—Billy—started to walk off, but they quickly blocked his path. One of them raised a hand high and waved. Their sweatshirts were inscribed with an icon of a blue horse and white lettering that said "Ponies Wrestling Staff." The coach who waved was about the same height as Billy, and the other, while shorter, probably was a solid 230 pounds.

"Problem here?" he asked.

Billy started to edge away again.

"Hang on," the taller man said. The other put his hand on Billy's arm. Billy shrugged it off but didn't move further.

The taller man asked Duane: "What happened here?"

"What happened?" Duane repeated.

Two teens, wearing sweatshirts with the same horse icon, came jogging up.

"Bryan, go see if Officer Pierson is around," the stocky man said. Bryan took off; the other teen remained.

"The police!" Billy said. "Whuffor. Just a little disagreement, is all."

"Bullshit!" Jeanine yelled. "You hit him for no reason. He didn't do nuthin'."

"Don't worry," the stocky man said. "The police will sort it out. Sir, are you all right?"

Duane lowered the tissue from his face and examined it. "I guess so. Did I fall?"

"He may have a concussion. Sir, do you know where you are?"

"What?"

"Do you know where you are?"

Duane peered out at the football field. He put the tissue back to his face. "Ball game. Browning."

"Duane, we're in Havre," Thao said. "Remember?"

"You might want to get him to a doctor. The hospital is just a couple of blocks from here."

"The hospital," Duane echoed. "I don't need a doctor. Did I fall?"

"Sir, who's the vice-president of the United States?"

"What?"

"Duane," Thao said. "Duane. This man is trying to find out if you have a concussion. Do you know who the vice-president is?"

Duane scrunched his eyes, maybe in concentration, or out of pain, or both. "Quayle?"

"Duane!"

"You should maybe just go on," the stocky man said, "and the police can catch up with you later."

"Yes, let's go. Duane, can you walk to the pickup?"

"Hell, yeah, I can walk...The pickup?"

Thao wrote her name and cell phone number on a piece of paper and gave it to the wrestling coach. As we took Duane by either arm and started to walk off, Billy grunted something at us. "Told you."

Thao took a parting shot over her shoulder. "Jerk! You're not so tough now, are you?"

Billy smirked and glanced toward the spot he'd walked from. The knot of people dressed in red was gone. He wiped his sleeve across his mouth and articulated the theme of the day: "Outnumbered, is all."

A few minutes after we sat down in the waiting area of the emergency room, I pointed out that Duane was bleeding out of his right ear. The staff quickly took him to an examination room.

"Can you go with him?" Thao asked.

"Of course."

"I'll call his family. I think he put their number in the phone…"

"Really? Do you think it's that serious?"

"His family here, I mean. We were supposed to meet them later on."

"We were?"

"Yeah. He didn't want to tell you. He wanted it to be a surprise."

"Why?"

"I don't know."

The doctor could have been the brother of the taller wrestling coach. His badge said Dr. Bradley, but he introduced himself as Brad. He had Duane sit up on a gurney and asked questions about his medical history: medications he was on (none), allergies to medications (none), and prior head injuries (he remembered falling off a stool as a kid).

"Where does your head hurt, Duane?"

"It doesn't hurt that much. I'm just kind of dizzy."

"So what exactly happened?"

"To my head?"

"Yes. How were you injured?"

"I'm not sure…."

"Was your friend there?"

"I … think so."

"Yes, I was there," I said. "A guy punched him in the face."

"Where in the face?"

"The nose."

"Did he hit him around the ear, do you think?"

"I don't think so. It happened pretty fast."

"Why did he punch him?"

"Who knows. Apparently Duane was talking to his girlfriend."

"That seems a rather drastic reaction. Duane, you like the ladies, eh?"

"I guess."

"You can lie back and make yourself comfortable. We're going to send you in to take some pictures, just to make sure you didn't crack your noggin."

"OK."

Brad left and soon after a technician entered, pushing a wheelchair. "Let's take a gander inside your head," he said.

"I can walk," Duane said.

"Doctor's orders."

They were gone for what seemed like a long time. There was nothing to read in the examination room except a grotesquely graphic poster of the human vascular system. Through the lone small window, I could see the sun sinking behind the roof of a dark house. I thought about going back to the waiting area, but decided I should be there when Duane came back. When they finally returned, Duane appeared to be on the verge of falling asleep in the wheelchair.

"He's tired," the attendant said.

"It's been a big day."

The technician eased Duane onto the gurney. He lay down with a sigh, and within two minutes he was snoring. It was the same soft snore I'd heard two nights ago in the RV.

When Brad came back in, he chuckled. "Amazing how comfortable a gurney can be," he whispered. He sat down, reviewed a few papers, and wrote some notes on a notepad. "OK," he said in a low voice.

"Is it serious?"

"I don't think so. The bleeding is just from a cut he somehow incurred inside his ear. But he still has a concussion, and you want to be careful with that. His nose isn't broken—just swollen. He doesn't need anything other than ice and Tylenol for that. And he needs to be kept quiet. Bedrest."

"For how long?"

"Overnight, of course, and I'd say all day tomorrow, too, depending on how he does."

"I'm not sure how. We're traveling…"

"If you want, he can stay here. We have the beds. It's prudent just to keep him quiet and watch him for a while."

"Sure. That makes sense."

"Fine. I'll have him moved to a room now. You're welcome to stay if you like, but I don't think it's necessary."

"I don't think so, either."

I found Thao in the hallway just outside the waiting room, talking to a couple. The woman was short, a bit chubby, with short gray hair. The man was also gray. He wore cowboy boots, and he grasped either side of the brim of a cowboy hat, which he held in front of his stomach. Thao introduced them as Merlene and Marlin Wolf.

"White Wolf," Merlene said. She extended her hand to me. "Marlin here is one of Duane's cousins."

"Oh, I'm sorry," Thao said. "White Wolf."

"Never mind, honey. We're used to it."

I shook hands with the White Wolfs. Their grips were equally firm.

"How's Duane?" Marlin asked.

"They think he has a concussion. Not serious. But they want to keep him overnight. You know, just to keep any eye on him."

"Oh, sure, sure," Merlene said. "That's best. Keep an eye on him."

"They took X-rays, of course."

"Oh, of course."

"So, what the heck happened?" Marlin asked. "This feller from Fort Benton cold-cocked him?"

"I think he's from Browning, actually. We just ran into him in Fort Benton first. But yeah, pretty much. I don't think Duane really saw it coming."

"Boy. What the heck," Marlin said, shaking his head.

"They're so damn wild over there in Browning," Merlene said. "And here we were all set to have a nice dinner with Duane and his friends. Of course, you can come on over anyway."

"Oh, that's so kind of you," Thao said. "But we couldn't impose on you after all this."

"It's not imposing," she said. "We planned for you. I've got the roast on the stove on warm. You've got to eat."

"We'll find dinner. Don't you worry about us."

"Well, if you're sure…maybe we could have you over tomorrow, if

Duane's better."

"Of course. That would be great."

Merlene said she and Marlin would stay with Duane for a while. We shook hands again, and Thao gave them her number. Just as Thao and I were walking out of the emergency room door, a Havre policeman showed up. He'd been searching for us. He wrote down in a small notepad, in meticulous cursive, Thao's account of the events. She concluded with, "You should arrest that guy."

"I already did. Drunk in public, and he has an outstanding warrant in Glacier County."

"And assault."

"That's another story. He says your friend threw the first punch."

"No way! All Duane did was put his hands up after the guy already hit him. Don't take our word for it, there were other people there."

"Yeah. We don't have a lot of facts. Only his girlfriend is talking, and her story's not all that consistent."

"What! She called him an asshole! She said he hit him for no reason!"

"She's not saying that now."

"What about the guys in the blue jackets? The bouncers or whatever?"

"The wrestling coaches? They did hear her. They didn't actually witness anything, though. They just heard someone yell that there was a fight."

"So…you're not going to do anything?"

"Hey, if your friend wants to press charges, we'll look into the facts of it. This guy's going to be in jail for at least another 24 hours."

"But it's just our word against theirs, then."

"Yeah, but the DA will probably take your word over theirs."

"Really? Why?"

"He just will. Believe me." He dug out a card and handed it to her.

"I'll talk to Duane about this," Thao said. "That guy really ought to be in jail for a while."

"He might as well join the crowd. We've got a whole tribe of them."

According to the cop, the best steak and best accommodations in town were at the same place, the Northern Lights Hotel on Highway 2. We checked in and headed straight to the restaurant, which held a fair number of post-game revelers in blue. There was no one in red.

"I guess the Indians lost," Thao said.

"I'm sure they made a valiant effort."

I ordered a bottle of wine, a Cabernet from Washington.

"A whole bottle? I can't help you too much with that. Maybe just a little bit."

"Rule of thumb: Don't order just a glass of wine in these little towns. The bottle will have been uncorked for days. Or weeks."

The waitress opened the bottle with some difficulty. As she filled our glasses nearly to the rim, Thao opened her notebook.

"Sorry," she said. "I just need to clean these notes up a little before I forget what I was writing down."

"Understood. Please, go ahead."

She nibbled at Saltines and drank her wine while skimming the pages. I surveyed the customers. Some of them ate with their jackets on. Almost all the men wore ball caps.

Thao sighed suddenly, and deeply, put the notebook away, and sat back in her chair. She stretched, pulling her arms back, which pushed her chest forward. She smiled at me, then assumed a serious expression. "I hope Duane is OK," she said.

"I think he'll be fine."

"What if he wakes up, and wonders—"

"Merlene and Marlin are there. He'll be fine. I wouldn't be surprised if he just sleeps all night. He was pretty out of it."

"That..." She leaned back toward me, and whispered, "…asshole…"

"Yeah. There was something about Duane he just didn't like."

She broke back into the smile. "But the cop. He thought he was Friday."

"What's that, now?"

"Hee. Sergeant Friday. You know. 'Dragnet.' 'Just the facts, ma'am.'"

"How do you know about 'Dragnet'? That's way before your time."

"Reruns. Daytime TV. How do you think I learned to speak English? 'I Dream of Jeannie.' And 'Bonanza.' 'Pa! Little Joe's horse just came back, and he ain't on it!'"

"If that's how you learned to speak English, it worked out pretty well. Football terminology aside, your English is excellent."

"Really? Do you think so?" She put her elbow on the table, and supported her chin with her palm. "I know it's not exactly perfect, like yours."

"Mine is far from perfect. Anyway, whatever the user's expertise, language has its deficiencies. The older I get, the less faith I have in it."

"That's an odd statement, coming from someone who's a professional writer."

"Someone who has been. Has been. But it's true. I'm becoming more and more convinced that language is humankind's primary vehicle for misunderstanding. In fact, this trip has provided abundant evidence of that."

She emptied her glass, and pushed it forward for a refill. "It has?"

"Thirsty tonight?" I filled the glass to the same level that the waitress did. "I thought you weren't going to help with this."

She took a healthy sip. "I just feel like relaxing a little. And it tastes good...Ample evidence how?"

"People say things and they mean something else. Or they want to say something, but say something else. On the other hand, in communication, there is no mistaking certain facial expressions or body or movements that are absent of language. It's like apes. Like when Billy set himself a certain way in the café in Fort Benton. I could see he was getting ready to throw a punch. So could Duane. That's why he backed off."

The waitress returned. Thao said to me, "You order for me. You know what I like."

I ordered two steaks.

"See? You know what I like. In the meat department."

The waitress glanced at me before she walked off.

"I think I have an idea what you like."

"Hee-hee!"

"You're feeling a little silly."

"Nothing wrong with that."

"No. Nothing."

"I'm glad you agree." She raised her glass, and I clinked mine against it. "So," she said, "speaking of Duane."

"Which I guess we were…"

"Yes. I have to ask you something. About him."

"OK."

She leaned forward and spoke just above a whisper. "Am I crazy, or did you goad him a little bit?"

"Did I … go to him?"

"No. Goad him. Remember, my English is excellent."

"Goad him into getting into a fight? Why would I do that?"

"You tell me."

"What makes you think I goaded him?"

"One, you were the one who pointed out that those women from Fort Benton were in the stands. Two, you reminded him that he'd said he was going to take their picture. Three, when we were in the stands and I said let's go get him, you wanted to wait."

"I was just helping him to do his job."

"Okayyy…"

"Also, I'm the one who spotted Billy walking up."

"Exactly. You saw him, but didn't say anything until it was too late for Duane to even turn around."

"You have a suspicious nature. You must be a journalist."

"Yes, it's a kind of curse."

"Why do you imagine that I would goad him into getting his ass kicked?"

She sat back. "Sounds crazy, doesn't it? Maybe you wanted me all to yourself? And Duane was the third heel?"

"Oh-my-god."

"Yeah. I think you might have a little crush on me."

"You just lay it all out, don't you? Also, it's third-wheel."

"Really? 'Wheel.'" She reflected on this. "OK. Anyway, lay it out, why not? I like you, too."

She pushed her glass across the table. I poured half of what was left into her glass, and the rest in mine. She raised her glass again. "To laying it all out." She took a sip and quickly put her glass down, seeming almost surprised. "Oh!" She whispered, "I have to pee."

"By all means. I'll just wait right here."

"Good idea."

She rose and walked toward the bar. As she walked slowly off, I saw that two or three of the diners in ball caps were following her progress.

The waitress came over. "Your steaks will be out in just a couple of minutes."

"Great."

She picked up the bottle. "Would you care for another bottle of wine?"

"No, thanks. I think we'll switch to water."

Our rooms were on the second floor, adjacent to one another. We walked from the elevator down the hall. A couple of times we brushed against each other. Her fragrance was the same as the night before on the battlefield. We came to my door first. She stopped when I did, and when I opened the door, she peeked inside. "I bet our rooms are identical," she said.

"Yeah, probably."

I leaned my shoulder against the open door. She was pushing up against me, as if to get a better view inside. Her face was inches away. Then it was even closer; she must have been on tiptoe.

"Well, goodnight," she said.

I could feel her exhalations touch my face, just the faintest quiver of air. Was it warm? My head, as if of its own volition, inched closer to her face. I had the sensation that I could descend into the twin black pools of her irises.

I took a step to the side, placing myself between her and the interior of the room.

"Didn't realize how beat I am," I said. "Goodnight."

200

I edged backward into the room, and slowly pushed the door. Just before it shut, her face suddenly changed, twisting into something almost grotesque…as if she'd just witnessed an unexpected, profound horror. After the door closed all the way, I thought I heard her gasp.

I shed my clothes in a daze, leaving them where they dropped on the floor. I hadn't lied—I really was beat. But I don't think it truly hit me until I shut the door in her face. At the moment a sharply-attuned dog like Frankie would be able to hear the air hissing as I deflated. In some spots faster than others. "Ah. Frankie," I murmured.

When was the last time I had a good night's sleep? It seemed like a long time. Three nights back. The night before she and Duane came lurching into my life in the RV. I flopped onto the bed like I'd been poleaxed, with the lights still on, and immediately conked out.

I don't know how long. It seemed like only minutes before I was awakened by a concussive *whoom*. It felt as though the room had vibrated, floor-to-ceiling. Earthquake? I listened for signs of panic in the hallway. It was so quiet I wondered if I actually had heard anything. Still, I thought, best to stay up for a bit, watch some TV, just in case. I turned it on, sank back onto the pillow and immediately fell back asleep.

Maybe 15 minutes later the room quaked again. I went to the open window. The room faced north, toward the railroad tracks, and I could see a freight train slowly gathering up momentum. The best motel in town was right by the railyard, where they were coupling cars in the middle of the night.

I staggered to the bathroom to take a leak. As I stood there, slightly swaying, I thought I could hear a faint thump. "Now what?" Yes, a persistent but not loud thumping. Someone was at the door.

I pulled on my jeans and walked to the door. "Yes?"

"Ross. Sorry. It's me. I can't sleep."

I opened it. She was standing in the hall in stocking feet, wearing the same sleeping clothes she'd worn in Great Falls. She was holding the green binder.

"Come in."

She hesitated. "It's so noisy."

"It's the trains. Come in."

She still hesitated. "I have some things I need to tell you."

"OK. Things?"

"Yes."

I gestured to the binder. "In there?"

"Yes. Partly."

"Come in, then."

I opened the door for her and, moving almost sideways, she came in.

13. Perfect Timing

'What day of the month is it?' he said, turning to Alice: he had taken his watch out of his pocket, and was looking at it uneasily, shaking it every now and then, and holding it to his ear.

—Lewis Carroll, *Alice's Adventures in Wonderland*

She went directly to the one chair in the room, pulled it over to the foot of the bed and sat. She was hugging the binder against her chest. "I need to talk to you."

I walked to the head of the bed, tossed aside the pillow and sat, my feet on the floor. "Did the trains wake you up?"

"Is that what that booming is?"

"Yeah."

"Oh. I wasn't sleeping anyway."

"Why not?"

She had put her hair in a ponytail, carelessly. A strand strayed from her forehead, across her eyebrow. She pushed it behind her ear. "You were right not to kiss me. I crossed the line."

"Which line is that?"

"You know. The professional line."

"OK. But you've been kind of flirtatious almost from the start."

"Flirtatious, or friendly. Either way, this was something else."

"Isn't it just a matter of degree? Either you're flirting or you aren't."

"Oh, c'mon. As if you never tried to charm someone when you were doing a story. I just got carried away. I don't know why."

"Yeah. A mystery, huh?" I gestured toward the binder. "So…you decided you're doing a story. About me."

She was still hugging the binder. "No. Well, not anymore. That's the point."

"I see. I actually didn't mind your flirting, by the way."

"I could tell."

"Was it that obvious?"

Her eyes were two perfect discs of obsidian. "I like you less when you are coy," she said.

"Ah. Right. So tell me about the story you're doing. I mean, not doing."

She slowly lowered the binder to her lap; the stray strand of hair fell back in front of her face. She opened the binder, snapped apart the rings, and removed some pages that were separated by tabs. There were only a few. She pulled her chair close to me and handed me a page.

It was a photocopy of a news story. The date was written in ink, between the headline and the text: June 7, 1982. Another cat had been found in an East San Jose neighborhood, shot with an arrow. Unlike the previous two this one was still alive. Its prognosis was uncertain. The owner wanted to know what kind of sick person would do such a thing. Police were asking for the public's help in identifying a suspect.

I put the page face-down in my lap and reached out. She showed me another page. A fourth cat had been shot. This one was dead. In addition to suffering the arrow wound, the animal had had its paws singed. A psychologist was quoted, saying a person exhibiting this level of depravity could very well transition from abusing animals to people. The police again implored the public for help.

Another page. The date of this story leaped forward seven years. The headline read that a local man had been arrested on a charge of child abuse. The story was written by one of the Herald cops reporters, a woman named Roxanne.

Roxanne's spot in the newsroom had been just a couple of desks down from mine, and I was there the day she wrote that particular story. I still could picture her as she labored over the writing. Ed was the editor. They went back and forth several times about the lead paragraph. "Why are we dancing around this? This motherfucker should be hung by the balls," Roxanne said.

"Yeah, but you can't really put that in the story," Ed said.

"Why not?"

In the end, Ed persuaded her that a simple, straightforward approach was best, relegating the sordid details to the end. These years later, the words were still familiar to me.

> A San Jose man was arrested on Tuesday on charges that he beat and sexually assaulted the four-year-old son of his girlfriend after the child had wet his bed.
>
> Jack McMahon, 22, was being held Wednesday in Santa Clara County jail in lieu of a $150,000 bond on felony charges of sexual assault against a child and corporal injury on a child.
>
> According to police, the child's mother took him to the emergency room of Mercy Hospital Monday night, saying he had fallen down the stairs. After the child was examined, hospital officials contacted authorities to report that the child's injuries and information he provided were inconsistent with the woman's account of what occurred. The woman—whose name is not being released by police—changed her story after police questioning, and provided information that led to McMahon's arrest.
>
> The woman reported that while she was working the evening shift at a convenience store, she left her child in McMahon's care. When she came home, she found the boy injured and semi-conscious. She has not been charged in the incident.
>
> The child remains hospitalized, listed in fair condition.
>
> Police spokesman Jason Escover said police still are reviewing evidence and statements, including indications that in the course of the alleged assault the child vomited, and then was forced to consume the vomit. Escover said additional charges may be filed.

"Hm," I said. "Whatever happened to Roxanne?"

"I understand that she decided she wanted to be a teacher. She went and got her credential."

"Wise of her. She wasn't really cut out to be a cops reporter. So they hired you to take her spot?"

"Yes."

"But you moved up to general assignment. Pretty quickly. They must like you."

"Sure."

She handed me two more pages. The first story said that prior to going to trial, McMahon pleaded guilty to felony charges of child abuse. The other charges had been dropped because the boy's mother had moved out of state and refused any further involvement in the prosecution.

On the second page, the quality of the reproduction was cleaner. March 2, 1995. It was a just-the-facts story reporting that McMahon had been found shot to death. Following this was a story from three weeks later, also written by Roxanne.

> A Herald columnist has been interviewed by police in the investigation of the death of a San Jose man.
>
> Doug Rossiter, whose column appears three times a week in the Metro section of this newspaper, was interviewed by police this week because his car appears on a surveillance video at a San Jose convenience store where Jack McMahon had shopped on the night he was believed to have been killed.
>
> Police Detective Robert Causey said the video did not show any interaction between Rossiter and McMahon. "We just wanted to know if Mr. Rossiter remembered seeing anything or anyone that might help us in the investigation," Causey said. "This is just a routine part of the investigation. We appreciate his cooperation, and hope for the same level of cooperation from anyone who may have information on this matter."
>
> McMahon was released from prison after having served five years for child abuse. His body was found March 1 near the parking lot of Mendoza's Tavern. Police had been called by the manager after a customer noticed McMahon's pickup sitting at the base of a slope near the tavern.
>
> According to the coroner, McMahon probably had died the previous evening, from a gunshot wound to the forehead.
>
> Police found a receipt inside the pickup from Larry's Liquors, time-stamped from the previous evening. A review of the store's video surveillance revealed images of McMahon buying cigarettes and beef jerky at about 10:40 p.m. on Feb. 28. In that same time frame, Rossiter's car is visible in the parking lot.
>
> Causey would not characterize the nature of any information obtained from Rossiter, but said the investigation was continuing and no suspects have been identified. "We interviewed Mr. Rossiter, but he is certainly not a suspect in this case," Causey said. "He isn't a person of interest."

I went back to the first couple of pages and scanned the stories. There was no mention of a suspect's identity in the cat abuse. It was "someone" and "whoever did this."

I held those pages up, lifted the others and held them side by side. "You seem to have made a connection."

"Yes."

I immediately recognized the next page she gave me: It was a photocopy of a page from a yearbook. A photo of a tight-lipped teacher was at the top, with the label, "Mrs. Simmons: Second Grade." Below this were five rows of five students each. I remembered exactly where to look. Bottom row, second photo from the left: Jay Rossiter.

A similar page was laid out almost exactly the same. At the top was the same teacher, but younger, with bushier hair. And she was smiling. This label said "Mrs. Simmons: Third Grade."

Thao leaned forward and pointed out a photo.

"Jacky McMahon."

The image was not clear—a lot of blond hair, a chin stuck out and the top of the head pulled back—but the name underneath was legible.

I swallowed. "Yeah, and…?"

Thao continued to say nothing. Her face was impassive, her lips pressed together. Three more pages, the last ones in the binder.

They were photocopies of just one long story. The headline read, "No thaw for cold cases," with the subhead, "Unsolved slayings stymie county investigators." The date noted on this page was six months ago, jotted next to the byline: Thao Nguyen.

The piece was divided into four parts, each one about a specific unsolved killing, with the names of the deceased used as segment titles. The title of the second segment was Jack McMahon.

I skimmed the story. It summarized McMahon's arrest for child abuse, the plea bargain and sentencing. A police investigator was quoted. It described McMahon's history with drugs, and speculated that his slaying may have been the result of a drug deal gone bad. Evidence gathered after the case suggested that McMahon also was involved in peddling child pornography, but police did not think that related to his slaying. There were no suspects in the case.

I held the pages out to her. She took them, tapped them smartly against the binder, and replaced them inside the rings.

"When I was doing the story…" Her voice quavered. She cleared her throat. "When I was doing the story, I talked to his mother. I wanted to know if she felt she'd been wronged, somehow, that maybe the police were treating her son's death like it didn't matter."

"Did you talk to his sister, too?"

"Yeah. Actually, it was the sister who sort of gave me the idea for the story. She wasn't really quotable, though."

"Ed hooked you up with her? The sister?"

"Yeah. Why?"

"Oh—" I shook my head. "Anyway, it's a good idea for a story. Even the dregs of society leave behind loved ones who grieve. They may be kind of badly nourished and they're smokers and their teeth aren't very good, but their grief is as real and as intense as anyone else's. So, was that the mother's complaint? The cops just blew it off?"

"Not really. Maybe a little. That's what the sister thought, and I kind of tried to steer the mom that way, but she didn't really go along. Apparently he'd been quite a handful, you might say, as a kid. I think he wore her out. It was like she was bitter toward him. She had this whole laundry list of his transgressions. He'd been arrested when he was just a kid, for shooting the cats with the bow and arrow. He spent some time in juvenile hall."

"She told you all this?"

"Yes. And there was a bunch of other things. Including breaking into a classroom—Mrs. Simmons' classroom—and vandalizing it."

"Yeah?"

"Yes."

"Did you talk to Mrs. Simmons?"

"Yes."

"And she told you about Jay."

"Yes."

"I see. And we finally get to the lede that's been buried all this time. Based on this body of overwhelming evidence, you concluded…what?"

She did not answer.

"…That I'm involved? That I killed him? I not only had proximity, which was shown with the surveillance video. I also had a motive? Proximity, motive, and any dumbass who can walk into a sporting goods store has the means."

She blushed, raised a hand and indicated the binder.

"I understand," I said. "You come along to a new workplace, want to make an impression, you have some background in the story from your previous job, then you find this out and you think, 'This is a fantastic story. Former columnist tied to slaying!' But no, think bigger: 'Former columnist a killer!' And not so much that romantic story about fleeing civilization. Right?"

"Yes." She said it so softly I could barely hear her.

"But you must have run this by the investigators you talked to for your story, right? Of course you did. But they waved it off as ridiculous. Because otherwise you wouldn't have come up here to—well, why did you come up here? That's the question I still ask myself, Thao. Did you think you would soften me up, and then when the time was right, confront me with your binder? After which I'd fall sobbing to my knees and confess, that yes, your brilliant deductive powers had exposed me, and now, because of your irresistible charm, I was now ready to reveal everything and turn myself in?"

Simultaneously, twin tears spilled from her eyes. She wiped them away and said something.

"What?"

She sniffed. "I said, 'I just wanted to talk to you.'"

"Of course, to talk. But you must have felt like you couldn't come up here without a bodyguard, if you were planning to talk to a murderer and all. So this *talk* we were going to have—you wouldn't have wanted to conduct that alone. Not with a homicidal maniac journalist. So you brought…Duane? The guy who messed up some Indian's fist with his face?"

"I just wanted to *talk* to you."

"Sure, have a chat. How the venom that coursed through my veins for those 10 years suddenly exploded in my skull and I hunted him down and lay in wait and shot him, thinking no one would miss him anyway because he's too broke to fix. And then drop everything and run to the middle of nowhere, as you described it. But what about Ed? Were you planning to just show up with this awesome unexpected scoop? Or did he know about this connection you found?"

"As far as he knows, I'm here doing a story on people emigrating from the plains states to the West Coast. And he thought as long as I was here I could ask you to help, and also see how you're doing. That's it."

"OK. I might buy that, because he is soft-hearted and soft-headed. But what I don't get is, did you really think that you would come all the way up here, thirteen hundred miles, track me down, shed a few tears at some point, and I would—" I stopped. Her eyes were dry now. "Oh...oh my god."

I laughed. "Oh, my god," I repeated. "You really are good."

"Meaning?"

"No, honestly. You're very good. *Tonight* was when I was supposed to confess. Right here, right now. Was that the plan?"

"What! What do you think I am? It's not that way. I told you. I crossed the line. I'm not doing this story. There is no story."

"All right."

"I'm not kidding." Instantly, two more tears traced the path from her eyes to her cheeks. She impatiently brushed them off. "Stop being such a prick."

The obsidian of her eyes glistened. I had an impulse to reach out and touch them.

"OK," I said. "OK. It's not like you completely tricked me. I had an idea all along you were up to something. By the time in Fort Benton for sure. I just wasn't certain what it was."

"You suspected I was quote 'up to something.' But you came along anyway."

"Yes. Yes, I did."

"So why."

"I told you why."

"Tell me why, really."

"You really want to know?"

"Yes!"

The emphatic way she said the word made me smile. Which, I found, made me relax. Which, in turn, enabled the human part of my brain to receive the reminder from the animal part that I was tired. When was the last time I'd truly slept? I'd just counted off the days a while ago…when did I do that?

"Hello?"

"Right, why did I come along. Thao, it's so simple; it's ridiculous. First off, very first thing, when we started talking about it in your RV, I realized I really needed to see the battlefield again. I needed to see what Joseph saw when he looked around at the hills, wondering where his children were. Wondering if this was the time to finally give up."

"But you could've done that on your own, any time. You didn't need us."

"And I also came, maybe the main reason, was because I'm alone. OK? I've been lonely. The only friend I have in the world is a dog that I got when somebody put up a piece of paper on a corkboard in the gas station in Vaughn. 'Jocko needs a home.' But as it turns out, a dog, for all of his many wonderful attributes, goes only so far. In that you can talk to him, and he'll try to understand you, but ultimately, when you reach a certain level, he's incapable. It's kind of like having a husband. A dog-faced husband. So sometimes I'd drive to Simms or Fort Shaw, just to see the faces of actual people passing by, going about their business. And you and Duane came along. And besides breaking up the boredom, I found you attractive, obviously, and you stirred certain feelings I hadn't had in a while. And when the body experiences those feelings, it says, 'More!' So even though I deplore any act or instinct of procreation on moral grounds, it seems I'm weak."

"I don't understand why you deplore…"

"I told you. For one thing, it makes a person act like an idiot. Like me.

Because it was just as you said. Even if I didn't do it fully consciously, I did set Duane up. Not just in Havre. I've been sizing him up and setting him up ever since he stumbled out of that RV on the first day you came. Which he immediately sensed, by the way. Remember that pencil-neck crack? And for another thing…"

"What?"

"…I'm repulsed by my own procreative urges. Maybe this is just my psyche punishing itself—but in some weird way, I've always had the feeling that Jay's death was nature's way of correcting my mistake. The mistake of me. I need to just dry up and blow away, like a tumbleweed."

"I don't want you to."

"Why not? Do you actually have an attraction to me? How can that possibly be? I'm not what you'd call handsome. Or attractive in any way."

"You're maybe a little attractive."

"Even so."

"OK, you're right," she said. "I agree. It's inexplicable. My past attractions have developed over a period of many months. Usually, I'm just friends with a guy first. For a long time. My attraction to you is very, very bizarre. It's bordering on insane. It's—"

"All right. I get it."

"—something I should maybe get counseling for."

"I said, I get it. So, it's not a story."

"That's what I said. I know you think certain things, or you say you do, that are kind of crazy. Maybe you've even done some crazy things. Like maybe you were even stalking Jack McMahon that night. But you are not a killer. You wouldn't point a gun at some guy and kill him. Having known you for all of four days, I can say that."

"You don't know anyone in four days, Thao. You just don't."

"I'm very intuitive."

"I believe it. That's what frightens me about you."

"C'mon. Nothing about me frightens you."

"Everything about you frightens me."

212

"You're insane."

"At least you've figured that out in four days."

"Pfft."

"OK. So you're not doing that story. So, now what?"

"So I'll go back to doing my real story, the story they sent me here to do. And the Joseph story, too. And Wood."

"Will Duane go along with that?"

"I do the story selection. Not Duane. Anyway, he never bought the idea in the first place. I know he thinks this is just some fantasy of mine, and he was annoyed by having to go chase you down and sneak in some photos of you and take time from the real story. Which is what he called it. I think he's learned to tolerate you. But now he's fully hooked into this Indian story."

"So we won't talk about it anymore?"

She pushed her chair back, and dropped the binder onto the chest of drawers against the wall. "No."

The binder lay in a careless diagonal. One edge had caught against the wall, leaving it slightly open. She reached down and nudged it over so that it lay flat. "Let's find something else to talk about. Transition to something lighter."

"Such as?"

"I don't know…Maybe we shouldn't talk at all. But I'm wide awake and you're going to have to deal with that. Let's see what's on TV."

"At this hour?"

"There's always something." She walked to my side. "Hand me that remote and move over."

I gave her the remote and one of the pillows, and scooted to the other side of the bed, my back against the headboard, legs on top of the bedspread. She placed her pillow against the headboard, undid her ponytail and lay her head back. This did not satisfy her. "Aren't you cold?" she asked.

"No."

"I am. I want to put my legs under the covers." She accomplished this without getting up. "Ooh. That's better." She clicked the TV on.

The Andy Griffith show, black-and-white. The lilting whistly theme song, Andy and Opie goin' fishin.' I tried to follow along, with some difficulty. In this episode, Floyd the Barber revealed he'd been corresponding with a woman he never met. In his letters, he had misrepresented himself as wealthy. Now the woman was coming to visit, and Andy was helping Floyd to concoct a fictional affluent lifestyle. Were the Mayberry goings-on always this convoluted? Thao obviously had seen the episode before. At one point she dug an elbow into my ribs. "Did you get that?"

"Hm?"

"Floyd says he learned 'Tempus edax rerum' from his Latin teacher in barber college. It's not an exact translation, though, is it?"

"I don't know. Do you speak Latin, too?"

"As much as any other girl who went to Catholic school. Hey, were you asleep?"

"Uh. Don't think so."

"Pay attention! You're missing the best parts."

"I'm trying."

But by the end, as Andy was uncovering the woman's secret motive, I may have drifted off for a few seconds. Then I felt Thao stirring, and there came the whistle-tune and the genial voice announcing another episode.

"Again? Is this the only guy on TV?"

"What do you mean?"

"Griffith. Matlock. Matlock was just on last night. Griffith and more Griffith tonight. It's the same guy, right?"

"Of course it's the same guy. First Andy Griffith, then Matlock."

"But now we're in Mayberry, and his hair is dark. He's gone backwards in time."

She put her hand on my chest. "Honey," she said, "that's the magic of TV."

The instant that she said the word—*Honey*—I felt something churn inside me, right above my stomach. It was both warm and heavy. I sucked in a quick breath.

"You OK?"

I could only manage a soft grunt.

She shifted, turning her torso to me.

"You are?" She peered at me. She reached her hand to my forehead. "You *are* cold. C'mon, get under these covers."

The heat from her hand seemed to penetrate into my forehead, through my skin to my skull, and deeper, to my brain...from which it seeped slowly downward...to my cheeks, my neck and my chest... and deeper, lower, into the warm spot above my stomach, and spreading from there in every direction, like dye injected into water. Was this like being hypnotized? But it wasn't just my brain—it was my whole body.

"Your hand is warm," I said.

She lowered her face to mine, closely enough for me to hear her softly inhale and exhale. "Mm-hmm."

I closed my eyes and inhaled. Her breath smelled sweet, like summer grass. *That* was the smell. I let myself sink into the scent of her. Alfalfa. Honey. Honey. Sometime in the summer outside the gas station in Fort Shaw, I had bought a quart jar of honey from a farmer, who said it came from his hives in an alfalfa field out by Dutton. I ate a little of it every day. In mid-September, after a hard frost, the honey crystallized in the cupboard. For a few days I ate a spoonful with my breakfast. One morning I put the jar in water and warmed it on the stove, and poured it on my oatmeal. The warm and fluid honey suffused the oatmeal until every grain was coated. Each molecule of every oat imparted the essence of honey. But that night the jar crystallized all over again.

"Hey, are you awake?" She touched my nose and chin.

"Yeah."

She reached down and put her hand inside my T-shirt, on my lower chest, settling exactly above the internal pool of warmth I felt. But her hand was warmer than that, much warmer.

"The honey," I said. "That oatmeal...remember that oatmeal?"

"Mm-hmm," she whispered. She brought her face even lower. Her lips were apart. I felt her breath in my mouth. I could taste it.

I opened my mouth, and her lips were against mine. I realized that I had imagined, or somehow sensed, that they would be very soft, but not this soft. Ocean foam sewn up in silk. I pressed my mouth against hers tentatively, not wanting to crush the soft lips. But she firmly kissed me, and then her tongue was inside my mouth. I felt her hair against my brow and eyelids. She drew back a little, and exhaled into my mouth. I felt it as much as I heard it—*puh-h*.

I reached my arm around her shoulders. She pushed herself up slightly. Just as her mouth was soft, the muscles in her shoulders were surprisingly firm. She lifted one hand, reached down and with a quick deft twist, freed the button of my jeans.

"Wait," I whispered. "Are you—I don't have…."

"Don't worry, honey. The timing is perfect."

Her hair was a dark curtain all around my face. She reached up with one hand to pull it back, but it fell back down. She lowered her face again. In her dark eyes, I sought the reflection of mine.

14. Backwards

And it was like a confirmation of their new dreams and good intentions when at the end of their journey the daughter was the first to get up and stretch her young body.

—Franz Kafka, *The Metamorphosis* (1939)

Thao fell asleep almost immediately. Her head was on my shoulder; I could feel the gentle rise and fall of her chest. The railyard continued to emanate its grinds and moans, but she was oblivious. My drowsiness had lifted, and for what seemed a long time I lay there contemplating the dark. Finally I reached the point where I came in and out of sleep, but I found myself entirely awake before sunrise.

When I got up, she stirred slightly and mumbled something. I couldn't tell what. I showered, taking my time. When I got out she had rolled over. She now faced away from the window, which had gone from black to dark gray. She lay on her stomach, her mouth open. I dressed quietly and went out.

I returned about an hour later, and she was lying in the same position. It was fully light. I resisted an impulse to brush back her hair. I went to the small table in the room, put a newspaper on it, and spread out some food from a paper bag—a couple of breakfast burritos, muffins and coffee.

"Ooh." She slowly sat up. "Food!"

"Hey. Good morning."

"What did you get me?"

"A feast from the fat of the land."

She rubbed the top of her head vigorously and unpeeled herself from the bed. Grabbing her sweatshirt and sweatpants from the foot of the bed, she swept them in front of her, and looked at me expectantly.

"I will avert my eyes."

"Pff. Too late for that," she said. But she turned her back to me as she pulled on the pants. If she was 32, she still had the butt of an 18-year-old. She did a slight wiggle.

"Nice."

"Think so?"

"Yes."

"Good. Let's eat."

We sat at the table. She peeled away the wrapping from her burrito, and took a large bite. "Mm."

"Hungry?"

"Yeah. Aren't you?"

I picked off a small piece of a muffin. "Not terribly."

She took another bite. "You're an early riser, huh?"

"Usually, yeah."

"Late riser, too."

"Oh—hah. That all depends on the company."

I felt her foot against my shin. "So…you enjoyed the company? Sir, do you think you are a good fit for this company?"

"I did enjoy the company. Very much."

"Are you sure?" She nodded toward the bed. "It's best to make sure, you know."

"I enjoyed the company…too much."

"Oh-kay…And…"

"I can't, uh—I don't have time. We should go see Duane. Then I need to catch the bus. It leaves at noon. Just down the street."

"The bus!"

"Yeah."

"Bus to where?"

"To Great Falls. From there I'll hop one that goes west. I should be home by 4."

She put her hands flat on the table, and leaned forward. "Really? It was that great, huh?"

"No, I told you. It *was* great. It was…" I thought my hands might be shaking. I put them in my lap. "I can't think of anything to say that wouldn't sound stupid. It was everything I thought it would be. It was what I dreamt of. I'm—I don't want to fall in love with you."

"Love! Who said anything about love?"

"I did. I just did."

She reached her hand across the table. I kept my hands in my lap. "Honey," she said softly. Her flawless fingers and nails. "Honey, it's too soon for love."

At first I just sat there. Then I burst into laughter. I grabbed her hand. She waited patiently to hear the joke. "No," I said. I squeezed her hand harder. "No, it's the opposite."

"Meaning?"

"It's too late for love."

"Yeah, duh, I get that, the opposite. But why?"

I let go of her hand, and gave it a quick pat. "What do you care? It's too soon."

"C'mon. Why is it too late?"

I picked at a piece of the muffin. "Have some muffin," I said.

She reached across and took the muffin from my hand, put it to her mouth, and took a big bite. "OK," she said, still chewing on it. "Forget love, then. Why are you taking the bus back today?'

"It's just time."

"So, it's time, all of a sudden. Well, let me drive you, for god's sake."

"No, you have work to do. And what would you do after you dropped me off? With your sense of direction, you'd end up in Pocatello. Anyway, don't you have an interview today?"

"I'll call her and reschedule." She took another bite of the muffin, and slowly shook her head. "Was it something I said?"

"No."

"Something I did?"

"No. It was something I did."

"You mean, something you did twice?"

"OK. Yeah."

"So, you're going to disappear? Just like that? I have news for you. You don't just walk out of my life, pal."

"I'm not disappearing. You know where to find me. If you want, pick a date and we'll connect on your way back. At Freddy's or wherever."

She again nodded to the bed. "And what about that?"

"I'm sorry. That was a mistake."

"A mistake. Do you make a lot of mistakes like that?"

"No. But I have made a lot of mistakes."

She suddenly, emphatically pushed the food away. "OK. Fine," she said. "Speaking of mistakes."

"Yes."

"I've been thinking about what we talked about yesterday. What you said."

"What, specifically?"

"About how someone wouldn't feel remorse over shooting Jack McMahon. That a person couldn't blame them."

"You have an interesting way of reconfiguring certain statements of mine. But when exactly were you thinking about this? We made love—pardon me, we had sex—after which you fell asleep until a half-hour ago, and we've been talking and eating since."

"I'm a fast thinker."

"Clearly. So what does this have to do with mistakes?"

"So what I was thinking was this. Let's say someone shot him because they thought that, gee, this guy is a menace to society. In fact, that's what you said, right? 'Too broke to fix.' Which anyone could understand. But then the person thought, *Omigod, what have I done? This was a horrible mistake. I can't just kill someone.* Why wouldn't they just own up to it?"

"Just off the top of my head, for one reason, they might have to go to prison."

"Maybe. Yes."

"Oh. So that's it," I said. "There it is at last. That's your redemption angle? Raskolnikov serves his sentence in Siberia. It would wrap up the story rather neatly. We hope, we *believe* that I will emerge an older but wiser man. Just a little scarred. Emotionally, of course. Not physically. Your readers would love an ending like that."

"You don't have to be so snarky about it. OK, I suppose some people wouldn't really want to go to prison."

"Yeah, probably some people wouldn't."

"Even though it might actually give them some sense of relief. Getting it off their chest. They could pay their debt to society, and get on with their lives."

"Maybe they don't feel that they owe any debt to society. To the world, yes. Not to society."

"That doesn't make any sense."

"I have never made any claims about my making sense. Listen, can we continue this hypothetical on the way to pick up Duane? I have to…"

"Oh, yeah. You have to catch the *bus*."

She called the hospital, and found out that Duane had already been discharged. He had left word for her that he was at the White Wolfs. Thao wrote the address on the back of her hand.

We agreed to meet in the lobby a half-hour later. I dallied, absent mindedly picking up what little mess there was and packing my few things. When I went to the lobby, she was already there, perusing a rack of postcards.

"You're quick," I said.

"I have to be."

The skies were sullen, mulling rain or snow. There was a light wind. I barely eased out of the parking lot onto Highway 2 when she started talking.

"Another thing about last night. What did you mean last night at dinner when you said you were a weed?"

"What? Oh…nothing."

"Oh, c'mon. You meant something. What?"

"Did you get directions to this place?"

"Yes. The front-desk clerk said you only turn twice. First, you go left at that light down there. What did you mean? 'Dry up and blow away.'"

I steered the pickup on a road that curved up a hill. "I think we were talking about Jack McMahon."

"Yes, but at the time, you were talking about you."

"I think you are somehow confusing what I said with something that Aunt Bee said."

"Stop it. What did you mean?"

"I don't know, Thao. I was tired. I was confused. Or bewitched."

"So, now I'm a witch."

"Yes. You put a spell on me. I'm just going to keep driving till you tell me to turn again."

She checked the writing on her hand. "Find Stone Road and go right. What did you mean?"

"God. I don't think I meant anything. Nothing I say means anything. Haven't you figured that out yet?"

She went quiet until we got to Stone Road, which lay on the outskirts of town just off of Highway 87. The street bisected a series of one-acre parcels. I drove slowly; some of the numbers were hard to see. Thao saw it first. It was a neat modular home, with an adjacent carport, in which were parked a white Ford pickup and a John Deere tractor.

"Keep going," she said. I went on about a hundred yards. "OK," she said. "Pull over here."

I did as she said, and killed the engine. She unbuckled her belt and crossed her arms. "I'm not satisfied with any of this, but we can't sit here forever because you have a *bus* to catch." She stressed the word in a way that suggested its actual existence was dubious.

"That's right."

"So we're meeting at Freddy's?"

"When are you going back to San Jose?"

"I should be done up here in three or four days. Say four days. Thursday."

"We can connect at Freddy's, then. Friday, dinner."

"Fine. And wait, one more thing."

"We kind of have to get going…"

"Yeah, yeah, the bus." She checked her watch. "We actually have plenty of time, it seems to me, because as far as I can tell you can get from one end of Havre to the other end in no more than 12 minutes."

"We might get kind of stuck at the White Wolfs for a while…"

"Oh, don't you worry, I'll get your butt to the bus on time." She turned fully toward me. "Why is the number on your door twelve thirty-one, which is the same as what your clock is stuck at?"

"Coincidence, I guess."

"Coincidence." She began to drum her fingers on her thigh.

"You're a journalist; you know how it is. You have to set a deadline of some sort."

"Deadline for what?"

"Otherwise nothing ever gets done."

"Deadline for what?"

"Unh. You sure ask a lot of questions."

"As you just said: I'm a journalist."

"All right, fine… You didn't think I was going to live out there in that shack forever, did you? I think we've both seen over the past few days that as a hermit, I suck. I just need to get some issues settled in my mind before the end of the year and decide whether to rejoin society."

"Issues like what?"

"Mm…."

"C'mon, like what? Whether you're so tired of the world that you can't rejoin it?"

I felt a sudden wave of nervousness, a childish sensation of having been caught at something naughty. I let it pass. "Tired," I said. The sound of the word lingered, pulsing in the cab of the pickup. "No. I'm not tired, not in that way. It's not like that William Carlos Williams poem where his grandmother is in the ambulance and she says she's tired of the trees. It's the opposite of being tired of them. Sometimes I think I just want to *be* them. Let me crumble into the ground and feed them and then become them. Or let the bugs eat me, let the mice eat the bugs, let the hawks eat the mice. And I can fly at last. Into the orange of the sun."

She contemplated this, her lips—her soft lips—flexed forward, as if in a pout. "You know, you're not the only one who's had bad things happen. You could be in Rwanda or somewhere."

"I'm not complaining."

"OK, so whatever your troubles, you need to tough it out. Remember the good in life."

"I think it's a fallacy that you have to tough it out. 'Be strong, endure your suffering.' The real strength, the greatest strength of all human strengths, is knowing when to give up, like Joseph did."

"Why don't you do something to improve the world, instead of giving up?"

"I don't buy this idea that we're supposed to try to improve the world. People have this obsession about, 'How will I be remembered? How will I make my mark?' I'll sire children and grandchildren to carry on my legacy. And to cry at my funeral.' People cannot accept the reality that whatever they do—invent the polio vaccine, plot the slaughter of three million Cambodians, sing 'Un Bel Di' at La Scala —in the grand scheme of things, against the vastness of time and the universe, it's insignificant. It is as lasting as a smudge in the dirt that was made a million years ago, by one ant, in an anthill of a million ants."

"There's an inspiring thought."

"I'm going to sell it to Hallmark."

"It's only human to strive to be something."

"Exactly. It's only human. I always thought Kafka had it backwards. He should have started, *A giant insect awoke one morning to find itself metamorphosed into Gregor Samsa.* And it would go on to describe the life of this mortified insect-turned-human. It might require some fine-tuning here and there. Like, when he gets pelted with fruit, it would have to be something mushier than apples."

"You can't just walk out on the world."

"It's not the world that troubles me. It's the people in it."

"And where does one go when one is so troubled by the people in the world? I'm assuming it's not back to your house in San Jose."

"San Jose? No, the opposite direction. One lights out for the territory."

"One lights…what? The Northern lights? Northern lights territory?"

"I meant—well, yes. The Northern territory."

"So you run away. That's only going to hurt the people who love you."

"Huh? It's too soon for love."

I barely had the words out when she barked, "Shut up!" I flinched. "I should slap you!" The anger on her face lingered for several seconds. She repeated: "What about the people who love you?"

"All right. In my case, really, there are maybe a handful of people who would miss me a little. Or fewer. And they would get over it quickly." She started to say something, and I raised my hand. "They would. Trust me on that. Frankie would probably miss me more than anyone. But in a while he'll forget it, and he'll be fine."

"You wouldn't even bring your dog?"

"Thao. I really do need to catch the bus."

"Fine. But we're not finished. We're meeting at Freddy's, Friday. Right?"

"We'll definitely connect."

"Promise?"

"I said we would." I reached out for her hand. She extended it in the royal fashion. I could see the White Wolfs' address in blue ink. I brought her hand to my lips, and kissed her palm.

Merlene answered the door. "Good morning, folks," she said. "Duane's been worried that you wouldn't find us. He's out back with Marlin. You make yourselves comfortable, and I'll get them. There's coffee cups on the kitchen counter, and the pot's on. Have you had breakfast?"

"We can only stay a minute," Thao said. "Ross here has to catch a bus this morning."

"Oh? Where to?"

"The Falls," I said.

"Gosh, it's too bad that you have to run off. We were hoping you could stay for some cinnamon rolls."

"We'd love to," Thao said, "but I think we—"

I interrupted her. "Oh, sure. We can stay for cinnamon rolls. We'd be crazy not to."

"That's fine. You make yourselves at home." Merlene pointed to the kitchen entrance, and headed to the back door.

After we heard the door close, Thao hissed, "What about the *bus*!"

"I still have time. Enough for a cinnamon roll. Just 10 minutes."

We heard Merlene beckoning Duane and Marlin. When Duane came in, Thao gasped, but quickly recovered. "He's back among the living!" she said. "How do you feel?"

He briefly touched his nose, which was still red and swollen. The lids above his two bruised eyes were droopy.

"Fine. Just a little headache is all. I'm good to go."

"Thank god. That guy, he punch-suckered you."

"How's that?" Marlin asked.

I interpreted: "She means sucker-punched. He kind of caught Duane off-guard."

"As soon as we drop off Ross at the bus station, we're going to the police to press charges," Thao said.

"The bus station?"

"Yeah," I said. "Time to get back."

"Is that right." Duane rubbed his temple.

"Yeah."

"I'm not going to press charges."

"Yes you are!" Thao said.

"No. Not worth the effort. I don't remember most of it anyway."

I could see that Thao wanted to argue the point, but she refrained. Merlene passed around cinnamon rolls. They were still warm. Before I was finished with it, Thao had eaten hers, and half of another. "These are the best cinnamon rolls I ever had," she said.

226

"You bet," Marlin said.

I caught Duane's gaze. "You showed me."

He rubbed his temple again. "What?"

I reached out my hand for him to shake. "You did. You showed me."

His eyes suddenly burned a hole through the fog. "I *did*, didn't I?" He laughed; it was the one and only time I heard him laugh. "I showed you!"

When the 10 minutes had stretched to 15, I winked at Thao. She announced: "Time to go! Those buses don't wait!"

"I think I'll just stay here," Duane said. "Get some rest."

The consensus was that this was a good idea. Marlin offered to drive us, but Thao said no, she'd drive. They talked out logistics. Thao would spend the rest of the day doing interviews, and if Duane was up to it, he'd join her later to take photos. At Merlene's insistence, she and Duane would have dinner and stay the night there. Depending on Duane, they might go back to the Prague museum the next morning, then head east on the Hi-Line.

I thanked the White Wolfs, clapped Duane on the shoulder and shook his hand again, and stepped with Thao out the door. The breeze had gained more of a sting now.

Thao took the keys. She had to adjust the seat all the way forward, and her eyes were just about level with the top of the steering wheel, but she quickly displayed a knack for maneuvering the truck.

"Where'd you learn to drive?"

"My dad used to have a gas station and a tow truck. I drove trucks all the time."

"You are full of surprises."

"Yep."

Marlin had given us the route, and said we'd get there in 10 minutes. We arrived in six. Thao pulled into a parking spot on the street that bordered the bus lot. A man wearing a cap and a short uniform jacket was tossing bags into the belly of the bus.

"You'd better hurry up and get your ticket," she said.

"I already got it. While you were sleeping."

"You did? You're fast, too."

"I have to be."

I reached for her hand again. The ink had smudged, and there were still flecks of white cinnamon bun frosting on it.

"I'll be seeing you," I said.

"Stop with the mushy talk, will you?"

I kissed the back of her hand, gripped it and looked into her wet eyes. "I'll be seeing you," I said again.

"You'd better be. Don't make me have to track you down. I know where to find you."

"Right. You can always find me there."

"You're staying, all of a sudden?"

"Nobody really ever goes anywhere."

"Don't b.s. me."

"I'm not. You'll be able to find me, no problem. I promise."

"You promise?"

"Yes."

I got out of the pickup and plucked my bag from the back. She jumped down from her side and paused with her back to me. She was wiping her face.

I came around and gave her a quick kiss, too quick for her to kiss back. "See ya."

When I boarded, there were four passengers already seated. Two Indians were slouched in the seats all the way in the back, on either side of the aisle, both with their arms crossed and eyes closed. In the front seat there was a young blonde woman, a silver-colored University of Montana Grizzlies sweatshirt visible under her coat. She was tending to a baby. I went halfway down the aisle, and sat on the side facing where Thao had parked the pickup. I was unable to stop myself from looking toward her. I raised my hand; she raised hers.

The Indians got off at Loma, but three more got on there. Two guys and a woman. They occupied the same row of seats the other Indians had vacated. Nobody else got off or on until the bus rolled into Great Falls.

I walked to Public Drug on Central Avenue and bought a pen, some paper and a box of envelopes. I took a cab to Freddy's, using the 10 minutes to write on the paper and stick it in one of the envelopes, on which I wrote "Thao N." The sign at Freddy's was pale in the daylight. I asked the driver to wait.

The waitress without eyebrows was standing near the entrance at the cash register. She smiled at me. "Hey there. Back again?"

"Yeah. Sorry for the disturbance the other night."

She waved her hand. Free from the stresses of the evening restaurant rush, she was positively affable. "Don't worry about it, hon. That little gal left a nice tip, and nothing got broke."

"No? Surely we broke something."

"Nope." She gestured to the dining room, which was almost empty. "It's all still standin.'"

"I guess I overestimated our potency. Listen, I was supposed to meet the two of them here again, but I can't make it. Can you give her—that little gal—this note?"

"Sure, you bet."

I handed it to her and went back into the cab.

In spite of its bulk, the bus rocked and creaked as it bucked the west wind, all the way to Simms. I got there with about an hour of good light left, and used most of it walking to the shack. When I got there, I went inside just long enough to put an X through four days on the calendar, grab the 4-Runner keys and head out.

When I pulled into May's place, Frankie was already at the fence, wagging his tail. He started running in a circle, which got the pack of a dozen dogs running around in the same circle, panting and fake-growling and jostling one another. I laughed. "Frankie!"

May came out and started to chat as though she'd been expecting me at that very time. We visited for a while. "I see he made some buddies?" Yes, May said, everyone was a buddy.

When we piled into the 4-Runner and pulled out, Frankie fell asleep, head in my lap, before we got onto the highway.

Jack McMahon is Good for It

February 1995

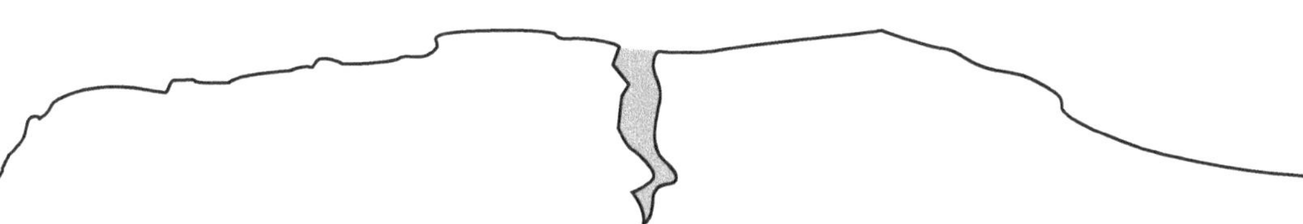

Rossiter froze as McMahon walked away from the door. It took just a second or two for the bulb's feeble yellow glow to disappear into McMahon's dark clothes. Now it reflected only dimly off of his hair and one side of his face. From the distance, this gave the effect of a disembodied head, floating away from the doorway toward the parked cars. As McMahon walked farther into the lot, his movement gradually became evidenced only by a vaporous glint of yellow, and the sound of steps on the gravel.

As the sound grew louder the pace slowed. Somewhere behind a gray van, maybe four vehicles away, the steps stopped. After a few seconds the gravel scraped once, twice, slowly. Then there was no sound.

"Over here," Rossiter said. The words broke up inside his throat, and emerged in a fragmented croak. He coughed. "Hey, over here."

Five seconds of silence. "What? Me?"

"Are you looking for your pickup? A Datsun pickup?"

The gravel scraped again. He heard McMahon come around the SUV. "Yeah. What did—"

"It's over here. Down that slope. I saw some guys push it down there."

McMahon was coming toward him slowly. The vapor took shape again: a light face atop a dark torso. "What guys? Who're you?"

"I was just parking my car when they pushed it off." Rossiter turned on

233

the flashlight and pointed the beam at McMahon's chest. McMahon flinched.

"What for? What's it doing way down there?"

"How would I know what for?" He put the beam to the tangle of tree branches stretching above the crest of the slope. "A prank or something. They looked like kids."

"What kids? Where are they?"

"Teenagers, I mean. They look like kids to me. They went inside, I guess."

McMahon had stopped about 12 feet away. "I didn't see no kids go inside."

"Well, they're not here." Rossiter started walking toward the slope. He pointed the beam again at McMahon. "Come on, it's over here. Do you want to get it or not?" He walked on. After he took a few steps, he heard McMahon walking behind him. A little ways farther Rossiter stopped and checked behind him. McMahon stopped, too. Mensa's was now out of sight. Rossiter continued down the slope to the pickup, with McMahon trailing. He shined the light over it. "Doesn't appear to be any damage."

McMahon was suddenly at his side. "Better not be." He glared at Rossiter. He went to the driver's side door and peered inside. "Better not be any fucking damage." He reached into his pocket and pulled out a ring of keys. "If there's damage I'm going to be pissed off."

Rossiter backed up three steps, reached behind him to pull out the .38, and put the light onto McMahon's face. He shifted the light to the revolver, then back to McMahon's face. In the light, the scar next to McMahon's eye glistened.

"What the fuck!" McMahon raised his hands. "Hey. I didn't mean pissed off at you."

Rossiter wanted to speak—Do you remember me?—but the words disintegrated. "Dooh—" He coughed again.

"C'mon," McMahon said. His hands remained up. "Oh. Dude. Are you with Jinx or somethin'? 'Cause I told him I'd pay him next week and he said it was OK. I said everybody knows that Jack McMahon is always good for it and he said OK."

Rossiter again tried to speak. The sound emanated from his mouth as barely a puff.

"Fuckin' A, man," McMahon said. "Does Jinx know you're doin' this? Because he said next week was OK." He moved his head back and forth, shying against the light. "You can call him. You better, cause he's gonna be pissed if he finds out about this. I'm not shitting you."

Rossiter shook his head.

McMahon lowered his hands a bit, and took a step forward, half-shutting his eyes against the probing light. "Dude, there's a baggie under the front seat, it's all that's left. The dude's paying me next week, and I'll pay Jinx soon as I get it. I swear." He moved sideways, clearing a path to the driver's door. "Go ahead, take it, motherfucker."

"I don't want it," Rossiter whispered.

McMahon lowered one hand slowly and reached into his back pocket. He pulled out his wallet, and threw it at Rossiter's feet. "There. It's like twenty bucks. So I'll pay him 980 next week."

Rossiter ignored the wallet.

McMahon's pale face went whiter. "C'mon," he said. "What does he want? My sister...she'll suck his dick again." He attempted a grin. "Tell him that. I'll make her."

"I…"

"Yeah, you, too," McMahon said. "She'll suck your dick or whatever. Really."

The revolver was growing heavy in his hand. "I'm sorry," he mumbled. He said it again, and this time it was clear. "Sorry." He pulled the hammer back with his thumb.

15. The Tiger Tales

Tempus edax rerum, tuque, invidiosa vetustas,
omnia destruitis vitiataque dentibus aevi
paulatim lenta consumitis omnia morte!

—Ovid, *Metamorphoses* (ca. 8 AD)

On Saturday I had an early breakfast of one-third of a can of beans and some dried apricots, and then, with Frankie riding shotgun, drove south on the gravel, about 20 miles to I-15. I headed south on the interstate, into the sudden hills that introduced the plains to the Rockies, and exited at Wolf Creek, which comprised a smattering of cabins and a bar/café. From there I took the frontage road about five miles to a plot of a half-dozen decrepit cabins on a hillside. I parked on a weedy, more or less flat area beside one of the cabins. This spot opened directly onto a trail that led into the thick pines. We exited the truck and headed up the trail, Frankie nosing an ecstasy of scents at every turn. The sky was clear and it was cool; I kept a pace that kept me warm without breaking a sweat. The trail eventually circled back to the west, and ultimately broke out of the pines onto red shale, and the banks of the Missouri. Cliffs of variegated red and rust climbed on either side of the river. We sat and rested for a while. Sometimes a trout going after a bug would crease the surface. Otherwise it was just the water, muscling slowly along. After a while we rose and went back the way we'd come.

I stopped at the lone restaurant in Wolf Creek and ordered a dinner of spaghetti with marinara and a bottle of Gallo Hearty Burgundy, the only available alternative to Mateus Rosé.

Frankie got a soup bone. They wouldn't take any money for it. I dawdled over the dinner and drank half of the bottle. By the time we were back on the road, it was completely dark.

When I eased the 4-Runner up the bumpy road to the shack, I faced the nose of it toward the front door. Sure enough, there was a piece of paper affixed to the door, gleaming in the light. I got out and slowly walked toward the door, the areola from my mini-flashlight encircling the paper. Even in the weak light, I could read the message from 10 feet away. In large, black letters, it said: "YOU LIED!!"

It wasn't until dusk the next evening that I realized the clock had been changed. I stared at the face of it for some time before it sunk in: The time now read 10:10. I laughed aloud when I saw it, startling Frankie. I went out to check the door. And there it was—I'd missed it the night before, and all that day: The numbers now said 1010. I leaned my back against the door, right against where the extra "0" would be, and took in the vista in front of me, the meek light washing out across the colorless grass. I let the feeling flow through me unchecked, the mixture of relief and some shame, but mostly relief. I waited there until that was all gone.

Anson first came around mid-November, on a day of light snow. He was driving a red Dodge pickup with bumper stickers from the past three Augusta Rodeos. He stopped the pickup at a respectful distance—about where Duane had first parked the RV four weeks earlier—and waited for me to come forward, with Frankie at my side.

I walked to the door of the Dodge. He rolled down the window and introduced himself as Anson Gustafson. Anson was the editor of the Simms school paper. The Tiger Tales. "This gal from out in California contacted me," he said. "At school. She asked the secretary in the office for the editor. Anyhow, her name is Thao. I can't say her last name."

"Nguyen."

"Yessir. And she sent me twenty-five dollars to come out here and give you this, so here I am." He indicated a manila envelope beside him on the horse-blanket seat cover. I could see the logo of the San Jose Herald on the envelope.

"Come on inside, Anson. No point in us both freezing out here."

Standing, Anson revealed himself to be a sturdy if somewhat pudgy young man, with the hope of a yellow mustache above his lip. He wore a jean jacket and a Seattle Mariners baseball cap.

Anson extended his hand. "Pleased t'meet ya."

I shook it. "Same here."

"Yessir."

We went in and sat at the table. Anson declined my offer of coffee. I could see that the envelope had my name written on the face of it. Anson placed it on the table. "She said she mailed another one to you, but didn't know if you'd get it, because it just went to general delivery at the post office."

"Sometimes I forget to go in for mail. I don't get much."

Anson slowly rotated to scan the interior of the cabin. He did the full 360 degrees. "Don't the mailman come out here?"

"Unfortunately, no."

The envelope contained newspaper tear sheets. There was a front-page story on the declining populations of the railroad towns of the Great Plains, and a Living Section cover story headlined "Under the Big Sky," with a story and photos of Shep and Fort Benton. A sticky note stuck to the front page read, "Chief Jos. story running next week. –Thao." I inserted the paper and note back inside the envelope.

"I'll certainly read this with interest, Anson," I said. "I appreciate your bringing it out to me."

"You bet," Anson said. He rose, and only then thought to remove his cap.

"Are you sure I can't get you something warm to drink?"

"Oh, no, that's all right." But he showed no inclination to head toward the door.

"Was there something else?"

"Oh…nothin'." He re-did the rotating room surveillance. "It's pretty nice here," he said, somewhat dubiously.

"Thanks."

"How are you?"

"I'm fine, thanks."

"Doin' all right, huh?"

"Yes. Sure."

"All right, then." He pulled his cap back on. "I guess I'll be going."

I walked Anson to his pickup. When he got in, I said, "You can tell her that. That I'm fine. I'm doing all right."

"Yessir," Anson said.

Anson came back two weeks later. He drove up just as the last light from the sunken sun was fading, and the cold day was transitioning into a frigid night. He was dressed for the weather, with a down vest over the jean jacket, and he'd exchanged the Mariners cap for a red Elmer Fudd hunting cap.

"Hello again, Anson."

"Hello again. Got another envelope for ya."

"Come on in."

Anson eased out of the pickup's bench seat, his down vest squeaking against the steering wheel like boots on snow.

I lit the kerosene lamp, and Anson walked to the chair where he'd sat the last time. He unzipped the vest halfway, tentatively. "Keep it kinda chilly in here, huh?"

"It is? Oh." I went to the stove, stepping around Frankie on his bed, and grabbed a couple of logs from the pile against the wall.

"You don't have to do that on my account," Anson said. "I don't want to be any trouble."

"No trouble at all. Sometimes I just forget. Glad you reminded me. Have a seat. The kettle's still hot. I'll dig out some tea."

Anson sat. "Never had it before."

"Really? You've never had tea?"

"Nope. Just coffee."

"No problem, I'll make you some coffee."

"I'd like to try the tea, if that's OK."

I poured water into a mug, threw in a stiff Lipton teabag, added some honey, and set the mug down on the table, next to one of the blue-and-white Currier-and-Ives saucers. "Let that steep for a couple of minutes—I mean, just let the bag sit there for two minutes or so. Then you take it out."

"Right."

The white envelope was on the table. I opened it. She'd sent the Sunday Living section, along with a folded typewritten note. The cover featured several color photos by Duane. One was a striking shot of Joe, just after the reenactment, standing next to the "surrender" monument, his head bowed, his hair windblown underneath the band. The portrait showed just enough of his profile to suggest both defiance and dejection. In the upper right corner of the frame, Duane had somehow caught a swallow frozen in flight.

"Look at that," I said. "He really knew what he was doing."

Anson examined the photo. "Yessir."

The main header of the page read:

The Surrender

The Soldier

The Speech

The Sorrows

Underneath that, the subhead:

Los Gatos pioneer Charles Wood transcribed one of the most famous speeches in American history; after that, the true tragedy began

There was a short copy block on the cover, and the text jumped inside, to two open pages, which also contained a short story on Wood and the cat statues in Los Gatos.

Anson sipped the tea, taking it in with plenty of air to cool it. "This ain't bad," he said. "Different." Anson touched the newspaper page. "Did she write all that?"

"Yes."

"Gosh. The Great Falls Tribune doesn't have that many color pictures in a week."

"She wrote the story. A photographer took the photos." I folded the pages back up.

"Two people come all the way up here to do that? That must've cost some money."

240

"I imagine it did. The Herald can afford it. Newspapers make more money than they know what to do with."

"Ha. Not ours."

"Your school paper?"

"We don't have no money at all." Anson again perused the page, shaking his head. "Mm-m. Hope I can do somethin' like that one day."

"You want to be a journalist?"

Anson blushed slightly. His mustache was more noticeable with this contrast against the pink flesh. "Yeah. I like to write. What I want to do…tell the truth, I'd like to go to school in Missoula. The journalism school."

"That's great. It's a wonderful career. It really is. And UM has a good j-school."

"Yeah. But my folks want me to go to MSU and study ag."

"Oh. Your folks farm?"

"Oh yeah. Wheat and barley. Tell the truth, I'd rather do somethin' else. Write for the newspaper. My folks don't get that at all." Anson spread his hand against the paper, smoothing it out. "'Story by Thao…' How did you say her last name again?"

"Nguyen."

"She seems like a pretty nice lady."

"Yes, she is. Very nice."

"Say." Anson touched the byline with a chubby forefinger. "I wonder if she'll talk to my mom about newspapers when she…" He stopped, and blushed again. "I mean…over the phone."

I studied his face.

"…Call her up." He could barely choke out those last words.

"Is she coming up here?"

"Pardon?"

I slowly pulled the page away from Anson, and folded it in half.

"Thao. She's coming up here?" The rosiness in Anson's cheeks deepened to near-red. "When? You can tell me."

"Ooh. Uh-oh."

"She won't mind."

"She asked me not to say."

"And you in fact have not said a word about it, Anson. I merely intuited it…I guessed it. So the cat's out of the bag. Not your fault. But listen. Here's the thing. I'd like to get the place ready for her. You know, make sure it's comfortable and warm. She's from California, so she's kind of thin-blooded." I smiled at Anson, and he cautiously smiled back. "And maybe we can schedule some time for her to talk to your mom."

"Really?"

"Sure. I bet she'd be glad to."

"The thing is, though…I promised her I wouldn't say nothin.'"

"And again, you have not said a word. Listen, how much is she giving you? You said twenty-five the first time? Did she give you another twenty-five for this?"

"Well…she did."

"I'll give you a hundred if you tell me when she's coming."

"You would?"

"Yep. It means that much to me. See, the thing is, I can't stand to be surprised. It drives me crazy."

"It does?"

"Yep. I'd pay a hundred bucks not to be surprised."

"I don't know if I'd feel right, though."

"But you're not breaking your promise. I figured it out, it's not your fault. But this way she'll still think it's a surprise. You get it? You're actually doing her a favor."

Anson took some time to consider this. "I guess so…in a way," he said slowly.

I went to the bookshelf, opened up a copy of *Ulysses*, and withdrew a hundred dollar bill. I placed it on the table next to the Currier and Ives dish. Anson picked it up cautiously.

"She said she's coming up on the 26th. Day after Christmas."

"Thanks, Anson. I appreciate that."

"Thank you, Mr. Rossiter."

I had Anson write down his home phone number for Thao before we walked out to the Dodge.

"Best of luck, Anson. I hope that journalism plan works out for you."

Anson hesitated at the open door of his pickup. "So…you're doin' all right," he said.

"Right. Fine as always."

When the last chrome-and-red glimpse of his pickup was gone, I went back inside and pulled out the note from Thao. It had been typed on a computer, and printed out.

Dear Ross,

I hope this story comes close to matching your expectations. I enjoyed the reporting and writing. Thanks for giving us the idea.

I have decided to forgive you for LYING to me about meeting us at the restaurant. We had a great meal of steak and ravioli, thank you for buying, and Duane was the perfect gentleman. The waitress gave him a Freddy's BASE BALL CAP. If you can believe that. He can be charming when he wants to be. I've found this to be even truer in his post-concussion state.

OK, I have not totally forgiven you. But I will on one condition: Whatever your deadline is for, I want you to put it off until the fall. That's why I changed your clock and address! Did you notice?? I hope that did not make you late for any appointments or make you miss your favorite TV program starring Andy Griffith.

My Dear Ross. I have learned that you can't stop crazy people from doing crazy things. However, you CAN stop a sane person from doing a crazy thing. So. Just in case you are considering doing something crazy—moving to Palm Springs, starting a rock band, becoming a dance instructor, whatever. I am asking you NOT to. At least, not till I talk to you. This is the LEAST you can do under the circumstances, if you know what I mean, and I think you do. I am going to try to make it up there, not sure when. CAN YOU PLEASE CALL ME. 408-920-5809.

The closing was handwritten in ink.

Love, Thao

I put my finger on the spot where she had written, "Love, Thao." I let it rest there for half a minute. Then I got up and changed the hands of the clock to 12:26.

"Come on, Frankie," I said. "Ride."

I drove into Fort Shaw, to the pay phone in front of the café, and called May.

Brandy McMahon and Jacky

May 1995

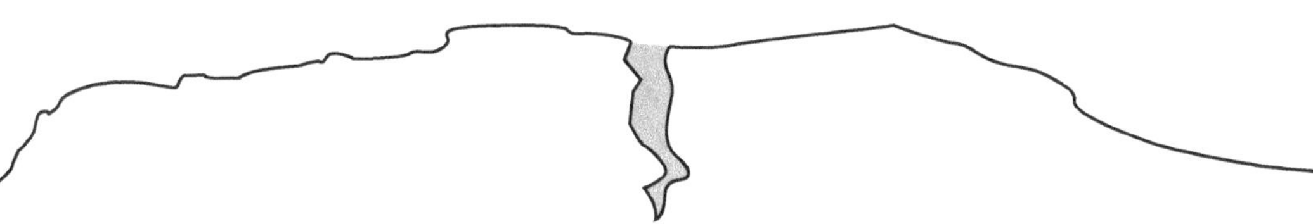

By this time, and unfortunately for the last time, Rossiter had found that if he immersed himself in an abundance of minutiae—which is readily found at almost any level of reportage—this immersion offered a strange comfort. All the facts and figures were trees. While it ran counter to the typical tenets of journalism and the daily gripes of Ed, Rossiter felt it was dicey to try to quantify, assess, or even proclaim the visualization of a forest, because so much depends on the point of view and inadequacies of the seer. Where does the forest begin and end? To say so requires a judgment. Ultimately, it was far more sensible and reassuring to reject any notion of seeing a forest, while acknowledging the conglomeration of individual trees, which themselves were solid and undeniable.

So it was that on this spring day, May Day, he had been out all morning on an interview for a column, speaking to a guy who lived in a residential tract adjacent to a little strip mall. The guy had been documenting the length of time that cops were parking at a sandwich shop in the mall. Not only that, when they made a left turn across traffic to enter the mall lot, they used their signals only 26 percent of the time. The guy knew that because, in the past 18 months, of the 228 instances he had recorded of the cops making a turn, only 60 such instances involved turn signals.

For the purposes of the column, Rossiter was mulling over the potential reader interest in all this. Not so much for the cops' transgressions as for the obsessive determination of the neighbor—reflected, for example, in the neatly penciled spreadsheet on which he'd recorded columns headed by the date, time of left turn, and whenever possible the identifying number of the cop car. The last column was devoted, down to the minute, to the length of time each cop spent in the sandwich shop: 1:23, 1:19, 1:01, and so on, but with a notable outlier (circled in red) of 3:17.

"*That* one didn't come out that entire time," the neighbor said. "I didn't go to the bathroom until I saw him come out and get back in his car."

Rossiter was reviewing the photocopy of the spreadsheet that the guy had provided him when Ed came by and pulled up a chair next to him. He gestured toward the city desk, where his desk was located. Rossiter could see the head of a woman seated in that area.

"Who's that?"

"Jack McMahon's sister."

"What…McMahon's sister?"

"Yeah."

He half-stood to get a better view. The woman's head was down. "What does she want?"

"She wants to talk to you."

"Really? Why?

She wants to talk to you about her brother. She has a copy of that column you wrote about being interviewed. She thinks the cops are blowing off the investigation."

"What does she want me to do about it?"

"She wants you to write about how they're blowing it off."

"And what? You think I should talk to her?"

"Would you mind? She's completely determined to talk to you. I already told her it would be inappropriate for you to write anything because you've had dealings with the cops on the matter."

"Right."

"But she doesn't care. She says she just wants to talk."

"She needs to talk to a reporter, not me. Isn't this Roxanne's last week? She can go out with a bang."

"I told her about talking to a reporter. But she's quite determined that it be you." Ed leaned closer and lowered his voice. "I feel kind of sorry for her."

"You are getting weaker by the day, aren't you?"

"Yes."

"You shouldn't even be in this fucking business."

"Stipulated. Tell you what. Talk to her for 15 minutes or whatever, and just send her back to me. You won't have to do a single keystroke."

"Christ. Bring her over."

When Ed introduced them, Rossiter extended his hand. "I'm pleased to meet you, Brandy, and sorry about your loss."

"I'm pleased to meet you," she answered in a flat tone. Her hand felt mushy in his. She was very thin. About six months pregnant. No ring on her finger. Pale, freckled. She'd dyed her hair black.

He led her down the hallway, past a long succession of prize-winning photographs lining the walls, which she ignored. There were more photos in the room. There was also a rectangular table around which four chairs were arranged. He pulled one out for her. She sat and scooted forward toward the table, like a schoolgirl at her desk, and put her purse on the tabletop.

He went to the chair opposite her.

"Would you like a soda?"

"No thank you." She put her hands on the table. One was flat; the other held a piece of paper.

"Water? Anything?"

"No thank you. I know you're busy."

He sat across from her, and placed a notepad and pen on the table. He left the pad unopened.

"I have a little time. What can I do for you?"

She opened her hand and showed him the paper. It was a folded-up photocopy of his column. "Can you write an essay about my brother?"

He glanced at the photocopy. He could see his column heading and part of the headline: "…**person of interest**."

"As I think Ed explained to you, I really can't, but maybe someone else can talk to you. What kind of…essay were you thinking of?"

She unfolded the paper. "That the police aren't doin' nothin.' I've gone to the station three different times and they keep sayin' that they're lookin' at their leads or whatever, but haven't found none."

"No?"

"I brought pictures, and they didn't even want 'em."

"Pictures? Pictures of what?"

"Pictures of Jacky."

She reached into her purse and pulled out a manila envelope. She hesitated, seeming to wait for a cue to reveal whatever was inside.

"Why would they need a picture of him? They know what he looked like, of course."

"For the file or whatever. Like, who he is. You know, so they can, like, spread 'em out and look at 'em, like they do on TV."

"Ah. So they weren't interested in doing that?"

"No way. They didn't care or nothin.'"

Her face reflected more resignation than bitterness. Rossiter could not connect this face to the little blonde girl in flip-flops, hiding behind the car when the school bus came.

"How do his other siblings feel?"

"Pardon?"

"Did he have any other sisters? And wasn't there an older brother?

"Haven't heard from him in 10 years. It's just me and my mom. We live with my mom. Did. Till he got killed, I mean."

"Oh—your mother. She's…."

"She don't hardly care."

"What about your father?"

"I don't remember him."

"Hm."

She waited for him to say something else. When he didn't, she said,

"Look Mr. Roster, I know my brother was not one of your upstanding citizens or nothin,' but he didn't deserve to get killed." She placed her finger on the photocopy, on a paragraph circled in blue ink, and began to slowly read it.

"The case presents an interesting quandary—" she pronounced it kondaree "—in that Mr. McMahon, who would not have been mistaken for a model citizen, nevertheless should be entitled under the law and by virtue of our better natures to a full and earnest investigation of his demise."

She looked up. "You wrote that, right?"

"Yes."

"Can't you write another essay that says the cops aren't doin' their job?"

When he did not answer, she reached back into the envelope and pulled out several photos. There were maybe a dozen, in varying degrees of fadedness. "See," she said. "This is him." She sorted them in what appeared to be chronological order, from an early pose—one of those Sears portraits—to one that appeared to be quite recent, a backyard barbecue snapshot.

Rossiter reached across the table and pulled the Sears portrait toward him. It showed a child of maybe 18 months. He wore a striped shirt, with a cartoon tot on the front, depicted as scampering along, cartoon clouds kicked up at his heels. The shirt said, "Eat My Dust!" Jacky's blond hair was carefully brushed to the side. There was a discoloration next to one eye, where they had tried to airbrush out the scar, without complete success.

"Jesus…he already had the scar."

She sniffled. "Huh?"

He continued to study the photo even as he reached for the box of tissues that sat farther down the table. He pushed it across to her.

"He had a scar on his face." He pointed at the photo. "At that age."

"Oh, yeah. You can see it in the picture."

"How did he get that, I wonder?"

She was dabbing at her nose with a tissue. "I don't know. I wasn't born yet."

"Oh. It was never discussed?"

"I don't remember. Why?'

"No reason." He studied the photo and then her blue-gray eyes. They were dry now and dull. "Can I keep this for a while? I'd like to make a copy."

"You can have it. There's a bunch more just like it at home."

"Thank you."

He tried to smile at her, but knew he was failing at it. She clearly understood that this was not a sign of encouragement—that in fact, his distorted mouth indicated something quite the opposite.

"I'll take you to Ed," he said. "He's interested in having a reporter talk to you."

She dropped her gaze to the table, folded the clipping back up, and started to gather up the photos. "Is it a reporter with his picture on the paper?"

"No. Not a columnist. A regular reporter. That's your best bet."

"Somebody who talks to me, but he talks to the cops, too?"

"Right. If she does a story, she'll have to get the side of the police."

"That woman? Who's been writing all that stuff in the paper about his record and stuff? Would she do that again?"

"Yes, probably, but that would be part of the story, wouldn't it? That, yeah, he had this background and all, but still—"

"I hafta go somewhere anyway."

"It doesn't have to be today…"

She got up, put the paper and photos back in the envelope, and returned the envelope to her purse. "'Kay."

She extended her hand across the table. He reached out and took it. It still felt mushy, but also surprisingly warm. He grasped it, lightly, until she pulled it back.

"'Kay, thanks," she said.

He picked up the Sears photo by its edges, pulled out his wallet and slipped the photo inside.

16. A Good Day Now

It was still dark when I woke up, suddenly, as if there had been a noise, like a door slamming. I lay there breathless, thinking, *no, there was no noise, my door is closed, I was dreaming.* I groped for the flashlight underneath my bed and shone it at the calendar. Everything was X'd up to December 26. I raised the light again, and again illuminated the calendar. Yes: December 26.

When I got up Frankie stirred, too. "You can sleep, buddy." But Frankie shook himself, and followed me to the door. I stepped outside, naked, and checked the sky: the fallen moon still insinuated itself from the other side of the butte. The temperature was 10 or 15 above. "Yep. Gonna be clear," I said to Frankie. When I started to shiver, I went back inside.

After some consideration, I pulled on a t-shirt, jeans and a pair of hiking boots, started a fire in the stove, and made coffee and oatmeal. By the time that Frankie and I ate, it was just getting light. I retrieved a stack of folded-up boxes from beneath my bed, and taped them into cubes. What books I had, I fit into two boxes. The blue-and-white plates went into another box, nesting in the newspaper pages of Thao's stories. There was still room, so I put the few glasses and cups in there, too. I jammed most of my clothes in the duffel bag, and the rest—along with some miscellany: the flashlight, a topo map, the Swiss Army knife, the oatmeal and coffee—in a paper bag. I rolled up the down bag with the pillow inside. I considered the cans of beans, lined stoically on the shelf, and decided they should stay.

The last box was for Frankie's things: the remainder of his canned food, his blanket and his blue rubber bone. Frankie observed the process with discernible consternation.

"It's OK, boy," I said. "This is yours. It goes with you."

I'd left three unsealed envelopes the night before on the table, alongside a couple of tacks. Two of the envelopes—one addressed to May, the other to Brandy McMahon—I now picked up and slipped into my back pocket. The third had THAO written in large block letters on the front. I removed the contents of that one. There were two pages, one inside the other, and a key. I took the outer one and read it again.

Dec. 25, 1996

Crown Butte near Simms, Mont.

Dear Ms. Nguyen:

As the direct result of your investigation into the matter, I hereby attest that on Feb. 28, 1995, I, Douglas Rossiter, shot and killed Jack McMahon of San Jose, California, in a wooded area down a short decline from the parking lot of Mendoza's Tavern outside San Jose. The weapon I used was a Charter Arms .38 caliber revolver, which can be found in a safe deposit box in my name at Cattleman's Bank on 10th Avenue South in Great Falls, Montana. The key is enclosed, just in case it's needed.

I want to stress that my action was not taken in self-defense, nor in any way related to any perceived threat by him toward me.

I acknowledge that my action undoubtedly caused pain and anguish among people known and possibly unknown to me. For that I apologize.

My motivation in this act was formed by the notion that I would be bringing about some measure of improvement to the world. I was wrong. The world is a finished entity; it cannot be further refined. Please notify the proper Authority.

Sincerely,

Douglas Rossiter

I reinserted the pages in the envelope along with the key, and put them and the tacks in the breast pocket of my T-shirt. I left the door open. It was a still morning, so the cool air did not come blustering in. Instead it seeped, invisibly and inaudibly, along the floor and into the corners, upward and outward, until it had compressed into every inch of the space.

I tossed the paper bag and duffel bag into the back of the 4-Runner.

Then the boxes. When that was done, I went to a flat rust-colored rock about fifty feet from the cabin. I removed the envelope and tacks from my breast pocket, and laid them underneath the rock.

Normally, if I were puttering about outside like this, engaged in unknowable human tasks, Frankie would be off somewhere, roaming around. But this morning he stayed close to the vehicle and watched me.

When it was all done, I opened the front passenger door.

"OK boy."

He jumped into the open door and sat.

I closed the passenger door, walked around and got in the driver's side. I faced him, and he immediately started to lick my face.

"Yes, bud." I put my hand on his neck and rubbed it. His usual reaction to a neck rub was to go all limp, his corporeal levitation restricted just barely by gravity. But now he stayed upright. "I'm just going to let it go right now because I can't be bawling at May's. OK? Now…hah, Christ…Now…Buddy, you are going to have the best time there. OK? You'll have so many pals. Not just some stupid human on two legs. I want you to enjoy every single second. Run, eat, pee, shit, chase the ball, chase your friends…All that. Sleep in the sun. And bark at the moon…Remember to bark at the moon, buddy." I kept rubbing his neck.

"Now…here's the thing."

With the change in the tone of my voice, Frankie cocked his head.

"Here is the thing. Do not go all Old Shep on me. Got it? I don't want anybody putting together a Fort Shaw museum with a diorama of you waiting faithfully outside this shack. Right? You live your dog life, and just leave all this to your dreams."

I leaned over and kissed him on the forehead. "You forget me and lead a great dog life. Got it?"

I choked out a sound that a dog might mistake for a laugh. Frankie raised his head at this. "That's right, bud!"

On the way to May's I drove below the speed limit, and let Frankie rest his head on my lap. But when I pulled into the driveway he suddenly sat up and issued a small *woof!*

"Thatta boy. That's my boy."

He woofed again, louder.

"There's your buddies. You show 'em who's the fastest."

I pulled to a stop. May was just inside the gate, with the dogs in a swirl around her long blue wool coat. Apparently it was pre-breakfast pee time.

I walked around and opened Frankie's door. He bounced out, but then hesitated.

"Come on Frankie!" May called. "Has he had his breakfast?"

The dogs noticed Frankie. They packed round the gate and started to dance and bark.

"Yeah. Over an hour ago."

"He can have a snack when these guys eat, so he doesn't feel left out. Come on, Frankie!"

Frankie was still at my side.

"OK, boy," I said softly. "Go on." Frankie took one step, glanced up at me again.

I waved my hand toward the gate where May was waiting.

"Come on Frankie!" May urged.

"Go!"

Frankie bounded to the gate, ran one circle around May to say hi, then plunged into swirl of the dogs. May let them play, but not too roughly. "Carli, nice. Rudy, be nice, now."

I pulled out the box and walked over to the gate.

"How you doing?" May asked. "You can just set that there. Luther will bring it in later. I can't believe you're out here in that T-shirt and no jacket."

"Oh, I left it in the car. I'm doing good. How about you?"

"Good." Her hand shaded her eyes against the glare of the low winter sun. "Everything OK?"

"Yep…How about you?"

"Sure. Just living paw to mouth, like always."

"Seem to be doing all right."

"We are."

"So you can accommodate this guy."

"You bet we can. He's a sweetheart, and he can stay as long as he wants."

"Glad to hear that. Like I said, I don't know how long I'll be gone. Maybe a while. So I'll get those funds in the mail to you. Go ahead and cash it for the full amount, and if there ends up being a balance, you can just refund whatever. Just cash out whatever I send."

"Well, don't be sendin' me no million dollars and then comin' around for a refund, because you won't find me. Or your dog. We'll be in Paris."

"It's no million dollars."

"Right. I just mean, it's not how I normally do business, you understand."

"I do understand, and I really appreciate it."

"OK. Do you want to leave a number in case I need to reach you?"

"I probably won't have one for a while. If there are any vet needs, go ahead and use whatever of the funds are needed. I trust him in your care completely. If you do whatever you think is best for him, I'll be happy."

"I will do that."

I stole one more look into the kennel. Carli and Rudy, a couple of matching terrier-like mutts, were leading the pack in an erratic trot down the fence. Frankie was following, a little unsure, trying to mimic the movements of the others.

I nodded once more to May—did she briefly shake her head?—quickly turned and went back to the 4-Runner.

When I got to Great Falls, I first went to the bank. A bespectacled middle-aged woman, pleasantly perfumed and subtly chewing gum, helped me with everything, from the safe deposit box to the grant deed. She assured me that the letters and the deed would go out that day with the mail. She was extremely efficient, and friendly to the required minimum, which included the parting remark, "You have a good day, now."

The Goodwill store was just a couple of blocks down 10th, on a side street. An Indian wearing a white pearl-snap shirt beneath a denim vest took the boxes inside. He came back out with a clipboard. He was a skinny guy, wrinkled, expressionless, and could have been anywhere from 40 to 60.

I extended a twenty dollar bill. "I don't need a receipt," I said.

"We ain't sposed to take tips."

"It's not a tip."

He took the bill.

"By the way, is there a phone in there I can use?"

He led me inside to a small, neat office, with a wood desk that had to be a hundred years old. It needed refinishing, but otherwise it was in excellent shape. He pointed to the phone on the desk and walked off.

I called Catholic Charities and arranged for someone to meet me at the bus station. I went back to the car and got the duffel bag, the paper bag and the rolled-up sleeping bag. I took them to the Dumpster and tossed them in.

The bus station was busy—post-Christmas travelers, frayed and tired, weighed down with bundles and bags. I sat near the front door, monitoring the time and mulling over what to do if Catholic Charities didn't get there before the bus left. But they came with 15 minutes to spare—an older man and a perky, heavy-set woman who did most of the talking—and it was all done in the space of 10 minutes. I signed the papers and gave them the 4-Runner keys.

"We don't normally receive a vehicle of quite this quality," the woman said. "We sure do appreciate it."

"I'm glad to know it. I hope someone makes good use of it."

"Oh, they will, I promise you that."

When they walked out, I threw my copies of the papers away.

The bus route pretty much traced backwards the trip that Thao, Duane and I had made into town that day back in October. Leaving downtown, the bus crossed the bridge over the Missouri, a ways downstream from Mike's RVs, proceeded along Central Avenue West, past the pawn shop with the polar bear on top, and climbed the ramp onto the highway. The land pushed past. It had been a dry December, and only a few vestiges of a late November snow lay here and there, in dissolute patches. There was more higher up, on Square Butte, and to the west, on Crown Butte.

When we got to Fort Shaw and the bus slowed, I checked out the house across the street from the diner. There was no one about, but I thought I saw a curtain twitch. It could have been just a flash of reflected light. The green VW was in the same spot it had occupied when I first saw it that day I pulled into the café parking lot a year-and-a-half ago. Any labor intended to achieve the end-result of locomotion apparently had been fruitless, or maybe merely indifferent.

The bus arrived in Simms just about the time I figured Thao's plane would be landing at the airport. Doing the math: It would take her 20 minutes to get a car, so craziest-case scenario, even if she came straight out and mastered any navigational issues, the soonest she'd arrive would be an hour. An hour was cutting it close. So, with nothing on my back or in my hands, I started walking at a healthy pace. There was a strong wind behind me, from the north, cold, but it propelled me down the road. Even though it was mid-afternoon, the sun was almost directly in my eyes. I instinctively lowered my gaze to the ground a few feet in front of me. I tried to raise my eyes, but each time I had to blink and look back down. The eyes are disconnected from the mind.

The wind blew sound to me: the rumbling of semis on the highway, a train whistle, the whinny of a horse somewhere. After a half-hour of walking, I heard a vehicle coming up from behind, a ways back. It was going along and suddenly throttled down. Must have just seen me. It was slowing, slowing, until it came abreast of me. It was a nearly new and quite dusty blue Ford pickup, carrying two Hutterites, a man and a teenage boy.

The boy lowered his window. "Hey. Y'need a ride?"

"Thanks, but I'm just going down a couple of miles."

The man leaned forward so he could see around the boy. "Little chilly out there, an' no jacket," he said. He pronounced the word in two distinct parts: *chee lee*. "Y'might as well hop in."

The boy pushed open the door and scooted over. I climbed in and shut the door. They had the heater going, and I immediately felt droplets of sweat emerge from my trunk and temples.

"Ya movin' along there purty good," the man said. He had a dark chin-curtain beard, which framed his doughy face.

"Yeah."

"Have a breakdown? Didn't see y'rig."

"Just got off the bus in Simms."

"Oh, yah."

"Just walking down to my place down here a ways. Over toward the butte."

"Oh, yah. That gate wit' the cattle guard?

"That's it."

"Yep. Thanks."

I got out, and the truck immediately started to roll away. I could see the reflection of the boy in the side-view mirror, necked craned, mouth slightly agape.

The drive saved me a good half-hour, so I allowed myself a slow pace to the rust-colored rock. I retrieved the envelope, took it to the cabin and tacked it onto the front door. The sunlight made the white of it gleam against the weathered wood. I skirted around to the trail and headed up toward the crest of the butte.

I stopped where the trail switched back, where the tree grew out from the rock. This distance was reasonable. If against all odds anyone happened to come along, there should be time enough to dash back down, yelling and waving, and prevent whomever from getting at the envelope on the door.

As I had many times before, I contemplated the base of the trunk, which had emerged from a gap in the rock about the size of a grapefruit. The base filled the space entirely; it could have been a post set in cement. The trunk grew almost horizontally out of the rock about three feet before it jutted upward— an arm extended, with a crooked finger pointing to the sky. In the west, the sun, descending into a nebulous blue-orange haze, sat just atop the glazed Rocky Mountain Front. Here on the southern crest of the butte I couldn't see Simms, but the road was visible. There were no vehicles at this hour on this day. The flat top of Square Butte was a few miles to the east. Low, broad, muscular, pointless. Just like this butte.

The moon was ascending on the other side. Nearly full.

The sweat I had worked up on my hike was now cold and heavy, and my t-shirt was getting stiff. I shuffled around a bit on the crusty snow. My ears were getting a little numb. I swung my arms back and forth against my chest.

"C'mon, Thao," I said.

I had felt so certain she would come, but now my mind was fogging with doubt. What if Anson had mixed up the date? That or any number of other things. A missed flight. Getting lost from the airport to here. That actually seemed more likely than her actually finding the place. If she didn't show, I would have to go back down. Right? My mental processing had slowed a fraction. Right? The cold was making my thoughts thicken. Like Jell-O that's been in the refrigerator for a while, but before it completely sets. I sorted out the possibilities, slowly: If she didn't come, I would go back down and just walk the letter into town and mail it. That would require buying a stamp. I patted my back pocket to verify that I still had my wallet. OK. If she didn't come, I would have to go back down, build a fire, stay in the cabin overnight, walk to town tomorrow to mail the letter, walk back here. I whispered this sequence aloud, twice.

A red pickup and a white SUV appeared on the road in tandem. They were moving to the south, slowly. The pickup looked to be Anson's. It went just past the cattle guard, stopped, and did a slow U-turn. The two vehicles remained side-by-side for a while. Then Anson's truck headed back toward Simms, and the SUV turned in and headed up the rutted road.

I retreated, squatting behind the flank of the rock.

The SUV creeped along, not stopping until it came up almost to the cabin. Thao got out and shut the car door. The sound reached me a second after I saw it close. She had graduated to warmer wear—a full-sized white parka. Her black hair spilled onto the shoulders of the parka.

I laughed a low happy laugh. I was shivering. The laugh itself shivered.

She headed to the front door, which put her out of sight. It was another thirty seconds before she reappeared. I could see white paper now in her hand. Rocking slightly to and fro, she slowly scanned the area.

I lowered my head.

She got back inside the SUV. She'd left it running. The exhaust circled lazily about the back of the vehicle. She would be reading the pages now—first the confession, then the letter I had written and read, and reread and rewritten, the night before:

Dear Thao,

I've taken so many shots at writing this that I've gone bleary. But no matter, by now I'm in the best state of mind of all in which to write, because I'll just say what I want and need to say, and I won't worry about whether it's perfect.

First off—yes, I moved up my deadline, because (1) I knew you were coming, and (2) why prolong the inevitable? Nothing is going to change. It's time to go.

Anson did not tell me about your plans. I extracted it from him against his will, and he felt terrible about it. Please don't be angry at him. Also, would you please contact his mother? He wants to be a newsman. Tell her to let him, if that's what he wants.

You will write your story. Columnist-turns-vigilante-turns-hermit-turns-fugitive or however you choose to do it. You did it—to my amazement even now, you sifted your way through all the piles of nonsense I've strewn about, and Found the Nut. I guess in spite of both of us.

I know you will write the story just right. You were correct, of course—it's really a good story. If I say so myself.

I sent a little money, a cashier's check, to McMahon's sister. Also a grant deed to my house in San Jose. Frankie is at the kennel. I sent May some money, too, and a grant deed to the butte property.

I can't tell you where I'm going now, of course. As I told you—I cannot bear the thought of incarceration. Please do not look for me. Anyway, for us—yes, darling, for us—this is where I am. Remember when I told you I'd be here and you said I lied? I didn't lie. I have peed and pooped and blown my nose here so much, and rinsed the dead cells off my skin, and bled in the dirt from cuts and scrapes, and maybe even cried a tear or two, that I'm part of the landscape now. I'm a droplet inside the cactus, a strand in the meadowlarks' nest, a molecule in the smell of the sage. If you ever really want to find me again, this is where I am.

I know you will live your life beautifully. I can't tell you how happy that makes me.

Give my best to Duane. What a blessing it was to have the two of you fall into my life. It was the most fun I've had in—I can't think of how long. Very long.

OK. Time to go. Lift your face, and I will be the breeze that kisses it.

By now I was vigorously shivering. I found that I had folded my arms tightly against my chest. The sun had set, and in the darkening dusk the dome light of the SUV glowed brighter and warmer. My teeth were chattering. A fast, steady clicking. Like the teletype machines they used to have in the wire room at the newspaper. When was that? Years ago. The '70s.

It seemed like it was taking her a long time to read the note. What was she waiting for?

The SUV would be warm. Thao would be warm. Her skin, her hands, her model's fingers. I could run down the slope and be at the SUV in no time. I would jump inside the door and she would feign being furious. Then roll her eyes and kiss me. We would go get Frankie. Go to Great Falls. Get a steak at Freddy's, get a room at the O'Haire Manor. Make love, sleep, make love again.

I shook my Jell-O brain, and willed my legs to rise. Every part of me seemed to be shaking. My knees would not quite straighten entirely, but I was able to rise up from behind the rock. The wind suddenly kicked up; maybe I felt it more because I was standing.

The door of the SUV opened and Thao emerged. The moon illuminated her movements. She was stretching and lifting her face toward the butte.

I slowly crouched back down, and tried to focus on her. Yes, she surely had raised her chin. She was scanning the slope, not fixing her gaze in any particular spot. Feeling certain she could not see me, I slowly, carefully, lifted my hand, about as high as my shoulder. It was in a fist. I unclenched it, so that my open palm was directed toward her. After a few seconds, as if of its own accord, the hand became a fist again.

I clambered back toward the deer trail and followed it over the lip of the butte. After a few more steps I peeked back to confirm that the cabin and the car were out of sight.

The moon lit the path. I went into a pained jog. My feet seemed to have disconnected from the rest of me; they were two stones attached to my legs. Even though the way was clear, and the ground flat, I stumbled several times, and fell twice. I scraped my hands. I saw that they were bleeding, but it did not hurt at all.

By now I was fully confident I would make it. Maybe a half-mile, and there would be a white shelf of rock to the right of the deer trail. I plodded forward, waiting for the moonlight to reveal something. And suddenly it was there, a little farther off the trail than I remembered, but as clear and reflective as a big patch of snow. It gave the illusion of bouncing up and down with my every step, and grew a little bigger each time. The trail veered left, and I went straight. When I got to the rock, I didn't speed up or slow down. I just ran off the edge and plunged into the ravine.

I opened my eyes and blinked. Closed them, opened them again. The moon was directly above. One eye was very blurry. I extracted my forearm from some scratchy brush and rubbed that eye. A flaked substance, like dried mud. I kept rubbing until it went away. There was something sharp against my back, but I couldn't move away from it. I realized that I couldn't move anything except my head and arms, and just barely because there was scrub brush all around me.

There was no sound at all except for my own breath. I listened to it for a time. It might have been a long time. Eventually I realized I was hearing something else. On a clear cold night such as this, sound traveled forever. Was it the wind? Or...a car? Yes, it was a car. Thao was still there, down by the shack.

I remembered: She had raised her chin as if to catch my scent. By now, if she were looking higher up, she would see the moon. This same moon. Our lines of sight were intersecting at the moon. At Jay's Man in the Moon!

264

Which Frankie was barking at in this very moment! I kept it in my vision, and started to feel the warmth of Thao's gaze, a sensation of heat, in my own eyes. And her dark irises—I could see them, two dark dots bouncing off the moon. The warmth made me want to take off my shirt, but I couldn't. I smiled; she smiled. Our smiles bounced off the moon: mine to her, hers to me.

There was something—a whoosh, a thump. Must have been her car door closing. I listened hard. The sound of my breath was an annoyance. I could make out the clunk of the SUV's tires going over the metal cattle guard. Then they were scrunching the gravel. She was leaving. She would be heading north, back toward Simms. Soon she was off the gravel, onto the pavement. Into town. Fainter, but yes, still audible. Now she was on the highway, the tires whispering on the blacktop. Going east, back toward Great Falls. The stabbing in my back had numbed. I groaned. The loudness of the sound surprised me. I let myself listen to my own breathing, in out, in out, but also to the sound of her tires on the blacktop, a circular rhythm like my breathing.

The driving sound stopped. I sucked in a gasp of air. Five miles down the road, she was stopping in Fort Shaw. She had got about as far as the café, but there was no sound of the café's gravel parking lot. No, she must have turned into the driveway of the Volkswagen house!

Silence. Then faintly, very faintly, came the sound of footsteps. Slow, deliberate steps, and lighter steps following. The bearded man, and his kid, walking to her car. I heard a squeak. *Scree.* Thao was lowering her window. Yes, down here at the bottom of the ravine, mustering all my concentration, I could hear the impossibly faint squeak of the foggy glass as it descended into the door. In a voice as faint as the squeaking window, in a tone that was even and unhesitant, she said something. From the inflection, I could tell that she was asking a question.

After a second or two, there came what sounded like a deep, rumbling laugh. A congenial laugh. And at the end of the laugh, the man said something. Spoke! But it was not the sound of a voice so much as muffled thump, a felt mallet lightly bouncing off the head of a bass drum. *Thunt…thunt.*

I raised my head as much as I was able. "What?" It was more of a thought than a whisper. I listened, trying to hear. I closed my eyes and lay my head back down. I could hear better if I closed my eyes. "What?"

There was the steady wind, blowing into the shrubs and tree branches of the gorge. I listened until I heard it again, plainly, without a doubt.

The man said:

You sing.

You sing… You sing.

After a time, Thao answered, briefly. *OK. Thank you.*

Her car backed up, back onto Main Street. The man was still repeating himself—*Sing…Sing…Sing*—even while she was driving away. As she headed eastward, she would be hearing the word over and over, rolled up in the sound of her tires on the road.

Acknowledgments

A version of Chapter 11, No More, Ever, was previously published as the short story "No More, Ever" in *Cirque Journal*, Vol. 10, No. 2, 2020.

***

Several people were kind enough to read various drafts of this book and offer helpful remarks: Karla Bolken (of Havre!), Susan Gordon, Barb Griswold and Janet Wells. My wife, Sandi, who is the best proofreader I ever had, found my usual quota of gaffes. I appreciate the efforts of the folks at Cirque Press. They do great work in providing an outlet for fine and underappreciated writing that comes out of the Northwest.

Special thanks to my former colleague Truong Phuoc Khanh, a first-rate newspaper reporter with an incidental genius for the malapropism and portmanteau, which inspired much of the dialogue in this book.

—LFS

About the Author

Larry F. Slonaker was born and raised in Great Falls, Montana, and graduated from the Medill School of Journalism at Northwestern University. He worked as a reporter and columnist at the *San Jose Mercury News*. He and his wife now live in California's Central Coast, on a place just large enough to accommodate a few horses, a few dogs and several (fixed) feral cats.

About Cirque Press

Cirque Press grew out of *Cirque*, a literary journal that publishes the works of writers and artists from the North Pacific Rim, a region that reaches north from Oregon to the Yukon Territory, south through Alaska to Hawaii, and west to the Russian Far East.

Cirque Press is a partnership of Sandra Kleven, publisher, and Michael Burwell, editor. Ten years ago, we recognized that works of talented writers in the region were going unpublished, and the Press was launched to bring those works to fruition. We publish fiction, nonfiction, and poetry, and we seek to produce art that provides a deeper understanding about the region and its cultures. The writing of our authors is significant, personal, and strong.

Sandra Kleven – Michael Burwell, publishers and editors
www.cirquejournal.com

Books from Cirque Press

Apportioning the Light by Karen Tschannen (2018)

The Lure of Impermanence by Carey Taylor (2018)

Echolocation by Kristin Berger (2018)

Like Painted Kites & Collected Works by Clifton Bates (2019)

Athabaskan Fractal: Poems of the Far North by Karla Linn Merrifield (2019)

Holy Ghost Town by Tim Sherry (2019)

Drunk on Love: Twelve Stories to Savor Responsibly by Kerry Dean Feldman (2019)

Wide Open Eyes: Surfacing from Vietnam by Paul Kirk Haeder (2020)

Silty Water People by Vivian Faith Prescott (2020)

Life Revised by Leah Stenson (2020)

Oasis Earth: Planet in Peril by Rick Steiner (2020)

The Way to Gaamaak Cove by Doug Pope (2020)

Loggers Don't Make Love by Dave Rowan (2020)

The Dream That Is Childhood by Sandra Wassilie (2020)

Seward Soundboard by Sean Ulman (2020)

The Fox Boy by Gretchen Brinck (2021)

Lily Is Leaving: Poems by Leslie Ann Fried (2021)

One Headlight by Matt Caprioli (2021)

November Reconsidered by Marc Janssen (2021)

Someday I'll Miss This Place Too by Dan Branch (2021)

Out There In The Out There by Jerry McDonnell (2021)

Fish the Dead Water Hard by Eric Heyne (2021)

Salt & Roses by Buffy McKay (2022)

Growing Older In This Place: A Life in Alaska's Rainforest by Margo Wasserman Waring (2022)

Kettle Dance: A Big Sky Murder by Kerry Dean Feldman (2022)

Nothing Got Broke by Larry F. Slonaker (2022)

Sky Changes on the Kuskokwim by Clifton Bates (2022)

Yosemite Dawning by Shauna Potocky (2022)

Between Promise and Sadness by Joanne Townsend (2022)

On the Beach: Poems 2016-2021 by Alan Weltzien (2022)

CIRCLES
Illustrated books from Cirque Press

Baby Abe: A Lullaby for Lincoln by Ann Chandonnet (2021)

Miss Tami, Is Today Tomorrow? by Tami Phelps (2021)

Miss Bebe Goes to America by Lynda Humphrey (2022)

www.ingramcontent.com/pod-product-compliance
Lightning Source LLC
Chambersburg PA
CBHW072211150726
48002CB00005B/1769